He turned to see the Vulcan intently working his medical tricorder. This caused Chakotay to look more closely at the nearest patient, who was swaddled in a soiled blanket, lying on top of a grass mat, surrounded by filth.

The man wasn't wounded—he had oozing pustules and black bruises on his face and limbs, and his yellow hair was plastered to his sweaty forehead. Although his species was unfamiliar to Chakotay, his skin had a deathly pallor, just like the Cardassian's had. Chakotay took a step away from him.

Another patient finally noticed the visitors. She propped herself up with some difficulty and began to crawl toward them. Others saw the away team as well, and a chorus of desperate voices rent the air. Some of their words were incoherent, but Chakotay could make out a few phrases as the people crawled forward: "Help us!" "Save me!" "Kill me!"

"What's the matter with them?" he whispered to Tuvok.

"A serious illness," answered the Vulcan with tight-lipped understatement.

Chakotay tapped his combadge. "Away team to transporter room. Beam us up, but on a ten-second delay. Get out of the transporter room before we materialize."

"Yes, sir," said the Bolian, not hiding the worry in his voice. "Is everything all right?"

"No," answered Chakotay as he stepped away from the advancing tide of disease and death. "It's not."

# STAR TREK
## THE NEXT GENERATION®

DOUBLE HELIX

BOOK FOUR OF SIX

# QUARANTINE

## JOHN VORNHOLT

Double Helix Concept by John J. Ordover and Michael Jan Friedman

POCKET BOOKS

New York   London   Toronto   Sydney   Tokyo   Singapore

An Original Publication of POCKET BOOKS

POCKET BOOKS, a division of Simon & Schuster Inc.
1230 Avenue of the Americas, New York, NY 10020

A VIACOM COMPANY

This book is published by Pocket Books, a division of Simon & Schuster Inc., under exclusive license from Paramount Picture.

ISBN: 0-671-03477-4

First Pocket Books printing July 1999

10  9  8  7  6  5  4  3  2  1

POCKET and colophon are registered trademarks of Simon & Schuster Inc.

Printed in the U.S.A.

For E.J.

# QUARANTINE

# *Chapter One*

THE *PEREGRINE*-CLASS SCOUT SHIP looked much like the falcon that inspired her design, with a beaklike bow and sweeping wings that enabled her to streak through a planet's atmosphere. Her sleek lines were marred by various scorch marks and dents, which left her looking like an old raptor with many scars. Larger than a shuttlecraft yet smaller than a cruiser, she was better armed than most ships her size, with forward and rear torpedoes plus phaser emitters on her wings.

Her bridge was designed to be operated efficiently by three people, allowing her to carry a crew of only fifteen. The engine room took up all three decks of her stern, and most of the crew served there. This proud vessel was state of the art for a scout ship—about forty years ago. Now she was practically the flagship of the Maquis fleet.

"What's the name of our ship?" asked her captain, a man named Chakotay. His black hair was cut short and severe, which suited his angular face and the prominent tattoo that stretched across half his forehead.

Tuvok, the Vulcan who served as first officer, consulted the registry on his computer screen. "She is called the *Spartacus*. The warp signature has aleady been modified."

Chakotay nodded with satisfaction. "I like that name."

On his right, an attractive woman who looked vaguely Klingon scowled at him. "Let me guess," said B'Elanna Torres. "Spartacus was some ancient human who led a revolution somewhere."

Captain Chakotay smiled. "That's right. He was a slave and a gladiator who led a revolt against Rome, the greatest power of its day. For two years, he held out against every Roman legion thrown against him."

"And how did this grand revolution end?" asked Torres.

When Chakotay didn't answer right away, Tuvok remarked, "He and all of his followers were crucified. Crucifiction is quite possibly the most barbaric form of capital punishment ever invented."

Torres snorted a laugh. "It's always good to know that my human ancestors could match my Klingon ancestors in barbarism. Considering what happened to Spartacus, let's not put him on too high a pedestal."

"It's still a good name," said Chakotay stubbornly. Like many Native Americans, he believed that names were important—that words held power. He didn't like having to change the name and warp signature of his ship all the time, but it was important to make their enemies think that the Maquis had more ships than they actually had.

"We've reached the rendezvous point," announced the captain. "I'm bringing us out of warp." Operating the conn himself, he slowed the craft down to one-third impulse, and they cruised through a deserted solar system sprinkled with occasional fields of planetary debris.

"Captain Rowan is hailing us on a secure frequency," reported Tuvok. "Their ETA is less than one minute."

"Acknowledge," answered the captain. "But no more transmissions until they get here."

While Tuvok sent the message, B'Elanna Torres worked her console. "There are no Cardassian ships in scanner range," she reported.

"Still I don't want to be here more than a couple of minutes." Chakotay's worried gaze traveled from the small viewscreen to the even smaller window below it. There was nothing in sight but the vast starscape and a few jagged clumps of debris. This area appeared deserted, but Chakotay had learned from hard experience that it was wise to keep moving in the Demilitarized Zone.

"They're coming out of warp," said Torres.

Chakotay watched on the viewscreen as a Bajoran assault vessel appeared about a thousand kilometers off the starboard bow. The dagger-shaped spacecraft was slightly larger than the *Spartacus,* but she wasn't as maneuverable or as fast. Like Chakotay's ship, her blue-gray hull was pocked and pitted with the wounds of battle.

"Captain Rowan is hailing us," said Tuvok.

"On screen." Chakotay managed a smile as he greeted his counterpart on the other Maquis ship. Patricia Rowan looked every centimeter a warrior, from her scarred, gaunt face to the red eye patch that covered one eye. Her blond hair was streaked with premature gray, and it was pulled back into a tight bun. Captain Rowan had gotten a well-deserved reputation for ruthlessness, and Chakotay was cordial to her but couldn't quite bring himself to call her a friend.

"Hello, Patricia."

"Hello, Chakotay," she answered. "The *Singha* is reporting for duty under your command. What's our mission?"

"Do you know the planet Helena?"

"Only by reputation. Wasn't it abandoned when the Federation betrayed us?"

"No," answered Chakotay. "The Helenites opted for the same legal status as the residents of Dorvan V. Instead of being relocated, they chose to give up their Federation citizenship and remain on the planet, under Cardassian rule."

"Then to hell with them," said Rowan bluntly.

Chakotay ignored her harsh words. "The Helenites have always marched to their own drum. The planet was settled by mixed-race colonists who were trying to escape discrimination in the rest of the Federation. There are some Maquis sympathizers on Helena, and we've been getting periodic reports from them. Two weeks ago, they sent a message that Cardassian troops had arrived, then we lost all contact. There hasn't been a transmission from the planet since then. It might be a crackdown, maybe even total extermination. For all we know, the Cardassians could be testing planet-killing weapons."

"They're not Maquis," said Rowan stubbornly.

Chakotay's jaw clenched with anger. "We can't just abandon four million people. We have to find out what's happening there, and help them if we can."

"Then it's an intelligence mission," replied Captain Rowan, sounding content with that definition.

Chakotay nodded and slowly relaxed his jaw. One of the drawbacks of being in a loose-knit organization like the Maquis was that orders were not always followed immediately. Sometimes a commander had to explain the situation in order to convince his subordinates to act. Of course, fighting a guerrilla war against two vastly superior foes would make anyone cautious, and Maquis captains were used to acting on their own discretion. Sometimes the chain of command was as flimsy as a gaseous nebula.

Captain Rowan's scowl softened for an instant. "Chakotay, the people on Dorvan V are from your own culture. Wouldn't it make more sense to find out what happened to *them* instead of racing to help a bunch of mixed-breeds on Helena?"

Chakotay couldn't tell if Rowan was bigoted or just callous. He glanced at Torres and saw her shake her head. "Good thing there are no psychological tests to join the Maquis," she whispered.

"Did you say something?" demanded Captain Rowan.

Chakotay cleared his throat. "She said the Helenites are not really, uh, mixed-breeds—they're hybrids, genetically bred. I've heard their whole social structure is based on genetics, the more unique your genetic heritage, the higher your social status."

"A facinating culture," added Tuvok without looking up from his console. Rowan grimaced, but remained silent.

Chakotay went on, "As for my people on Dorvan V . . . yes, I'm worried about them. But that's a small village, and they've chosen to live in peace with the land, using minimal technology. They're not much of a threat, and of no strategic value, either—the Cardassians will probably leave them alone. But Helena was a thriving Federation planet with millions of inhabitants and a dozen spaceports. When they go silent, it's suspicious."

"How do we proceed?" asked Captain Rowan.

Chakotay gave her a grim smile. "Have you ever played cowboys and Indians?"

\* \* \*

Observing the planet on the viewscreen, Captain Chakotay was struck by how Earth-like it was, with vast aquamarine oceans and wispy cloud cover. Helena had small twin moons that orbited each other as they orbited the planet, and he could see their silhouettes against the sparkling sea. Small green continents were scattered across the great waters, but they seemed insignificant next to all that blue. The lush hues were accentuated by a giant red sun glowing in the distance.

On second glance, Chakotay decided that Helena looked more like Pacifica than Earth. Here was yet another beautiful planet stolen by the Cardassians, while the Federation looked the other way.

"One ship in orbit," reported B'Elanna Torres. "A Cardassian military freighter. They use those for troop transports, too, and they can be heavily armed."

Chakotay nodded and spread his fingers over the helm controls. "Let's keep it to one ship. Tuvok, as soon as we come out of warp, target their communications array with photon torpedoes and fire at will. I don't want them sending for help."

"Yes, sir," answered the Vulcan, who was preternaturally calm, considering they were about to attack a ship that was ten times larger than they were.

"Then hit their sensor arrays, so they have to concentrate on *us*."

"What about their weapons?" snapped Torres. "I hope you aren't planning to take a lot of damage."

"No more than usual." Captain Chakotay smiled confidently and pressed the comm panel. "Seska, report to the bridge for relief."

"Yes, sir," answered the Bajoran. She was only one deck below them, in the forward torpedo bay, and Chakotay heard her footsteps clanging on the ladder behind them. Now if B'Elanna had to go to engineering, they were covered.

The captain hit the comm panel, and his voice echoed throughout the ship. "All hands, Red Alert! Battlestations."

Like the falcon that inspired the *Peregrine*-class, the *Spartacus* swooped out of warp, her talons bared, spitting photon torpedoes in rapid bursts. Plumes of flame rose along the dorsal fin of the sturgeon-shaped Cardassian freighter, and dishes, deflectors, and antennas snapped like burnt matchsticks. Shields quickly compensated, and the next volley was repelled, as the lumbering, copper-colored vessel turned to defend herself.

Phasers beamed from the wing tips of the *Spartacus*, bathing the freighter in vibrant blue light. Although damage to the hull was minimal, the enemy's sensor arrays crackled like a lightning storm. Despite her damage, the freighter unleashed a barrage of phaser fire, and the *Spartacus* was rocked as she streaked past. With the larger ship on her tail, blasting away, the Maquis ship was forced into a low orbit. A desperate chase ensued, with the blue seas of Helena glimmering peacefully in the background.

"Full power to aft shields!" ordered Chakotay.

"Aye, sir," answered Torres.

They were jolted again by enemy fire, and Chakotay had to grip his chair to keep from falling out. From the corner of his eye, he saw Seska stagger onto the bridge and take a seat at an auxilary console. There was a worried look on her face.

"We can't take much more of this," said Torres.

"Making evasive maneuvers," answered Chakotay.

Zigging and zagging, the Maquis ship avoided most of the Cardassian volleys, but the larger ship bore down on them, cutting the distance with every second. Chakotay knew he would soon be in their sights, but his options were limited this close to the planet. He had a course to keep . . . and a rendezvous.

The two ships—a sardine chased by a barracuda—sped around the gently curved horizon and headed toward the blazing red sun in the distance. On the bridge, Chakotay pounded a button to dampen the light from the viewscreen, the glare was so bright. But if he couldn't see, they couldn't either. He felt the thrill of the hunt as he prepared to use one of the oldest tactics of his ancestors.

A direct hit jarred them, releasing an acrid plume of smoke from somewhere on the bridge. The ship began to vibrate as they started into the atmosphere.

"Shields weakening," reported Tuvok.

"Just a little longer," muttered Chakotay. He made another sharp turn, but quickly veered back toward the sun. The Cardassians increased their fire, as if worried that she would escape into the planet's atmosphere. Since the *Spartacus* wasn't returing fire, they had to to assume she was trying to land on the planet.

"They're powering up a tractor beam," said Torres urgently. "Their shields are . . . down!"

"Now!" barked the captain. Tuvok's hand moved from the weapons console to the comm board, while Chakotay steered his craft vertically into the horizon, trying to present a small target. The Cardassians had swallowed the bait, and now the trap snapped shut.

A Bajoran assault vessel streaked out of warp in the middle of the sun's glare. Chakotay knew the *Singha* was there, but he could barely see her on the viewscreen. The Cardassian vessel didn't see her at all, so intent were they upon capturing their prey.

With her shields down, the freighter's bridge took a direct hit from a brace of torpedoes, and lightning crackled along the length of her golden hull. The freighter went dark, but she lit up again as the *Singha* veered around and raked her hull with phasers, tearing jagged gashes in the gleaming metal. The Cardassians got off a few desperate shots, but the *Singha* raced past them, unharmed.

"Aft torpedoes," ordered Chakotay. "Fire!"

With deadly precison, the Vulcan launched a brace of torpedoes that hit the freighter amidships and nearly broke her in two. Chakotay cringed at the explosions that ripped along her gleaming hull, and he made a silent prayer on behalf of the fallen enemy. They were more arrogant than smart, but they had died bravely. Fortunately, that trick always worked on the arrogant. At a cockeyed angle, spewing smoke and flame, the massive freighter dropped into a decaying orbit.

Chakotay piloted the *Spartacus* into a safe orbit that trailed behind the dying ship. "Hail them."

Tuvok shook his head. "Their communications are out, and life support is failing. They have about six minutes left before they burn up in the atmosphere."

The cheerful voice of Captain Rowan broke in on the comm channel. "That was good hunting, Chakotay, and a good plan. What's next?"

"Enter standard orbit and see if you can raise anyone on the planet. We're going to take a prisoner, if we can."

He tapped the comm panel. "Bridge to transporter room. Scan the bridge of the enemy ship—see if you can find any lifesigns."

"Yes, sir." After a moment's pause, the technician answered, "Most of them are dead. There's one weak lifesign—"

"Lock onto it and wait for me. I'm on my way." The captain jumped to his feet. "Tuvok, grab a medkit—you're with me. B'Elanna, you have the bridge. Keep scanning the planet, and try to raise someone. Seska, you have the conn. Keep us in orbit."

"Aye, sir." The attractive Bajoran slid into the vacated seat and gave him a playful smile. "This looks like a nice place for shore leave. What do you say, Captain?"

"I'll put you on the away team," promised Chakotay. He took another glance at the viewscreen and saw the smoking hulk of the freighter plummeting toward the beautiful blue horizon.

The captain led the way from the clam-shaped bridge to the central corridor, which ran like a backbone down the length of the *Spartacus*. He jogged to the second hatch and dropped onto the ladder with practiced efficiency, while Tuvok stopped at a storage panel to pick up a medkit.

Dropping off the ladder, Chakotay landed in the second largest station on the ship after engineering: the combined transporter room and cargo hold. Not that they had any cargo to speak of—every spare centimeter was filled with weapons, explosives, and photon torpedoes, stacked like cordwood.

He drew his phaser and nodded toward the Bolian on the transporter console. The blue-skinned humanoid manipulated some old trimpot slides, and a prone figure began to materialize on the transporter platform. Chakotay heard Tuvok's footsteps as he landed on the deck, but he never took his eyes, or his phaser, off the wounded figure.

It was a male Cardassian, with singed clothes, a bruised face, and bloodied, crushed legs. With their prominent bone structure and sunken eyes, most Cardassian faces looked like skulls, but this one looked closer to death than usual.

"According to his insignia, he's the first officer," said Tuvok.

The Cardassian blinked his eyes and focused slowly on them. When he realized where he was, he wheezed with laughter. "Are you trying to save us?"

"Lie still," answered Chakotay. He motioned Tuvok forward with the medkit, but the Cardassian waved him off.

"Too late," he said with a cough. The Cardassian lifted his black sleeve to his mouth and bit off a small black button. Before anyone could react, he swallowed it. "I won't be captured . . . by the Maquis."

"What are you doing on this planet?" demanded Chakotay. "Why don't you leave these people alone?"

A rattle issued from the Cardassian's throat, and it was hard to tell whether he was laughing, crying, or dying. "You beat us . . . but all you won was a curse."

The Cardassian's bloodied head dropped onto the platform with a thud, and his previously wheezing chest was now still. Tuvok checked the medical tricorder and reported, "He has expired."

Chakotay nodded. "Beam his body back to his ship. Let him burn with his comrades."

"Yes, sir," answered the Bolian. A second later, every trace of the Cardassian officer was gone.

The captain strode over to the transporter console and tapped the comm panel. "Chakotay to bridge. Have you or the *Singha* raised anyone on the planet?"

"No, sir," answered Torres. "But we detected a strong power source that suddenly went dark. It could be a Cardassian installation."

"Are you picking up lifesigns on the planet?"

"Lots of them," answered Torres.

"Pick a strong concentration of lifesigns and send the

11

coordinates to the transporter room. Tuvok and I are going down."

"Okay," answered Torres. "Did you get a prisoner?"

"For only a few seconds—we didn't learn anything. Chakotay out." The captain reached into a tray on the transporter console and grabbed two Deltan combadges, one of which he tossed to Tuvok. The *Spartacus* was so small that they seldom needed combadges while on the ship; they saved them for away teams.

"I've got the coordinates," said the Bolian technician. "It appears to be the spaceport in the city of Padulla."

"Fine." Captain Chakotay jumped onto the transporter platform and took his place on the middle pad. Tuvok stepped beside him, slinging the medkit and tricorder over his shoulder.

"Energize."

A familiar tingle gripped Chakotay's spine, as the transporter room faded from view, to be replaced by a cavernous spaceport with high, vaulted ceilings covered with impressive murals. The captain expected to see a crowd of people, but he expected them to be standing on their feet—not lying in haphazard rows stretching the length of the vast terminal. This looked like a field hospital, thrown together to house the wounded from some monstrous battle. Coughs and groans echoed in the rancid air.

His first impression was that the Cardassians had wreaked terrible destruction on the people of Helena, and he started toward the nearest patient.

"Captain!" warned Tuvok. "Keep your distance from them."

He turned to see the Vulcan intently working his medical tricorder. This caused Chakotay to look more closely at the nearest patient, who was swaddled in a soiled blanket, lying on top of a grass mat, surrounded by filth.

The man wasn't wounded—he had oozing pustules and black bruises on his face and limbs, and his yellow hair was plastered to his sweaty forehead. Although his species was unfamiliar to Chakotay, his skin had a deathly pallor, just like the Cardassian's had. Chakotay took a step away from him.

Another patient finally noticed the visitors. She propped herself up with some difficulty and began to crawl toward them. Others saw the away team as well, and a chorus of desperate voices rent the air. Some of their words were incoherent, but Chakotay could make out a few phrases as the people crawled forward: "Help us! Save me! *Kill* me!"

"What's the matter with them?" he whispered to Tuvok.

"A serious illness," answered the Vulcan with tight-lipped understatement.

Chakotay tapped his combadge. "Away team to transporter room. Beam us up, but on a ten-second delay. Get out of the transporter room before we materialize."

"Yes, sir," said the Bolian, not hiding the worry in his voice. "Is everything all right?"

"No," answered Chakotay as he stepped away from the advancing tide of disease and death. "It's not."

## Chapter Two

It was the morning of his twelfth birthday, and his father had promised him something special—a trip to the Yukon Delta National Wildlife Refuge to observe Kodiak bears fishing for salmon. Living in Valdez, Alaska, did have its advantages, and so did having a father who was important enough in the Federation to command his own shuttlecraft and pilot. Will wasn't exactly sure what his father did in outer space—only that it involved diplomacy and lots of traveling. He tried hard not to resent the time he had to spend in boarding schools and living with other families, who were always eager to do a favor for Kyle Riker.

That was why it was so special to wake up in a mountain cabin on the slopes of Mount Waskey and see his dad waving to him from the meadow, where a gleaming shuttlecraft waited. In the distance, snowy peaks shimmered like amethysts and diamonds against a lustrous pearl sky. To the north, the Tikchik Lakes gripped the vast land like fingers of mercury. Will took a breath, delighting in the musky pine scent. The cool breeze carried sounds of trickling water from the snow thaw, along with the calls of terns and geese. And there was his dad, waving to him from the shuttlecraft.

The gangly twelve-year-old strode across the frozen grass, which crunched satisfyingly under his boots, and he watched as his father inspected the small craft. Although it was a shiny new shuttle—with warp drive—Kyle Riker never took the condition of his ship for granted. When something needed to be done, like inspection before a take-off, he didn't hesitate to do it himself. His dad got things done, no matter what the cost, and Will figured that was his true value to the Federation.

"Hi, son!" he said jovially as the boy approached. Kyle Riker was a tall, robust man with a square jaw, piercing eyes, and a strong handshake. Women loved him, and he was a commanding presence wherever he went, even the Alaskan wilderness. Will was in awe of him.

"Should I wake up the pilot?" asked the boy.

"No, let him sleep. I can fly us for a short jump like this. I'd have to tell him exactly where to go, anyway, and this will be easier." His dad circled the craft one more time, looking for damage to his shiny ship. "By the way, happy birthday."

"Thanks."

"Are you ready to go see the bears? I know a salmon run where they almost always show up. And I packed us a picnic lunch."

"Great!" In reality, Will would be thrilled if they did nothing but sit in the cabin and talk, he saw so little of his dad. But everything that Kyle Riker did had to be an occasion. A mere visit wasn't enough—they had to travel hundreds of kilometers to observe the largest bears in the world.

Dad opened the main hatch of the shuttle. "Jump in. Take the co-pilot's seat."

Will did as he was told, and he was excited to sit at the front of the cockpit, gazing at the amazing array of instruments and sensors. It seemed incredible that they could take off in this small vessel and travel all the way to the stars. More than anything else, that's what Will wanted to do.

His dad settled into the seat beside him and started punching buttons and flipping switches. The instrument panel blinked impressively, and the impulse engines began to hum.

"I wish we had time to hike there, or ride horses," said Kyle. "But we don't, so this will have to do."

"I think it's great," replied Will. The question of time saddened him a bit, because there was never enough of it. "When do you have to go back?"

"Tomorrow." Kyle began his preflight checklist.

"How come you can't stay longer?"

His father scowled, looking slightly resentful of the question. "I'm supposed to be on Rigel II in four days to negotiate with the Orions, and you don't keep Orions waiting. Hang on—here we go."

With a roar of thrusters, the shuttlecraft lifted off the ground and streaked into the pale blue sky, leaving the frozen meadow far below them. They swooped over lakes, forests, and mountains, heading northwest toward the ocean, which glittered in the morning sun like the aurora borealis.

Will knew he shouldn't bother his dad with a million questions, but it might be months before he saw him again. With childlike directness, he pointed to the brilliant sky and asked, "How come you live out there, and I live here?"

"Don't you like it in Alaska?" asked his dad with surprise.

"Sure, it's okay." Will didn't mention that he had never lived anywhere else, so he didn't have anything to compare it with. "I'd like it more if you lived here, too."

"Well, I do live here . . . officially."

"But you're never here."

His dad's scowl deepened. "Are you trying to spoil this trip? I'm here now, aren't I? And I came a long way for your birthday."

Will knew he should shut up, but he had always spoken his mind. And this had been bothering him for a long time. "Dad, why can't I live with you . . . out there?"

Kyle laughed. "On a starbase? In a little five-by-five room, with no scenery at all? It's okay for me, but I'm only there a few days every couple of months. It's just a place to hang my hat between assignments. And the places I go are often dangerous. Believe me, Rigel II is no place for a child. Besides, you need to have some stability in your life, with your school and friends."

"I need to have my dad around," said Will bluntly. "I feel like an orphan sometimes."

"I don't need this," muttered Kyle Riker. "I drop everything and travel twenty light-years for your birthday, and for what? To get chewed out?"

Will hung his head. "I'm sorry, Dad. I'm glad you're here, I really am. But it's just that . . . when you're here, it makes it worse later . . . when you go away."

His father nodded sympathetically, but he kept his eyes on his instrument panel. "You know, Will, I didn't plan for your mother to die when you were so young. The plan was that you would have a home and at least one full-time parent. But it didn't happen that way. When you were little, I stayed close to home and tried to raise you as best I could,

17

but a man only has so much time to make his mark in the universe. This is my time."

Will started to argue that it was also *his* time, that the months they were separated could never be recaptured. But the twelve-year-old didn't have the words or the experience to debate his father. He would often look back and see that his dad had probably decided at that moment to desert him entirely. If it was painful to return home for brief visits and then be separated, he must have figured it would be less painful to never come home at all.

"Lieutenant Riker," droned a voice, "when I clap my hands, you will awaken. You'll feel fine and well rested, and you'll remember what you told me."

A sharp sound jolted the man who called himself Thomas Riker. He blinked at the counselor and remembered where he was—not cruising above the Alaskan wilderness but in a consultation room aboard the *U.S.S. Gandhi*. Dr. Carl Herbert was a skilled ship's counselor, and he had hypnotically regressed Riker to his childhood during the session. It was hard for Tom to come back from that simpler time, before everything had turned to crud.

He mustered a smile. "I'm sorry, Doctor, what did you ask me?"

"You said something about how your father had decided on your twelfth birthday to abandon you a few years later. Do you really think that's true?"

Tom shrugged. "Who knows? That was the only time we ever talked about my feelings. I saw him less and less after that. The last time I saw him I was fifteen years old."

"However, it is true that Will Riker has seen your father since then and made amends."

Riker scowled. "That's not *me*. Although we may be

physically identical, we're two different people. You can't compare us."

"Sorry." Dr. Herbert pursed his lips and frowned deeply. "I only meant that perhaps *you* could make peace with your father, too."

"That other Riker has had lots of opportunities I never had, and that was one of them." The bearded man stood and paced. "Are we here to talk about my father?"

"No. We're here to talk about you." The counselor folded his hands in front of him. "Lieutenant, you have some very serious issues with abandonment. First, you fear your mother abandoned you, although you know logically it wasn't her fault. Then your father actually *did* abandon you—an act which you've never forgiven or forgotten. Then Starfleet accidentally marooned you on Nervala IV—for eight years. It could be said that your own double rejected you, and that might be the most devastating of all."

"So you're saying I probably should be in therapy for the rest of my life," grumbled Tom. "I'll agree to that, if you'll just clear me again for active duty."

Now it was the counselor's turn to rise to his feet and begin pacing the nondescript chamber. "Lieutenant," he began slowly, "we're about to patrol the Demilitarized Zone, with a good possibility of seeing action against the Maquis. And you were heard voicing pro-Maquis sentiments."

Riker took a deep breath, trying to stay calm. "In every other mission I've ever been on, we're supposed to discuss the pros and cons of using force. Since when is asking questions a treasonous crime?"

"Since it's the Maquis," answered Dr. Herbert with a sigh. "You're right, they're not like any other enemy we've ever faced. They're *us*—former Starfleet officers and colonists. We have to be sure that everyone on bridge duty is unquestionably loyal to the Federation."

"And what makes you think I'm not?"

"Your background," answered the counselor sympathetically. "We've talked about your issues with abandonment, and who has been more abandoned than the settlers in the DMZ?"

Tom laughed. "You know, Doc, if Commander Crandall heard you say that, you'd be confined to quarters the same as I am."

The counselor frowned. "Commander Crandall is just doing her job."

Riker sucked in his cheeks, careful not to speak his mind. As far as he was concerned, Emma Crandall had had it in for him since the first day he arrived on the *Gandhi. She thinks I'm after her job, just because that other Riker is the most famous first officer in Starfleet. She's been looking for an excuse to stick me in the doghouse, and this is it.*

"I think I have a way out of this," said Tom, slumping back into his chair. "I want to transfer over to the medical branch. That will get me off the bridge and away from Emma Crandall. It will also allow me to pursue a career that is different than my double's. I won't even be able to help the Maquis, except to heal them if they get sick."

"It will take you years to become a doctor."

Riker sighed. "One thing I learned during my eight years on Nervala IV—patience is a virtue."

Dr. Herbert took a padd off his desk and began to make notes. "I'll recommend your transfer to medical—and your reinstatement—but it will have to be approved by Commander Crandall."

"There's always a catch, isn't there?" replied Tom Riker.

\* \* \*

Two hours later, Tom was sitting in his quarters, watching a video log of Kodiak bears fishing for salmon in a wild Alaskan stream. That day with his father, on his twelfth birthday, they hadn't actually seen any bears, although they had hiked several kilometers along a beautiful stream. His dad had been disappointed, but not the boy—he could see bears anytime, but not his father. They had sat on the bank of the stream, eating their picnic lunch, while his dad talked about the far-flung worlds he had visited, and the incredible species he had known.

One thing his father and he could both agree upon: there was no place like outer space. Kyle's enthusiasm had instilled in the boy a burning desire to see those strange planets and people. In fact, the young Riker had outdone his civilian father by joining Starfleet. If possible, he would see even more amazing sights and do more amazing things than his dad had ever dreamed of. Although Kyle Riker hadn't realized there was a competition going on, there was.

Unfortunately, that wanderlust and ambition had been severely dampened by the long years spent on Nervala IV. Now Tom Riker didn't know what he wanted, except to be something different than Kyle Riker or the man called Will Riker.

On the viewer, he watched the great brown bears, who stood almost four meters tall, as they frolicked like cubs in the rushing stream. Catching leaping fish with a swipe of a claw wasn't easy, and the bears often failed. But they looked as if they were having fun. He realized that life wasn't worth it unless fun was involved. Unfortunately, Tom couldn't remember the last time Starfleet had been fun.

A chime sounded at his door, and Riker turned off the viewer. "Come in!"

The door slid open, and a slim woman with short dark hair entered his quarters. Under different circumstances, he could have been attracted to Commander Emma Crandall, but that had never been an option on the *Gandhi*. He jumped to his feet and stood at attention behind his desk, trying not to show the loathing he had for the ship's first officer. She was capable, but she never seemed to have any fun.

"At ease, Lieutenant," she told him in a tone of voice that did nothing to put him at ease.

"Yes, sir." Tom put his hands behind his back and remained standing.

Crandall scowled. "I've seen the counselor's report, and I'm frankly amazed. You want to toss away years of training and bridge experience in order to start a new career in medicine? I don't get you, Riker."

He opened his mouth to reply, but realized that he might make things worse. Then again, how could things be worse?

"Permission to speak freely?" he asked.

Crandall's scowl deepened, because she really didn't like her officers speaking freely. "Very well."

"Commander, you've never understood me, and you've always been wrong about me."

She began to protest, but Riker kept talking while he had the chance. "You think I'm interested in your job, and at one time, I would have been. But I've been through an experience that you can't begin to understand. I had eight years stolen from my life and career . . . and given to someone else. You think I'm a threat; others treat me like an imposter. To everyone, I'm an oddity. Face it, my chances of rising very far in the command structure are dim.

"I need to do something different, something that will make me stop dwelling on my own problems. If I can help other people, maybe I can help myself. In medicine, I'll have a chance to start over, without leaving Starfleet."

Crandall's expression softened a bit, and for the first time in almost two years, she looked at him with sympathy. "You have too much experience to be an orderly in sickbay, but I have a related job you could do. Although it's medical, it also requires command skills."

Riker leaned forward. "I'm listening."

"In addition to our patrol duties, we have to deliver medical teams and supplies to the observation posts along the DMZ. Some of them have been deluged by refugees. The captain thinks it will be more efficient to have a personnel shuttlecraft do these runs instead of the *Gandhi*. So we need a medical courier. You would be in command of a crew of two—yourself and the co-pilot."

Riker smiled gratefully. "Well, we all have to start somewhere. I'll take the job, Commander. Can I have Lieutenant Youssef?"

"Our most experienced pilot?" said Crandall, bristling at the very idea. "I think not. We have a new pilot on board, name Ensign Shelzane—you can teach her the ropes."

Riker nodded. "Thank you, Commander. I won't let you down."

"I hope not. You leave at sixteen hundred hours for Outpost Sierra III. Report to main shuttlebay." Emma Crandall started for the door, then turned back to give him a half smile. "If you want to wear a blue medical tunic instead of a red one, it's okay with me. In a way, I envy you, Lieutenant. Sometimes I think I'd like to make a change."

"You'll be promoted to captain soon," Riker assured her. "Just be patient."

Emma Crandall stiffened her spine and put on her command face again. "One more thing: try not to get into any discussions about the Maquis. I will admit, I made an example of you, so that the talking wouldn't get out of hand. I'm sorry about that, but it was necessary. On this ship, we don't set policy—we follow orders. Like it or not, the Maquis are the enemy until further notice."

"Yes, sir," answered Riker. He hadn't sympathized or thought all that much about the Maquis until recently, when everyone just assumed he must be a sympathizer. This oppressive atmosphere was another good reason to get off the *Gandhi.*

"I'll stay far away from the Maquis," promised Lieutenant Riker.

*My first command,* Riker thought ruefully as he inspected the squat, boxy craft known simply as *Shuttle 3.* A Type-8 personnel shuttlecraft, she accommodated a maximum of ten people, including crew, in very tight quarters. *Shuttle 3* had warp drive and a transporter, but no weaponry. According to the manifest, they would be transporting six members of the med team, plus the two crew. What worried him were all the boxes of supplies and equipment the shuttlebay workers kept loading onto the small craft. With all that weight on board, he feared she might handle sluggishly in a planet's atmosphere.

Rounding the bow of the shuttle, the lieutenant caught sight of his reflection in the front window. He looked quite dashing in his blue and black tunic, denoting his transfer to the medical branch. A new ship, a new uniform, and a new assignment that would actually do some good in the galaxy—maybe his life was turning around. Tom hadn't felt so hopeful since the day he had been rescued from Nervala IV. He tried not to think about how quickly all those hopes had been dashed.

"Lieutenant Riker?" said an inquisitive voice. He turned to see a diminutive, blue-skinned Benzite female. She was the first Benzite he'd seen who didn't rely on a breathing apparatus hanging from her neck.

"You must be Ensign Shelzane," he said with a charming smile. "Pleased to meet you."

She nodded formally. "Thank you, sir. I've been on the *Gandhi* for a month—it's odd that we haven't met before."

"Well, I've been incognito for a couple of weeks," explained Riker. "You're a shuttlecraft pilot, I presume."

"Class two rating," she answered proudly, "although I haven't logged that many hours of solo flight."

"You will on this assignment, because I intend to get my beauty sleep."

Shelzane forced a polite laugh. "Yes, sir. Are you also a doctor?"

Riker smiled and plucked at his blue tunic. "No, I'm just a . . . a medical courier. Here come the doctors."

He pointed to six more people in blue uniforms who had just entered the vast shuttlebay. They strode briskly between the parked shuttles, and Riker was struck by their youth. Like the young Benzite in front of him, they were just starting their Starfleet careers, and they did everything with self-important urgency. He wanted to tell them to slow down, to live more in the moment. But youth must be served.

Maybe he was a fool to think he could start over at this late stage of his career, but what did he have to lose? Maybe he was nothing but a glorified shuttle pilot, but it felt bigger than that. This mission felt like a step toward destiny, at least personal destiny.

After the introductions were made, Riker and Shelzane shoehorned their passengers into the cramped compartment, then they took their seats in the cockpit. A row of seats had been pulled to make room for the supplies, and the passengers were practically sitting in each others' laps. Every spare centimeter was taken up by crates and boxes. Riker was glad it was only a twenty-hour trip to Sierra III, because they would be at each others' throats if they had to spend any more time in these tight quarters.

During his preignition checklist, Riker tried to think like his father and not miss anything. They weren't over the allowed weight for the craft, but they were darn close. He whispered to Shelzane, "I think we need to compensate for all the weight we're carrying. What if we open the plasma injectors in the main cryo tank to give the impulse engines a little boost."

The Benzite looked at him with alarm. "Sir, that is somewhat unorthodox. It would also cut down our fuel efficiency by twenty or thirty percent."

"As soon as we're away from the *Gandhi*'s gravity, we'll go back to normal," he assured the worried ensign. "Don't worry, I'm used to doing things on the fly."

The Benzite gulped. "I hope you're the one taking us out of dock."

"Yes, and you'll be glad I boosted the engines when I do."

A few minutes later, the preparations were complete, and Riker tapped his comm panel. "*Shuttle 3* to bridge, requesting permission to launch."

"Crandall here," came the businesslike response. "You are cleared for launch, *Shuttle 3*. Lieutenant, I'd appreciate it if you returned in one piece. We've got lots of supplies that need to be delivered. Good fortune to you."

"Thank you, sir," answered Riker cheerfully. His fortune hadn't been all that good, and he was ready for a change in that department. For Commander Crandall, these few words were as close as she had ever come to bubbly enthusiasm. He punched up a wide view of the area on his viewscreen and kept it on during the launch.

The *Galaxy*-class starship hung suspended in space among the dazzling stars, appearing much like her better-known sister ship, the *Enterprise.* Double doors slid open atop the immense saucer section, and a tiny shuttlecraft darted out, looking like an insect escaping from an open window. The Type-8 shuttlecraft cruised to a distance of several thousand kilometers from the *Gandhi,* then with a flash of light, she disappeared into warp.

# Chapter Three

LIEUTENANT RIKER CUT impulse engines and slowed the
shuttlecraft to a stately drift through a sea of widely scattered asteroids. Some were only a few meters wide, while
others were several kilometers wide. Slowly they approached a monstrous rock that was over eight kilometers
in diameter. It was as dark as obsidian, yet its center
appeared even darker. Riker needed a few seconds to realize that the asteroid had a mammoth hole in its middle, at
least one kilometer across. In comparison with the black
asteroid and the blackness of space, the chasm looked even
darker—like a black hole.

Despite the deserted appearance of this region, these
were the correct coordinates. "Open up a secure channel,"
he told Shelzane.

"Yes, sir," replied the fish-faced, blue-skinned Benzite, working her board with webbed fingers. "Channel open."

He tapped his panel and said, *"Shuttle 3* to outpost, this is Lieutenant Riker from the *Gandhi,* requesting permission to dock."

"Permission granted," answered a pleasant female voice. *"Shuttle 3,* are we glad to see you. Take dock one, the first open dock to starboard."

"Thank you."

"We're lowering shields and force field. Proceed when ready."

With a flash of light, the dark cavity in the asteroid turned into a blazing neon pit. Pulsing beacons guided the way to a mammoth spacedock within, and the walls of the chasm glittered with sensors, dish arrays, and weapons. Trying not to be distracted by the remarkable sight, Riker spread his fingers over the conn and piloted the tiny shuttlecraft into the glowing heart of the asteroid.

"Well, it's about time," muttered one of the doctors behind him.

Riker ignored the crack, as he had ignored so many others during the past twenty hours. Although the ship's sensors claimed that life support was working flawlessly, he could swear that he was beginning to *smell* his passengers.

At least Ensign Shelzane had proven to be skilled, even-tempered, and unflappable. He had to give Commander Crandall credit—she was a good judge of personnel.

As they cruised toward the landing dock, Riker glanced around the cavernous installation. He was somewhat surprised to see several unfamiliar and battered ships docked at the rear bays; they didn't look like Starfleet vessels. This was supposed to be a secret outpost, but it looked more like a junkyard at the moment.

Shelzane noticed it, too, and her pale eyes darted to Riker before going back to her instruments. The lieutenant concentrated on the docking, although a first-year cadet could have hit that huge target. They sat down with a gentle thud, and the umbilicals began to whir.

When Riker heard the clamps latch on to the shuttle's hatch, he sat back in his chair and smiled at Shelzane. "We made it in one piece . . . without killing any of the passengers," he whispered.

The ensign nodded. She couldn't really smile, but her heavily lidded eyes twinkled with amusement. "This job will test my social skills more than my flying."

When the hatch opened, the medical team gathered around the exit, anxious to get off. *Nothing like twenty hours in a shuttlecraft with eight strangers to give one claustrophobia,* thought Riker. *Welcome to Starfleet.*

Without warning, the lights in the great cavern went out, eliciting gasps from the passengers. Once again, the void in the asteroid was as black as space, only without the glistening stars to give it some cheer. Seen from afar, the shuttlecraft glowed like a feeble lantern in a great hall.

A few of the passengers thanked him as they filed out, and Riker nodded pleasantly. He held nothing against them—in many respects, it was easier being a crew member than a passenger on a trip like this. At least he had been occupied. From eight years' experience, he knew how hard it was to pass the time when nothing needed doing and physical activity was difficult.

He and Shelzane shut down all but essential life support on the small craft, then they followed the medical team into the corridor. The last member of the team was just passing through a force-field security gate that demanded positive

30

identification. Riker stepped back to let Shelzane go first, but she stepped back and deferred to him.

*Oh, well, there's nothing else I can do,* thought Riker. He placed his hand on the security scanner, and the computer's feminine voice declared, "Commander William Riker, access granted."

Shelzane looked quizzically at him. *"Commander* Riker? Did you receive a promotion during the trip?"

"Hardly," muttered the bearded man, making sure the med team was some distance down the next corridor. "It's a long story. On the return trip, I'll tell you about it. Let's just say that Starfleet security systems have a bug in them where I'm concerned."

He walked through the gate and waited for Ensign Shelzane to gain admittance to the outpost. "How long do you think we'll be here?" asked the Benzite.

"Maybe long enough to get a meal," answered Riker. "They're expecting us back as soon as possible for more of these runs. I'm afraid this assignment is going to be hectic but not all that exciting."

"We'll see," answered the Benzite cheerfully.

As the party stepped off the dock, they were met by two officers, both wearing the red uniforms of command. One was a bald-headed Deltan and the other was a tall, antennaed Andorian. Since both were male, neither one could be the friendly female with whom Riker had spoken earlier, he noted with disappointment.

The Andorian conducted the medical team down one corridor, while the Deltan nodded politely to the new arrivals. Two gold-shirted technicians strode into the landing dock behind them, and Riker assumed they would take charge of the cargo.

"Hello, Lieutenant Riker. Welcome to Outpost Sierra

III," said the Deltan, with a slight smile. "I'm Ensign Parluna. I believe we met once aboard the *Enterprise.*"

Riker scowled. "That wasn't me."

"But weren't you first officer—"

"You're mistaken," said Riker brusquely. "Now if we could get a bite to eat, and maybe a walk to stretch our legs, we'll be on our way."

The Deltan nodded, but his hairless brow was still knit in puzzlement. "As you wish, sir. However, our commanding officer, Captain Tegmeier, was hoping to meet with you and ask a favor."

"A favor? We're just medical couriers—what could we do for your CO?"

"I'll let her ask," said Ensign Parluna. "But I will show you something on our way. Will you please follow me."

As they walked down a long doorless and windowless corridor, Riker could feel both of the ensigns looking curiously at him, wondering how Ensign Parluna could be mistaken about meeting him. For a while after being rescued from Nervala IV, he had taken the time to explain to people why they didn't know him, even though they had met someone who looked exactly like him. Now he didn't waste words. *Let them investigate his record and figure it out.* He hated being so brusque, but it did no good reliving his misfortune over and over again.

The Deltan took a left turn at a junction in the corridor, and they finally came to a row of doors. He opened one marked "Recreation," and Riker wondered if they would interrupt the CO during her exercise period. As soon as he got a glimpse inside the room, he knew he was wrong.

The room was full of bedraggled, sorry-looking people—men, women, and children—several of them dressed in rags. A few of them glanced at the visitors, but most stared straight ahead with vacant eyes. A handful of children were playing board games and watching video logs, but most of the people looked bored and disillusioned. Riker glanced at Shelzane, and he could see the young officer was deeply affected by the sight. Without saying a word, the Deltan ushered them out and closed the door.

"Refugees," he explained. "And these aren't even the wounded, sick ones—the ones who survived Cardassian torture and starvation. They're in sickbay, which we've had to enlarge twice. That's why we need the supplies and med team."

"I thought this was supposed to be a secret outpost," said Riker.

The Deltan sighed. "So did we. As you can see, the secret is out. They've been flooding in here ever since the treaty drove them from their homes in the DMZ."

"That's terrible!" blurted Shelzane.

"The price of peace," muttered the Deltan. "The awkward thing is that we can't let them leave here, because it's a secret base, even though everybody apparently *knows* about it. I mean, we can't let them leave in their own ships, most of which wouldn't get very far, anyway. So we have to impound their ships and hold them, until we can find official transportation to get them back to Earth . . . or wherever."

Riker crossed his arms. "I bet I could guess what this favor is."

"Let's go to the commissary," said the Deltan with forced cheer, "and you can have that meal you so richly deserve. The captain will join you there."

The lieutenant nodded, knowing he didn't have much choice. If these pathetic refugees were the price of peace, he wondered if it was worth it.

\* \* \*

As he gobbled down the finest steak he had ever gotten from a food replicator, Riker watched Shelzane pick at the purple leaves on her plate. He felt sorry for the young Benzite, who evidently hadn't seen much of the cruelty and capriciousness of life. One moment, a person is on top of the world, living high in a Federation colony or on a sleek Starfleet vessel, and the next moment, he's wearing rags, staring at the ceiling, abandoned. Thomas Riker felt sorry for the refugees, but he had seen too much in his own eventful life to be shocked by their plight.

Shelzane glanced up, catching him looking at her. "What's going to happen to them?"

"They're going to start over," answered Riker. "They've lost everything, but they're still alive. A lot of people in the DMZ weren't so lucky. When it comes down to it, all we've got is our wits and tenacity."

"But Starfleet should try to help them," insisted Shelzane.

Riker shrugged. "On most issues, Starfleet employs Vulcan logic: the needs of the many outweigh the needs of the few. You'd better learn that, Ensign."

She peered intently at him. "You're very cynical, Lieutenant."

"Just realistic. I was once idealistic like you. It's good to be like that for as long as you can, but I have a feeling that this assignment is going to break you of that."

Shelzane looked down at her plate and whispered, "They say that some Starfleet officers are going over to the Maquis—to fight against the Cardassians in a hopeless cause. I feel sorry for the refugees, but I can't imagine ever doing something like that."

"Me neither," agreed Riker. "I don't think I could ever

feel that strongly about something. As you say, I'm too cynical." He took another bite of steak.

"Around here, cynicism is good," interjected another feminine voice.

Riker looked up to see an attractive blond woman approaching their table. Since she was wearing captain's pips, he jumped to his feet, certain he was about to meet the commanding officer of the outpost. Shelzane did the same.

"Relax," said the captain wearily. "We don't stand on ceremony around here. What good would it do us? I'm Captain Alicia Tegmeier."

"It's a pleasure," said Riker, recognizing her friendly voice from his initial contact with the outpost. "I'm Lieutenant Riker, and this is Ensign Shelzane. Won't you have a seat?"

"Thank you."

"We were a bit surprised to see the scope of your refugee problem," Shelzane explained.

"So were we," answered the captain. "We were hoping the *Gandhi* herself would come, and we could off-load the refugees, but it didn't happen that way. So now I've got to beg—can you take a few of them back to the *Gandhi* with you?"

"Certainly," Shelzane answered quickly.

Riker shot her a glance, and the Benzite lowered her eyes, knowing she had answered out of turn. Riker sounded very cautious as he remarked, "It's not really in the purview of our mission to transport refugees. However, if you ordered us to do so, we'd have no choice."

Captain Tegmeier slumped back in her chair and waved her hand. "Then I order you to take as many as you can. I'm sure I'll get chewed out for that by the admiralty, but I welcome an opportunity to explain the situation to them.

Having a secret outpost overrun with refugees is a bit of a security risk."

"We only have seating for six," said Riker. "How will you choose who goes?"

"We have two pregnant women in the group," said the captain. "I'd like to send them first. We're not exactly equipped for dealing with newborn babies here. A young couple showed up yesterday, and they claim they have intelligence to report, but they will only tell an admiral. There are several orphaned children—I'd like to give two of them a break."

Riker shook his head in amazement. "How long can you cope with this?"

"Not much longer, but we've been assured that Starfleet will eventually pick them all up. Then we'll relocate this asteroid. At least now we can cope with the medical problems, thanks to you." Captain Tegmeier gave him a warm smile.

"I wish we could stay longer," answered Riker with sincerity.

"We could use you," replied Tegmeier. "We have to stay on constant vigil—not only are there the refugees, but the Cardassians are experts at sneaking in and out of the DMZ. By the time we've discovered them, they're usually gone."

"We'll report back on the conditions here," said Riker.

"I wish you would."

With her napkin, Ensign Shelzane daintily wiped the tendrils around her mouth. "I'm ready to go when you are, sir."

"Right." The handsome lieutenant managed a smile and pushed himself away from the table. "Is the cargo off the shuttle?"

"Yes, it is," answered Captain Tegmeier. "Do you want to interview any of the passengers you'll be taking?"

"No, I trust your judgment. It's been a short but pleasant visit, Captain."

"I'd like to encourage you to come often. Have a safe journey back, Lieutenant . . . Ensign." She turned and strode through the commissary, nodding encouragment to the officers she passed.

Riker began to think that his new assignment would be a good change of pace. Out here on the edge of the DMZ, he had no bizarre history or hierarchy of command to deal with—he was just a medical courier bringing much-needed supplies. He would make his deliveries and go on to the next post, like the pony express. There would always be new people to meet.

He smiled at Shelzane. "I think I'm going to like this job."

The ensign looked thoughtful. "It's fortunate that Benzites require little sleep."

"Good, then I'll let you take the first shift."

Ten minutes later, they were sitting in the cockpit of *Shuttle 3,* going over the preflight checklist. In the cavernous interior of the asteroid, it was still eerily dark, and the windows of the shuttlecraft looked opaque. Without passengers and cargo, the cabin almost looked spacious, and Riker wished it would stay that way for a while. However, it was not to be.

The hatch opened, and a security officer stuck his head in. "Lieutenant Riker, are you ready to receive your passengers?"

"Sure. I hope they're not expecting a starship."

"This is better than they're used to." The security officer stepped aside, allowing two small Bynar children to enter the cabin. Whether they were actual siblings was hard to tell, but the two of them had bonded in their desperate situation; they held hands as if they were inseparable.

"Sit up front," Riker told them with a smile, "so you can watch Ensign Shelzane pilot the ship."

"Thank you," they replied in unison, speaking so softly they could barely be heard. They both squeezed into one seat, and Riker didn't bother to separate them.

The Bynar children were followed by two females, both obviously in the advanced stages of pregnancy. One was Coridan, judging by her distinctive hairstyle—half of her head sheared and the other half with straight, black hair down to her shoulder. She looked morose, as if resigned to some horrible fate, and she slouched to the back row of seats without a word. He guessed that the other woman was human, until she smiled at him and shook her head.

"Actually I'm a Betazoid," she said.

"I've always gotten along well with Betazoids," he replied.

"I can tell you have great affection for us."

Their conversation was cut short when a young Tiburonian couple entered the cabin, holding hands as tightly as the Bynar children had. With their bald heads and elephantine ears, they looked more alien than the others, and Riker recalled that Tiburonians had a reputation for being brilliant but difficult. These two looked wary.

"We were told we'd be going to a large starship," said the male.

"You will be, as soon as we get there," answered Riker. "I understand you have some intelligence to report."

"But only in a face-to-face meeting with an admiral," insisted the female.

"I've found admirals highly overrated, but we'll find one for you. Have a seat, please."

Once all the passengers were situated, Riker turned to address them. "I'm Lieutenant Riker, and this is Ensign

Shelzane. I know all of you have had a tough time, and I would like this trip to be as pleasant as possible. But we don't have many amenities on this shuttlecraft, and the quarters will be tight. In other words, you'll basically have to sit there and not make demands on us. If you do that, I promise we'll get you to our starship as quickly as possible."

"How long will the trip take?" asked the dour Coridan.

Riker glanced at Shelzane, who consulted her computer screen. "If the *Gandhi* stays on course and schedule, it should be about twenty-six hours," she reported.

"The sooner we get going, the sooner we'll arrive." Riker tapped the comm panel. "*Shuttle 3* to operations, requesting permission to leave."

"You are cleared," replied a businesslike male voice. "Please maintain subspace silence in the vicinity of the station."

Beacons suddenly illuminated the depths of the great chasm, and hydraulics whirred as the docking mechanism retracted from the hatch. Riker sat back in his seat and smiled at Shelzane. "Take her out, Ensign."

"Yes, sir," replied the Benzite, sounding eager to prove herself. With considerable skill, she plied her console, and the tiny craft lifted off the dock and moved gracefully through the neon pit. Riker crossed his arms and closed his eyes, planning on getting a little shut-eye.

Once the tiny shuttle had cleared the opening of the chasm, the brilliant lights abruptly went off, and Outpost Sierra III again looked like nothing but a craggy rock floating in the vastness of space.

Thomas Riker laughed and shook his head, then he put the computer padd down. For the third straight time, the

Bynar children had beaten him in a game of three-dimensional tic-tac-toe. "You guys are too good for me."

They gave him identical, enigmatic smiles and looked at one another with satisfaction. "We thank you," said one.

"For the game," finished the other.

"Would you like to play each other?" he asked.

"That would be—"

"Pointless."

Riker nodded and looked back at the other passengers on the shuttlecraft. They were a surly lot, except for the pregnant Betazoid, who occasionally flashed him a smile. The rest of the time she sat in contemplative silence with her hands folded over her extended abdomen. He didn't expect refugees who had been driven from their homes to be exactly cheerful, but they might be a bit more grateful for the ride back to Federation space.

Then again, maybe they didn't know what they were getting themselves into. Most of them had probably been born in what was now the DMZ, and they had lived all their lives there. To them, the Federation was a nebulous concept, especially now that it had seemingly deserted them. He wondered whether the two pregnant women had spouses and families to help them, or whether they were as alone as they appeared.

"You're wondering about me," said the Betazoid woman with a wan smile. "I happen to be alone, although not for long." She patted her ample girth.

"I'm sorry," said Riker. With the others watching and listening, he wished he were also telepathic, so they could continue this conversation in private. But privacy was hard to come by on *Shuttle 3*.

"I've never seen Betazed," said the woman. "Have you?"

"It's beautiful," he assured her. "The garden spot of the

Federation, with the friendliest people I've ever met." He paused, thinking about Lwaxana Troi. "Even too friendly."

She nodded eagerly. "I always meant to go there one day. I didn't think it would be . . . under these circumstances."

Unable to say or do anything that would change the circumstances, the lieutenant turned to his co-pilot. "How are you doing, Ensign? Getting tired?"

"It's only been three hours," answered the Benzite. "Perhaps in two hours more, I could use relief."

"Just let me know when you're ready. That short nap refreshed me."

The young Tiburonian male rose to his feet. "Is it all right if I stretch my legs?"

"Sure," answered Riker, "but there's not much place to go."

"I realize that." With two steps, he stood behind Riker and Shelzane, gazing with interest at the ensign's readouts. "Where are we, approximately?"

"We have just passed the Omicron Delta region," she answered.

"Then we're still fairly close to the DMZ."

"Yes. That is where the *Gandhi* is patrolling."

"Are you a navigator?" asked Riker.

The Tiburonian nodded. "In a way, I am. I was studying stellar cartography at the university on Ennan VI . . . until the Cardassians burned it down."

"I'm sorry," said Shelzane.

He scowled. "If you two keep saying you're sorry for every wrong committed against us, that's all you'll ever say to us. At some point, we have to stop feeling sorry for ourselves and get on with life."

"That's a good attitude," replied Riker, giving him a sympathetic smile. "We'll do what we can to help you."

"I know you will." The Tiburonian again studied the

readouts with a scholarly interest. "Our speed is warp three? That's very fast for a craft of this size."

"Common for a Type-8 shuttle," answered Shelzane.

The Tiburonian sighed. "Where I come from, we only had impulse shuttles. Had we ships like this, more of us might have survived."

"Kanil," said the female Tiburonian, "there's no sense talking about it."

"No, I suppose not." His shoulders drooped, and he turned to Riker. "I don't suppose you have any food on board?"

Before the lieutenant could answer, there came an awful groan from the rear of the shuttlecraft. He whirled around to see the pregnant Coridan gripping her swollen stomach and writhing in her seat. The Betazoid woman staggered to her feet and tried to comfort her, as did the female Tiburonian, while the Bynar children looked on with eerie calm.

Immediately, Riker reached under his console, opened a panel, and grabbed a medkit. His worst fear was that he would have to deliver a premature baby, when he knew very little about delivering babies and less about Coridan physiology. But a groaning, pregnant woman demanded action. He glanced at Shelzane, who gave him a nod, as if to say she would handle the shuttle while he handled the medical emergency.

He vaulted to his feet and muscled his way past the Tiburonian male, who seemed rooted to the spot, unable to move. When he reached the distressed woman, she was panting, and her eyes rolled back in her head. The other women stepped away to allow him room, although what he was going to do for her he didn't know.

"Are you in labor?" he asked urgently. "How far along are you?"

"Not . . . far . . . enough," she muttered through clenched teeth. "The pain . . . the *pain!*"

"I can do something for the pain." Riker opened the med-kit and reached inside for a hypospray. While he loaded the instrument with a painkiller, he felt a slight shudder, as if the shuttlecraft were coming out of warp. He turned to tell Shelzane that she didn't need to leave warp—it was better to keep going. That's when he saw the Benzite lying unconscious on the deck, with the Tiburonian seated at the conn.

"What the—"

He never finished the sentence, because the Coridan grabbed him by the shoulders with incredible strength and forced him headfirst into her lap. He struggled, but the young Tiburonian woman also attacked him; the two of them forced him onto his back and jumped upon him like women possessed.

Riker didn't like hitting women, but his instincts took over. He lashed out with his fist and smashed the Coridan in the mouth, sending her oversized body crashing back into her seat. Then he gripped the Tiburonian by the throat and tried to push her away, while she clawed at his face.

From the corner of his eye, he saw the Betazoid fumbling in the arms locker, pulling out a phaser pistol. Whose side was *she* on? Or were they all hijackers! He didn't have time to figure it out.

Riker grabbed the Tiburonian and yanked her around like a shield just as the Betazoid fired at him. The young woman took the full blast of the phaser set to stun, and she fell upon him like a dead weight. With adrenaline coursing through his veins, Riker tossed her off and scrambled to his feet, just as another phaser blast streaked past his head. He saw the Bynar children crouched behind their chairs, watching with wide eyes.

"Don't resist!" ordered the Betazoid, aiming her weapon to get another shot. "We won't hurt you!"

The only weapon at hand was the medkit, and Riker threw it at her with all his might. His aim was good, and the metal box bounced off her head with a thud, causing her to collapse to the deck. Riker dove for the discarded phaser and came up with it just as the Coridan jumped on his back. She was as determined and as strong as a sumo wrestler, and she shoved his face into the deck. Twisting around, he smashed her in the mouth with an elbow, and she slid off his back with a groan.

Riker crawled out from under the dead weight and staggered to his feet. He checked to make sure that the phaser was set to low stun before he fired at both her and the Betazoid.

With all three women immobilized, he turned his attention to the Tiburonian male, who was furiously working the shuttle controls. "Move away from there!" he ordered hoarsely. "Or I'll shoot!"

When the man didn't move immediately, the lieutenant drilled him in the back with the phaser, and he sprawled over the conn. From the stationary stars visible through the window, Riker realized that they must have come to a full stop.

The only ones left to subdue were the Bynar children, and they seemed content to stare at him with a mixture of curiosity and fear. *What kind of world is this?* Panting heavily, Riker stumbled into the cockpit to see how much damage the hijackers had done. He knew the Maquis were desperate, but to hijack an unarmed shuttlecraft was ridiculous!

He bent over Ensign Shelzane to check for a pulse and make sure she was still alive. She was, although a contusion on her skull was staining her blue skin with violet blood. Lying on the deck beside her was a length of metal pipe, obviously the weapon the Tiburonian had used to disable her. At least he had put down the hijacking and gained control of the ship—for the next several minutes. He had to act fast before the attackers came to.

Keeping an eye on the Bynar children, he set down the phaser pistol and grabbed the medkit to attend to his wounded comrade. Just as he loaded a hypospray with a coagulant, Riker felt a peculiar tingle along his spine. In the next instant, he realized it wasn't peculiar at all—it was a sensation he had felt many times. A transporter beam had locked onto him!

Riker reached for the phaser pistol, but his hand had already started to dematerialize—he couldn't close his fingers around it. Helpless, he stared at the Bynar children, and they stared back like porcelain dolls, until everything in the shuttlecraft faded from view.

# Chapter Four

LIEUTENANT RIKER MATERIALIZED not on a transporter pad as he expected, but directly inside an old-fashioned brig, with bars across the door. He charged forward and smashed into the bars, rattling them but not doing any real damage. The outer door whooshed open, and a wild-eyed Klingon woman entered, wielding a Ferengi phaser rifle.

At least she *looked* Klingon, although closer inspection led him to wonder, because her forehead ridges were not very pronounced. But the contemptuous scowl on her face sure made her look Klingon. "Back away!" she said with a snarl.

"Or what?" he demanded. "You'll hijack my shuttlecraft? You've already done that. But maybe you want to torture me—see if I know anything."

"The captain will be here in a moment," she replied. "Just shut up until then."

"What vessel is this? Are you Maquis . . . or something else?"

"This is the *Spartacus*," said an authoritative male voice.

Riker turned to see a commanding figure in a tan jacket enter the brig. He stared, because it appeared as if the dark-haired man had a maze tattooed on his forehead. Whatever outfit this was, it sure wasn't Starfleet.

"I'm Captain Chakotay," said the man, meeting Riker's hostile gaze. "And, yes, we are Maquis. Despite that, we mean you no harm."

"People keep telling me that," muttered Riker, "but somehow I don't believe it. You cracked open my co-pilot's skull, and you attacked us without provocation."

"Your co-pilot is receiving medical attention right now." Chakotay gave Riker a grudging smile. "And it sounds like you defended yourself fairly well. I'm glad we backed up our infiltration team, but we can't afford to leave anything to chance."

Riker shook his head in disbelief. "All this to hijack an unarmed shuttlecraft? If that's the scope of your ambition, it's a wonder Starfleet pays any attention to you at all."

"Shut up!" snapped the Klingon woman, threatening him with the phaser rifle.

"Stow it, B'Elanna," ordered the Maquis captain. "He's got a right to be angry. Don't worry, Lieutenant, it's not you or your shuttlecraft we want. It's your cargo."

"What cargo?"

"Aren't you carrying medical supplies?"

"We were, but we're empty on our return trip."

Chakotay scowled in anger and stepped over to a comm panel beside the door. He slammed it with a clenched fist. "Chakotay to bridge. Do we have a report yet on what they found on the shuttle?"

"Yes, Captain," answered a calm male voice. "We found only personnel—our own and the shuttlecraft's co-pilot."

"You're sure of that?"

"Yes, sir. No supplies were found on the shuttlecraft, other than standard-issue medkits. The wounded parties have been transferred to the *Singha* for medical attention."

From the captain's clenched jaw, Riker assumed this was very bad news. "All that trouble for nothing," he grumbled. "Chakotay out."

"Not for nothing," said the woman called B'Elanna. She glared at Riker. "We still have *him* and the shuttlecraft. And he's a doctor."

Riker shook his head. "No, I'm not—I'm just a medical courier who was in the wrong place at the wrong time. But I don't get this—if your people needed medical attention, why don't you just join the refugees? You could turn yourselves in."

With a heave of his broad shoulders, Chakotay stepped closer to Riker. "It's not us. We've got several million people in extreme danger who can't be moved. B'Elanna, open the cell door."

"What?" asked the Klingon in shock.

"Let him out. If we're going to help them, the lieutenant has got to help us of his free will."

Looking as if she disagreed wholeheartedly with this decision, the woman stepped back and pulled a lever on the other side of the room. She kept her phaser rifle trained on Riker as the bars retracted into the bulkhead.

"I'm not joining the Maquis," declared the prisoner as he stepped forward.

"I'm not asking you to," said Chakotay. "I'm asking you to help us save millions of lives. I presume that's why you joined the medical branch—to save lives."

Riker remained tight-lipped, unwilling to admit that altruism had only been one of several reasons, and maybe not the most important. He had already decided to say and do as little as possible, while waiting for a chance to escape.

The Klingon woman scowled. "Do you have a name, Starfleet?"

His lips thinned, because Riker knew he was on shaky ground. Anything he did to help these people could land him in a brig for the rest of his life, but antagonizing them could get him killed. *Better to keep my mouth shut.*

B'Elanna walked over to the comm panel and hit it with her fist. "Torres to bridge. Tuvok, have you tapped into the shuttle's computer yet?"

"Yes, I have," answered the same efficient voice that had answered them before.

"What's the name of our guest in the brig?"

"The computer identifies him as William T. Riker."

Chakotay blinked with surprise and stared more closely at his prisoner. "Are you the same William T. Riker who served aboard the *Enterprise?*"

Riker's jaw clamped shut, and he took a deep breath. Unfortunately, if he admitted to being *that* Riker, his chances of escape from this crew would be nil.

"Come on, Starfleet, answer," said B'Elanna Torres, leveling her phaser rifle at him. "Every prisoner of war is allowed to give his name, rank, and serial number."

"I'm not the Riker who serves aboard the *Enterprise,*" he finally answered. "In a transporter accident on Nervala IV, I was duplicated. My double left the planet and went on to serve aboard the *Enterprise,* while I got stranded there for eight years. I was only rescued two years ago, and now I'm assigned to the *Gandhi.*"

"You expect us to believe that?" scoffed Torres.

"I don't really give a damn what you believe!" snapped Riker. "What are you people but a bunch of two-bit space pirates? I find *you* hard to believe."

Torres started to swing the butt of her phaser rifle at his head, but Chakotay gripped the rifle and stopped her. "Calm down! We haven't got time for this. Whether he's William Riker or Santa Claus, it doesn't matter—he's the only link we've got to the medical supplies we need."

Breathing heavily, the woman tried to shake off her anger, but a fire still burned in her dark eyes. Despite his status as her enemy, Riker couldn't help but feel a kinship with this volatile woman. Like him, she harbored a bitterness and anger that couldn't be easily assuaged.

"What race are you?" he asked.

"I'm half-Klingon and half-human," she answered with some resentment. "I guess we're both freaks."

Chakotay waved his hand impatiently. "There's time to get to know each other later. Right now, Lieutenant Riker, I have to show you something."

"What if I don't want to see it?"

"I think you'll want to see it, because after you do, I'll let you go."

"Just like that?"

"Just like that. You can't do us any good stuck in this cell, but you can save a lot of lives if you're free. Let's go." The captain led the way out the door, and Riker followed, conscious of B'Elanna Torres at his back, aiming her phaser rifle at him.

After walking a few meters down a narrow corridor, Chakotay came to a ladder embedded in the bulkhead, and he climbed upward into a small hatch. With a glance over his shoulder at Torres, Riker followed the captain, and they emerged in a longer and wider corridor. Riker got the impression that the *Spartacus* was a rather small vessel, no more than a scout ship or an assault craft.

Chakotay strode down the corridor like a man with pressing matters on his conscience and time running out. He carried himself like a Starfleet officer, and Riker wondered whether he had ever served in Starfleet. Perhaps he had previously captained a merchant ship. What made a proud, competent man like this turn into a rebel in a ragtag fleet? These were the first Maquis he had ever met, and Captain Chakotay, at least, didn't fit his preconceptions.

B'Elanna Torres, on the other hand, was more the kind of person he thought would be attracted to the Maquis. She seemed a bit unstable, low in self-esteem, and angry at life. In short, she was damaged goods. Her Klingon side probably relished the prospect of dying a glorious death battling the imperious and callous Federation.

Riker knew he was damaged goods, too—a freak, as Torres had called them both. But he still had some ambition and loyalty to the Federation. Sure, the Federation was run by fallible beings who could make mistakes, but it was still the greatest hope for peace in the galaxy. He couldn't imagine what Chakotay could show him that would turn him against everything he believed in.

They entered a compact, clam-shaped bridge, and a Vulcan swiveled in his chair to glance at Riker before turning back to his instruments. *A Vulcan Maquis?* Of course, Vulcans could go mad—he had heard of it happening. Maybe everyone on the *Spartacus* was mad, even the dignified Chakotay.

Through the narrow cockpit window, he saw a Bajoran assault vessel off the bow, as well as his own star-crossed shuttlecraft. What could the Maquis hope to accomplish

51

with these three little ships out here in the middle of nowhere, a stone's throw from the DMZ? Like the attack on his shuttlecraft, this whole thing was surreal.

"Before you show me anything," said Riker, "I want to make sure that my co-pilot, Ensign Shelzane, is all right."

"Tuvok, hail the *Singha*," ordered Chakotay, "and have them put Ensign Shelzane on screen."

"Yes, sir."

"While he does that," said the captain, "let me ask you if you've ever heard of a planet named Helena."

Riker nodded. "I know it was on a list of planets in the DMZ that were turned over to the Cardassians."

"Yes, but it wasn't evacuated like most of the Federation colonies. The Helenites chose to stay and live under Cardassian rule, but something terrible has happened there."

"I have located Ensign Shelzane," interjected the Vulcan.

"On screen."

Riker turned with interest to the small viewscreen spanning the front of the bridge. The blank image switched to a view of a bustling sickbay, and Ensign Shelzane was lying on an examination table with a fresh bandage around her head. Upon seeing Riker, the blue-skinned humanoid sat up weakly.

"At ease, Ensign," he told her. "Have you been treated well?"

"As well as can be expected, I suppose. What happened to the shuttlecraft?"

"The passengers attacked us, stopped the shuttle, and then we were intercepted by these two Maquis vessels. Cooperate, but remember that you're a prisoner of war."

"Yes, sir. Are we going to be held long? Or exchanged?"

"I don't know." Riker glanced at Chakotay, who stepped in front of the screen.

"You and Lieutenant Riker will be released soon, along with your shuttlecraft," promised the captain. "Please try to rest. I'm sorry that our methods were violent, but Starfleet won't negotiate with *us*, only Cardassians." He motioned to the Vulcan, who ended the transmission.

"Satisfied, Lieutenant?" asked B'Elanna Torres.

Riker shrugged. He wasn't going to argue with someone who was aiming a phaser rifle at him.

"Tuvok," said the captain, "put on the vid log and explain matters to the lieutenant."

The Vulcan tapped his console. On the viewscreen appeared a beautiful, aquamarine planet, sparkling in the vivid light from a distant red sun. The surface of the planet had to be ninety percent ocean, with small green continents scattered across its vast waters. Riker had seen many Class-M planets, but none more lovely than this one.

"Helena," said Tuvok matter-of-factly. "It was a thriving world, inhabited by over four million people, mostly of mixed-species ancestry. The only thing that has protected them so far is the relative isolation of population centers on the various islands and continents."

The image shifted to a modern city street, which appeared to be deserted, despite sunny blues skies and balmy weather. Some kind of dead animal lay in the gutter, and there appeared to be a hunanoid corpse sprawled in an open doorway. Trash and leaves skittered across the empty thoroughfare, borne by a gentle breeze. It was an eerie scene, reminiscent of a planet ravaged by warfare, only without the full-scale destruction.

"This is the city of Padulla," explained Tuvok, "as we observed it four days ago. The streets are deserted, because a devastating plague has struck this continent. The disease is similar to anthrax, only several times more deadly and contagious. It is caused by an unusual combination of three prions, which are transmitted by air, water, saliva, and other bodily fluids."

Now the view changed to the interior of some cavernous hall, where sick people lay in haphazard rows stretching the length of the room. It wasn't a hospital, so Riker had to assume the hospitals were all full. Coughs and groans filled the disturbing scene. Two visitors in white environmental suits moved among the sick like ghosts, or angels. When the video log showed close-up views of dying people with distended stomachs, blackened faces, and open sores, Riker had to look away.

"I get the picture," he muttered. "But the Cardassians must have the technology to deal with this. As you said, it's now a Cardassian planet."

"The Cardassians have abandoned them," answered Tuvok, "except to station ships in orbit to stop any attempt by the inhabitants to leave the planet. Cardassian troops on the ground have destroyed ships and spaceports and shut off all communication with the outside. A quarantine is in effect, and the entire populace has been left to die."

"Maybe the Cardassians did this," suggested Riker. "They're not above using biological warfare."

B'Elanna Torres shoved him in the back with her weapon. "You're a cold fish, aren't you? It *is* biological warfare, only the Cardassians didn't do it."

"How do you know that?"

"Because it's the same plague that nearly wiped them out on Terok Nor four years ago." When Riker gave her a questioning look, she added, "It's now called Deep Space Nine."

Chakotay shook his head. "We don't know that for sure, B'Elanna."

"Oh, don't we? When we've conquered almost every disease known to science, how could an illness with the exact same symptoms pop up again? And look at the way the Cardassians have reacted. They don't want any part of that planet, except to bury it."

"She's right," said another feminine voice.

Riker turned to see a tall, attractive Bajoran standing in the corridor. She stepped onto the crowded bridge, her nose ridges furrowed with concern. "I'm sorry to interrupt, Captain, but I couldn't help but to listen. B'Elanna is right—this is the same plague that struck Terok Nor and the work camps on Bajor, I'm sure of it. I recognized the symptoms the moment I saw them. Only this version seems to spread even faster."

"Thanks, Seska," said B'Elanna with relief. "There's too much at stake here to ignore the past. Going over Starfleet records has made me think that this plague has appeared several times before—in widely separated areas of the quadrant. There was a similar plague on Archaria III, and it affected people who are half-human and mixed-blood. Then came Bajor, and a virus linked to it hit the Romulan royal family just two years ago. What are the chances of that?"

She peered into Riker's eyes. "Ask yourself, why *this* planet? Why *now?* Helena is as advanced as any planet in the Federation, but it's been cut off, abandoned. Nobody cares what happens there. You couldn't pick a more helpless place. But we still have time to help them, because of the distances across those huge oceans."

Riker sighed and held out his hands. "I'm one medical courier with a shuttlecraft. What do you expect me to do?"

"The Maquis are warriors, not healers," said Chakotay. "We're rounding up all the doctors and nurses we've got, but we only have a handful of them. Plus we don't have enough drugs or research equipment to do the job. *You* have access to everything we need."

Riker felt trapped on the cramped bridge, torn between doing his duty and doing what was right. His preconceptions about the Maquis had crumbled even further, and he felt as if he understood them. They were not wild-eyed pirates and opportunists; they were people trying to help other people. The Federation had abandoned the colonists in the DMZ, but the Maquis hadn't—it was as simple as that.

"Is there a drug that's proven effective against this disease?" he asked.

"To a degree," answered Tuvok. "According to Starfleet records, Tricillin PDF can prolong life, but it is not a cure. When the prions combine into a multiprion in the host's body, death can result in as quickly as forty-eight hours. The multiprion can be removed via a transporter biofilter, but that is extremely time consuming. The best way to stop the spread of the disease is to find the transmission vectors and shut them off. That is precisely what the Cardassians are doing with their quarantine."

"What about the Cardassians?" asked Riker. "If they've decided to let everyone die on that planet, won't they fight you?"

"Leave the Cardassians to us," said Chakotay. "They can sneak one or two ships into the DMZ, but they can't send a fleet without alerting Starfleet and violating the treaty."

"At least the treaty is good for something," grumbled Torres. "So will you help us?"

Riker paused before answering, although he knew he would say yes. His first duty was to reclaim his shuttlecraft and his co-pilot and get away from these people. After that, when he had time to think about it logically, he would decide how far to go in helping them.

"All right," he murmured. "Do you have those records you've been talking about?"

Tuvok nodded and pulled an isolinear chip from his console. "This also contains the video log you saw."

Riker took the chip, but as he withdrew his hand, B'Elanna Torres caught his wrist in a tight grip. "Can we trust you, William T. Riker?"

He didn't pull his hand away, because her touch was warm and charged with life. As he gently pried her fingers from his wrist, he gave her a charming smile. "Call me Tom."

"Okay, Tom." She smiled back, but it wasn't a friendly look.

"We'll meet you right here, at these coordinates," said Chakotay. "How soon do you think you can get back?"

He shrugged. "I would guess two or three days. I'll have to fake a requisition or divert supplies going somewhere else."

"If we see anything but a shuttlecraft coming toward us, we'll head into the DMZ," warned Chakotay. "And the deaths of millions of people will be on your conscience."

"I've already got a lot on my conscience," said Riker. "Can I go now?"

Chakotay nodded. "Seska, will you escort him to the transporter room?"

"Yes, sir." The Bajoran motioned to Riker, then led the way into the corridor.

When they were gone, Chakotay remarked to Torres, "Do you know how much help he can be to us?"

"You mean, with medical supplies?" she asked.

"Not just that. If he can impersonate the first officer of the *Enterprise,* he can gain admittance anywhere. The possibilities are endless. We have to try to recruit him."

"I thought we just did."

"I hope so," said Chakotay, his eyes narrowing.

In the briefing room of the *Gandhi,* Captain Azon Lexen and Commander Emma Crandall sat in stunned silence after viewing the video log and hearing Riker's story. In addition to the three of them, two other people were present: Ensign Shelzane and Lieutenant Patrick Kelly, an expert on the Maquis. Captain Lexen was a Trill joined with a symbiont who had lived six lifetimes, and even he appeared at a loss for words.

Finally Emma Crandall scowled and turned to Shelzane. "Do you corroborate Lieutenant Riker's story?"

The Benzite gingerly touched the small scar on her head. "I can't corroborate all the details, but I know we were attacked by the passengers. Looking back now, I can see that the distress of the pregnant woman was a diversion. When Lieutenant Riker went to attend to her, one of the other passengers must have hit me on the head. I only know that I woke up in sickbay on a Maquis ship with this head wound.

"But I believe Lieutenant Riker must have acquitted himself fairly well, because the passengers who revolted were also receiving medical attention." Shelzane glanced at Riker, and he gave her an appreciative nod.

"I actually regained control of the shuttle," he explained. "But before we could leave, the Maquis ships arrived and transported me directly to their brig."

"And then they showed you this video log and told you about the plague on Helena?" asked Crandall, sounding suspicious.

"After they found out we weren't carrying any medical supplies," Riker added. "That's all they were looking for."

"Did you hear the names of any of these Maquis officers?" asked the captain.

"No," lied Riker immediately. He didn't know why he lied about that, except that he felt oddly guilty about betraying the Maquis' confidence. Perhaps Chakotay, B'Elanna Torres, and the others were known Maquis, but if they weren't, he wouldn't be the one to identify them.

"What can you tell us about their ship?" asked Captain Lexen.

Riker shook his head. "It was small, older, nothing special. They weren't about to show me around. I've told you the truth, sir. I can't imagine that sending a med team and supplies to Helena will give the Maquis any strategic advantage, and it could save millions of lives."

"So you want to collaborate with the enemy?" Crandall asked snidely.

"I want to save lives," answered Riker, appealing to the captain. "If we don't cooperate, they'll just keep attacking our ships until they get what they want. And if any sick Helenites escape from the planet and reach Federation space . . . I don't need to tell you what might happen."

The Trill pursed his lips and rubbed the dark spots on his right temple. "I'm inclined to agree with you, Lieutenant, but I can't *order* anyone to go on a mission like this. You would have to depend upon the Maquis for protection, not us. We'll brief the medical teams, and if anyone wants to volunteer, you can take them. That is, if *you* wish to volunteer."

"I do."

"Count me in, too," said Shelzane, nodding her fishlike head resolutely.

"Sir, I strongly advise against this course of action," declared Commander Crandall.

"Duly noted." Captain Lexen rose to his feet. "These are strange times, and they require strange deeds. Lieutenant Riker, take a shuttlecraft and strip all the Federation signage; requisition the supplies you need. I myself will brief the medical staff and ask for volunteers."

"Yes, sir," replied Riker. "You should also tell Starfleet to get those refugees off Outpost Sierra III, and give them all a good interrogation."

"Good idea. If you confront Cardassians, say you're on a private, humanitarian mission, or say you're a Helenite. Don't pose as members of the Maquis or Starfleet unless you have to. Wear civilian clothes, and take as many precautions as you need. Dismissed."

After the captain had left the briefing room, Crandall stopped Riker and whispered, "I don't know what you're up to, but I'll break you if you betray us."

Riker stared her down. "I figure there's a good chance you won't ever see me again. I'd love to kiss you before I go."

Crandall stared at him in shock, utterly speechless, but there was a yielding in her eyes that made him smile with victory. "I thought so." He strode away, still grinning.

Gul Demadak laughed heartily as he watched his grandson cling to the back of a Cardassian riding hound. The giant canine galloped around the show ring on the grounds of Demadak's estate, totally oblivious to the young boy who gripped his shaggy fur and screamed. The hound was well trained; the boy was not. The stocky Cardassian looked up, noting that the sky was a beautiful shade of amber, and the breeze was hot and sulfuric. It was a wonderful day on Cardassia Prime, and he wheezed a laugh as he reached for his mug of hot fish juice.

"Hold on to him, Denny!" he yelled, using his grandson's nickname. If the boy fell off, he wasn't too worried, because the ground in the ring was cushioned with several centimeters of black volcanic sand. Besides, Denny could use a little toughening.

Sure enough, the lad slid off the withers of the giant hound and plowed headfirst into the black sand. For the first time, the hound took notice of the boy as he doubled back to lick the sand off his face.

"Get back on!" shouted Gul Demadak from the sidelines. "You can do it, boy!"

He heard footsteps behind him, and he turned to see his servant, Mago, shuffling toward the ring. The old Cardassian looked more bent and cadaverous than usual, and there was a worried look on his scaly face.

Since Demadak had given orders not to be disturbed on his vacation, he rose to meet the old man with a mixture of irritation and concern. "What is it, Mago?"

"Sorry to interrupt, Sir," said the old retainer, lowering his head reverentially. "Legate Tarkon from the Central Command is on the emergency channel."

"Tarkon, eh?" Demadak tried not to show his apprehension over this bit of news. Tarkon was an old friend and comrade, but he was also his superior in the pecking order of the Central Command. He would never say it aloud, but Tarkon had become something of an annoyance since his recent promotion.

"I'll take the call. Watch my grandson, and make sure he doesn't kill himself."

"Yes, sir."

"And get him back on that hound!" ordered Demadak as he strode toward the house.

"Yes, sir," muttered the old man with resignation.

Upon reaching the house, the gul went to his private study and locked the door behind him. Although his wife and daughter were out, there were other servants in the house, and Demadak had not gotten where he was by being careless. Plastering a confident look onto his angular face, Demadak approached the communications console.

On the screen, Legate Tarkon scowled with impatience. "You kept me waiting."

"I'm glad to see you, too," said Demadak with forced joviality. "Thank you for bothering me on my vacation. I was having entirely too much fun."

"This is an emergency."

"What?" scoffed Demadak. "Has the Federation swarmed across the Demilitarized Zone?" The DMZ was *his* responsibility, and he resented anyone telling him how to manage it.

"Nothing quite so dramatic . . . yet. The Detapa Council summoned me this morning—they're very worried about that plague planet. What is it called?"

"Helena."

"Yes. They found out about our losing our troop transport, and they know the Maquis have taken charge."

Demadak laughed out loud. "The Maquis couldn't take charge of a garbage scow."

"The Detapa Council is worried about the civilian population if that plague gets loose."

"It's not going to," declared Demadak irritably. "We have a spy on the lead Maquis ship, and she informs us that they aren't planning to evacuate any of the Helenites. Even the Maquis aren't that stupid. Besides, where would they take them? But they are trying to cure the disease, and it's worth giving them a chance to do that. After all, we still have a garrison of soldiers on Helena, and we'd like to keep them alive."

Legate Tarkon warned darkly, "There's a faction on the council who would like to dispense with halfway measures and just destroy the planet."

"I'm sure there is. There's always a faction who want to destroy things, but in this case it's entirely unnecessary. It could also plunge us back into war with the Federation."

Tarkon shook his head worriedly. "You had better be right about this, my old friend, or no power in the galaxy will be able to protect you."

"Of course I'm right," insisted Demadak with more confidence than he felt. "As we've seen before, panic is worse than plague. The Detapa Council has no business meddling with military policies in the DMZ. Tell them to go back to reforming the nursery schools."

Tarkon chuckled, obviously relieved by Demadak's bravado. "I won't tell them that, but I will tell them that the situation is under control."

"You do that. I'll be back at headquarters in two days, and I'll file a report myself. Demadak out." As soon as the image of Legate Tarkon faded from the screen, so did the smile on Demadak's face.

His bony brow knit with concern, the Cardassian went to his door to make sure that no one was in the vicinity. He closed it and double locked it. Then he went to his communications console and set it for a low frequency that was seldom used, except for antiquated satellite transmissions. There was a satellite in orbit around Cardassia Prime that was thought to be inactive. In truth, it was a subspace relay employing technology that was far more advanced than anything the Cardassians possessed.

Demadak's fingers trembled as they paused over the console. Even though his transmission would be encrypted and indecipherable to anyone but the intended recipient, he chose his words very carefully:

"Problem on test site. Outsiders present. Will try to delay overreaction from masters. Suggest you proceed to quick conclusion." He signed it with his codename, "Hermit."

When he sent it, a lump lodged deep in his throat. Demadak knew that his message would not be well received, and his secret benefactor would be very angry. Very angry, indeed.

# *Chapter Five*

A CLEAR, GREEN OCEAN stretched before Echo Imjim like the facet of a gigantic emerald. Vast beds of seaweed shimmered beneath the glassy surface, looking like the fire inside the immense jewel. Echo spied a buoy far below them, and small, frothy waves lapped at the alien object floating in their midst. Elsewhere, a school of flying fish broke the surface and arced back into the water like a ghostly ripple. Otherwise, nothing disturbed the glistening calm of the West Ribbon Ocean.

The only sound in the cockpit of the sea-glider was a gentle rush of air through the struts and ailerons. Echo felt as if she could fly forever on this sweet air current, but she knew she had to get lower, even if it meant losing the current. She edged the antigrav lever down, putting the craft into a dive. The sea-glider swooped like a graceful albatross over waters that were now lime colored.

When the seaplane dropped down to about twenty meters above the surface, its pontoons looked liked webbed feet bracing for a landing on the water. But Echo had no intention of landing out here—she was just hoping to avoid Dalgren's sensors by flying below them. At least she still had the easterly wind she needed to stay on course to the west.

As a glider pilot since the age of ten, Echo couldn't believe that she had to sneak from one continent to another. In her opinion, the air currents and the lands they blessed should be as free to travel as the breeze. There had never been borders on Helena before; overnight, freedom had vanished.

Over the rush of air, she called to the back of the cockpit. "Are you all right, Lumpkin?"

"Sure, Mommy!" answered Harper. The ten-year-old boy fidgeted in his seat, but he was content to stare out the porthole at the glistening sea and wispy clouds. He had always been a good passenger, even as a baby, recalled his mother. "We're flying awfully low, aren't we?" he asked.

She laughed nervously. "It only looks that way. Good currents down here." Her son knew too much about antigravity gliding for her to lie to him for very long. He would be suspicious when she didn't go higher to look for faster, safer air currents. She sure hoped they could sneak into Dalgren without anyone throwing a fit.

*What is the big deal? We aren't sick, and we don't even live in Padulla!* It was only happenstance that they had gotten stuck there while making a private delivery. After all, they *lived* in Dalgren. She knew she had broken the new regulations; but they had their own transportation, and they should be allowed to go home.

Echo shook her antennae and peered out the porthole. Unlike a full-blooded Andorian, her skin was not blue but a wrinkled gray, thanks to her Mizarian ancestry. However, she was much taller and stronger than any Mizarian who ever lived, and she could thank the blue-skinned side of her family for that.

She glanced at Harper, who was also gray but with blunted antennae and smoother features, thanks to the Troyian blood of his father. Ever since she heard about the plague, Echo had been watching her son like a seabird watches the kelp, but she had seen no signs of illness. If anything, he looked like he was going through a growth spurt.

"There's a flock of gliders," said Harper, pointing upward.

"What?" Scrunching lower in her seat, Echo peered into the glare of the reddish sun. High in the sky, at eleven o'clock, came what looked like a formation of snowy egrets, wending their way lazily in her direction. Echo checked her sensors and established that they weren't birds, unless birds had twenty-meter wingspans and were made of cellulose. She counted five approaching sea-gliders.

They must have spotted her, too, but they stayed at their high altitude, riding air currents that carried them toward her. If need be, sea-gliders could use a ripple of antigravity to keep momentum against the wind or in still air, but the constant diving and climbing made even the strongest stomachs revolt. Most glider pilots refused to use antigrav for that, preferring to climb or dive very little, only to find the best currents. It wasn't only a point of pride, although it was that, too. Gliders simply made better time—and the gravity suppressors exhausted less fuel—when they rode the natural air currents. Fuel consumption was a critical factor in a long haul over a vast ocean.

"Climb the wind and ride it," was a popular phrase among glider pilots. That's what Echo would normally have done, but this trip she was trying to hide. Despite what she saw, she still hoped that the flock wasn't coming after her and her son. With gliders on her tail, she wouldn't be able to go straight to Astar, the capitol of Dalgren. She would have to make for some more isolated port, hoping they wouldn't follow a lone glider for days on end.

Her radio crackled, making her jump. Echo peered at the device embedded in her console, surprised that they would communicate directly with her. It was a terrible breach of etiquette, since neither one of them had waved a wing to indicate a willingness to chat. Of course, this probably wasn't a chatting opportunity.

"Unknown glider, turn back," warned a stern voice over the radio. "Traffic from Padulla to Dalgren is not permitted at the present time."

Echo looked with embarrassment and fear at her son. She had told him that they might have to do some unpleasant things to be safe, and one of those things might include lying. But the scrawny ten-year-old gave her a brave smile, which was all she needed.

She flicked the switch and replied, "Glider *Golden Wraith* to unknown flock, we're *not* coming from Padulla— we're coming from Santos. And we're *residents* of Dalgren, born and raised there."

"That doesn't matter—all traffic has to be rerouted," warned the stern voice coming from the peaceful flock high above them.

*Hmmm, this is serious,* thought Echo, but she tried not to show how serious it was in her demeanor. "We're not even going to Dalgren," she replied snidely. "We're going to fly right past . . . on our way to Tipoli."

"You're going to turn back."

"Excuse me, but you don't own these skies," she snapped at the faceless voice. "I've been flying this easterly current since you were in diapers! We're not sick—we haven't been in Padulla. We should be free to go wherever we want!"

There came a tense pause, and Echo let her bravado fade for only an instant. She smiled confidently at her son, but he was starting to look anxious. "Maybe they'll see reason," she said, "and do the right thing."

The radio crackled. "You will turn back right now," warned the voice, "or we will force you into the sea."

"Or you'll *kill* me and my son!" she muttered, although she kept the radio mute. They had given her a long pause, and now they were going to get one in return. While they waited, Echo used her sensors to scan the air currents above them. She had already decided to make a run for home before she turned back to a place where everybody was dying.

Before the flock could respond, she activated the elevators on the tail section, turned antigrav to full, and soared upward. The golden nose cone sliced through the clouds, until she found a southerly flow that was fast but wouldn't take her terribly far off course. With any luck, they might conclude that she was turning around, not running.

"Glider *Golden Wraith,* turn to heading—" Echo flicked the radio off before it became even more annoying.

With embarrassment, she shouted back to Harper. "We tried to talk reasonably to them, but they weren't being reasonable. So we'll just go around."

"We're breaking the law," said Harper knowingly. "You said we should never break laws."

"Just this once, because we haven't got much choice." She flashed him a grim smile.

The ocean had turned a teal color directly beneath them, where a cold current made the kelp scarce. As she climbed, Echo could see the rainbows of color in the West Ribbon Ocean. It swirled this way and that in various shades of green and blue for ten thousand kilometers, until it struck the third largest continent on Helena—Dalgren. She could now see land with her superior vision, but it was little more than a bead of rust on the shimmering horizon.

*So close, yet still too far! If only we had left right away!* Echo tried not to chide herself for getting caught up in events over which she had no control. Yes, she and Harper didn't have to take three extra days to visit friends and relatives in Padulla. Somewhere in that brief period, the plague had exploded and become a major part of life, even supplanting the Cardassians in the news. Padulla was the hardest hit, or so they said. Certainly, the plague had been nothing but distant rumors on Dalgren when they departed nine days ago.

Now vigilantes ruled the skies and waters, keeping away everyone, even native Dalgrens. But that gave Echo hope, because it meant that her home was still relatively free of the plague. If they could just reach it and slip back into the current of life . . . before it was too late.

"They're coming lower," warned her son, who was straining in his seat to get a better look.

"Keep your seat belt on," she ordered him, knowing she might have to make some erratic maneuvers. In normal times, sea-gliders were never armed, but these weren't normal times. Five planes could force one plane from the sky, but they would have to be fools to try that. Then again, fear and panic made people do foolish things, thought Echo, as she continued to flee from the flock of gliders.

After thirty minutes of intense piloting, the prey and the

hunters were at the same altitude, about 400 meters above the gleaming ocean. Laterally, only one kilometer separated her from the lead glider. She couldn't hear their pleas over her radio, as she had long ago turned it off, but she imagined that they were now begging her to turn back. Land was getting closer and closer—Dalgren was a spill of brown and dark green across the turquoise horizon.

Echo banked slightly and turned toward the west. Without warning, some kind of missile shot past her window and streaked off into the ocean, leaving a red plume of smoke. Had that been a warning shot?

"Clones!" she shouted, shaking her fist at them. With a cringe, she glanced at her son.

"They're going to shoot us down, aren't they?" asked Harper.

"No!" she answered through clenched teeth. "They're not going to shoot at us, because I know where the pipeline is. Hang on!"

She cut the antigrav and went into a steep dive, being careful to keep her hand near the airbrake paddles and spoilers. There would be no more fooling around, no more running or hiding—she was headed straight for home.

Another missile streaked by the left wing of the glider, coming much closer. She had a feeling that one *wasn't* a warning shot. Warfare had been unknown on Helena for hundreds of years, so she had to hope that these makeshift armaments were none too deadly or accurate.

"Why don't you put out a distress signal?" asked Harper.

His mother nodded thoughtfully. "That's not a bad idea. We *are* in distress, and I'm not going down quietly."

She flipped on the distress signal, on all channels. The gliders pursuing her were probably the Coastal Watchers, the ones charged with answering distress calls at sea. *That's some irony,* thought Echo, *when the rescuers become the attackers.*

Leaning on the airbrakes, Echo pulled the craft out of its dive, and it skimmed the gentle waves of the turquoise sea. She smiled with satisfaction upon seeing the pipeline just under the surface of the shallow water; it looked like a flaw in the great jeweled facet, yet it carried much-needed fresh water. She swooped so close to the pipeline that she felt as if she could lean out the window and spit on it.

As she expected, that dissuaded her pursuers from shooting wildly at her, but her evasions had given them time to close the distance. Two of them were diving toward her position from high altitude. *Maybe they really are going to drive us into the sea!*

Harper looked out the window with awe, having never seen his mom fly this close to the water, except when landing. And then she would be going at a much reduced speed. There was just one problem—the air currents were slower at low altitude, and her pursuers could close the distance by staying in the upper currents. Echo still maintained the innocent hope that just by reaching land she could escape. Once she and Harper were on Dalgren, she rationalized, no one could keep them off.

Flying only meters above the water forced her to concentrate intently, and Echo didn't see them coming until Harper shouted, "Mom! On the right!"

She glanced over to see a large sea-glider swerve into view. Its wing nearly clipped hers, and she had to tap her joystick to edge away from the sky hog. Then she saw the other one crowding her on her left—he shook his fist at her. *Are they so insane that they would wreck themselves to stop us?*

No matter how close those idiots came, Echo couldn't

worry about them—the water was still her prime concern. At this speed, she'd be dashed into splinters if she hit it. The three gliders swooped over the smooth jade water, looking like three albatrosses fighting for the same school of fish.

Finally the plane on her right disappeared from view, and she didn't have time to follow it with her sensors. With a thundrous jolt, something hit the roof of her glider. Echo wrestled her controls to maintain altitude and not plunge into the sea; after a struggle, she managed to level her wings.

Seething with anger, she decided, *Two can play at that game! And my hull is stronger than your pontoons.* Tapping the antigrav lever, she rose rapidly and crunched into the struts, floats, and underbelly of the craft riding her. Hanging on to the joystick with both hands, she bucked like a bronco, dumping the unwanted rider.

"Mom!" shouted Harper.

Echo glanced out the window in time to see the attacking glider spin off, its undercarriage badly damaged. Fluttering like a wounded pelican, the glider hit the calm water and sent up a tremendous plume. The plane wasn't completely destroyed, but it looked fairly well shattered. Echo felt a pang of grief, because she had never been the cause of an accident in her thirty years of flying.

"Now we're in trouble," said Harper. It was an accurate assessment.

Echo scowled. "Maybe they'll realize that if we can fly this well, we're not sick."

The other glider on her left now moved away to a respectful distance, and Echo relaxed a bit at the controls. She continued to follow the pipeline toward the shimmering silhouette of land in the distance. At this point, she would normally feel relieved and happy to be so close to home, but today the sight of Dalgren only brought her dread. *What's going to happen to me and Harper? To all of Helena?*

Without warning, a missile slammed into her right wing, shearing it off. Only her quick reactions on the antigrav lever kept them from plowing immediately into the ocean. Instead the glider shot upward like a leaf caught on the breeze, then it lost its momentum and slowly spiraled downward, a wounded bird.

The glider creaked, trying to hold together, and the air howled ominously in the struts and ailerons. Harper screamed, but the torrent of rushing air drowned him out. Echo tried all of her controls, but none were responsive— the seaplane was in its death dive.

Looking out the window only made her head whirl as fast as the scenery, and Echo shrieked. She tried to reach back for her child, but he was scrunched down in his seat. "Oh, my Lumpkin . . . I'm so sorry!"

# Chapter Six

AS HER SEA-GLIDER SPIRALED toward the pristine ocean, a tingling came over Echo's body. She wondered whether this was the Mizarian Calm of Death she had heard so much about. The woman reached back to grab her son's hand one last time, but his slight body shimmered like a mirage, breaking apart before her eyes. She gasped at the unexpected sight.

The glider plunged erratically into the jade water, striking like a lopsided bullet and spewing a lopsided splash. Splinters from the sleek craft rained down upon the choppy waves, but Echo and Harper weren't aboard.

Mother and son stood huddled together on the transporter platform in what looked like a cargo hold full of medical equipment. The entire room looked like a laboratory, with modular clean rooms and research facilities crammed into its tight confines. They were confronted by four strange creatures dressed in elaborate environmental suits.

Harper shivered and gripped his mother's chest. "Are they . . . are they Cardassians?"

"I don't think so," she answered, unsure about that. Echo tried to stand upright and show some dignity, but she couldn't let go of her son. She remained hunched over his frail form.

"We answered your distress call," said a businesslike male, as he stepped forward and aimed a tricorder at them. He studied the device intently, not about to make any quick pronouncements.

"Federation?" asked Echo hopefully.

"Hardly," snorted a strong feminine voice. "We're Maquis."

Harper brightened instantly. "All right! Can I join you?"

"Harper!" snapped his mother, cuffing him on the antenna.

Another man chuckled. "I hope, by the time you're old enough, the Maquis won't be needed."

"They show no symptoms of the disease," said the man with the tricorder. "They check negative for the multiprions. Either they were uninfected, or the biofilter removed them. They may still be carrying individual prions."

"We haven't been sick!" declared Echo. She hugged Harper defensively. "Look, just beam us down somewhere on Dalgren, and we'll be going. And . . . thanks for saving our lives."

"Please dispose of your clothing," said the officious man. "After your fumigation, we will furnish you with new garments."

"Just a minute!" barked Echo, stepping in front of her son to protect him from these disguised pirates. "What if I don't want to strip naked?"

"You don't have to." The other man stepped forward and removed his hood, showing himself to be a human with odd markings on his forehead. "In our haste, we've gotten off to a bad start. I'm Captain Chakotay, and this *is* a Maquis ship. But we're not here to fight anyone—we're only here to deal with this disease. If you help us with some information, we'll innoculate you and your son . . . and help you get home."

"We don't need—"

"Weren't the other aircraft trying to kill you?"

"Uh, yeah," admitted Echo, scratching her wrinkled gray skull. "I'd heard they weren't permitting people to travel from Padulla to Dalgren, but I didn't really believe it. Now they've destroyed my sea-glider . . . my transportation, my livelihood."

"We've got transportation." Chakotay motioned to the figure with the tricorder. "Tuvok, you had better get to the bridge and check on Riker."

"Yes, sir." The officious man peeled off his environmental suit, revealing himself to be a Vulcan. With several long strides, he dumped the suit in a bin and exited from the cargo hold.

"B'Elanna, you and Dr. Kincaid can help our guests get cleaned up." The captain turned to her, as if expecting her to furnish a name.

"Echo Imjim," she said apologetically. "And my son, Harper."

The boy clicked his heels and saluted sharply. "Permission to come aboard, Captain."

Chakotay smiled and returned the salute. "Permission

granted. I'll brief the two of you after you've changed clothes."

The woman named B'Elanna removed her hood, and Echo gasped aloud. Harper only stared. "Oh, by Mizrah!" said the glider pilot. "Are you what you appear to be?"

B'Elanna frowned and put her hands on her hips. "And *what* do I appear to be?"

"Half-human and half-Klingon."

"Good guess," muttered the magnificent female Maquis. "And why is that so special?"

With a start, Echo realized that the other Maquis had no idea what they had in this B'Elanna woman. "It's a rare combination," she explained. "You are very unique. We haven't had any success convincing Klingons to breed with us."

B'Elanna scowled. "My father had no such problems."

Suppressing a smile, Captain Chakotay broke in. "Can we use this to our benefit?"

"Yes! Make sure that she leads any delegation to Dalgren, or anywhere on Helena." Turning her gaze to the unique woman, Echo almost felt like bowing.

"That's exactly the sort of information we need," said the captain, heading toward the door. "We'll have a briefing session after you've changed."

*Handsome man—for a human*, thought Echo. She had never wanted another child, loving Harper so much and knowing her profession didn't lend itself to family life—but a purebred human mixed with her lineage would produce an admirable child.

*Right*, she thought miserably. *In another fortnight, we'll probably all be dead.*

When Chakotay reached the bridge, Tuvok glanced at him, and Seska gave him a quick smile. On the screen was a view of the graceful blue curve of Helena's horizon, as seen from orbit. The planet looked serene yet vibrantly alive, kept that way by an enlightened populace. Yet hidden within those wispy clouds, balmy seas, and dimpled land masses was a deadly enemy committed to wiping out all humanoid life.

"Lieutenant Riker has set up Clinic One on Padulla," reported Tuvok. "Visual contact will be possible in seventy-five seconds."

"Bring it up when you can," ordered Chakotay. Like everyone else, he wanted to see some concrete results for all their foolhardy effort. Being in the Maquis often felt like being Sancho Panza in the service of Don Quixote. Would they do some good today? Or were they risking their lives in order to swat at flies on a corpse?

While they waited, Seska leaned back in her seat and looked at him. "You know what I said about wanting to go on shore leave? Never mind. I know where my duty is—right here."

"That's big of you," said the captain with a grim smile. When times got tense, he welcomed the Bajoran's dark sense of humor. In truth, he would need Seska on the bridge, with B'Elanna down on the planet's surface.

"In range," reported the Vulcan. With a flash, the viewscreen revealed a static-filled image with several blurry figures moving about. In a few seconds, the image cleared to make it plain that they were inside a portable geodesic dome. People stood patiently, waiting for inoculations from the efficient medical team. A couple of the medical workers were Maquis, but the majority were Starfleet.

The equipment and facilities were first-rate, thanks to Riker. The lieutenant had gotten everything they needed, but in small quantities, due to the confines of the shuttle-craft. Chakotay still found it hard to believe that Riker had stolen all this stuff, but he wasn't going to question a gift. The man had accomplished his mission, and that command-ed Chakotay's respect. The captain couldn't really be sure of the loyalty of those around him, so he had to trust in their character.

Riker sat down in front of the viewer, a satisfied grin on his bearded face. "As you can see, Captain, we're open for business, and it's booming! The word has gotten out in only a few hours. We're offering inoculations of Tricillin PDF and a wide-spectrum antiviral compound—the same thing all of us got. It should prolong onset—and relieve symp-toms—until we can do more research.

"If we catch anyone within forty-eight hours of contract-ing the disease, we're using the transporter biofilter in the shuttlecraft to remove the multiprions."

He was jostled slightly by two confused patients, and Riker lowered his voice to add, "Being on the outskirts of the city was a good idea. We're only getting those people who are still relatively healthy. As soon as I can get away, I want to take the shuttle and find any local doctors who can tell us how this developed."

"Be careful," warned Chakotay. "Wear the suits in the city—it was hit hard."

"We will. What about Clinic Two?"

"We're getting ready to beam down to Dalgren," said the captain, "but it doesn't sound like the plague has hit there very hard. They're more interested in keeping people *out*."

"Are you sure that's where you want to set up?"

"Yes, because we need a control site with relatively few cases—that's the best way to isolate and track them. At least that's what Dr. Kincaid says, and Tuvok agrees."

"Well, we're swamped here," said Riker, being jostled again. "I'll report in later. Away team, out."

Tom Riker rose to his feet, feeling very claustrophobic in the crowded dome. Although few of the patients appeared outwardly sick, he was cognizant that they could be. Plus the Helenites were alien in appearance and dress—each one an amalgam of various species, each person dressed in a colorful, billowing costume with ribbons and braids. It was as if they were headed for a masquerade party. Although Riker had served with numerous humanoid species, he found it disconcerting when he couldn't identify people by species. Perhaps that was the point, he thought ruefully.

When he looked more closely, he could see that many of the Helenites' ornate garments were soiled and tattered. In their haunted eyes, he saw that their comfortable lives had been blasted apart. They were either ill, grieving, or in shock; they hadn't yet reached panic, but their dignity was starting to slip. He smiled at them as he passed, but the Helenites were lost in their contemplations of death.

Riker strode out of the portable dome into the golden sunshine and flower-scented breeze of late afternoon on Helena. He took a deep breath of the sun-drenched air, then held his breath when he realized that it probably contained the deadly prions. He reminded himself that he was now in the medical division—his main concern was other people's health, not his own. If he were serving on the bridge in a battle, he wouldn't be worried about his life, only doing his duty. It had to the same here, on this strange front.

Fighting this enemy was harder, he decided, than fighting a well-armed, advanced starship. At some point, a starship would reveal itself and stand to fight—but their tiny enemy would always stay cloaked, if they let it. Now that the clinic was set up and people were being helped, Riker knew he had to find a way to go on the offensive.

He strode toward the unmarked shuttlecraft, formerly called *Shuttle 3,* where people were also gathered. Only they were waiting for friends and relatives to exit the small craft, not enter. He saw Shelzane escort a very weak patient to the hatch and hand her over to her waiting friends. There was much bowing of heads and many expressions of gratitude, and the thin Benzite looked gratified herself.

"Bed rest," she cautioned the patient. "Check back with the doctors in forty-eight hours."

Riker hated to interrupt this heartwarming scene, but he felt the need to keep moving. "Ensign," he whispered to her, "wrap this up, because we have to leave."

"Leave?" she asked in horror. "But I have more people to bring through the biofilter."

"They'll have to wait."

"Some of them can't wait," she insisted. "Tomorrow will be too late."

Riker guided Shelzane back into the shuttlecraft, away from the curious eyes and ears of the patients. "We're logistical support," he reminded her, "not doctors. Don't make me order you."

"Technically, you can't order me," replied the Benzite. "Since we're here on an unofficial, private mission, Starfleet chain of command doesn't apply."

Riker sighed. "Okay, bring through one more. Then we've got to gather information."

"How about *two* more?" she begged.

He nodded with resignation and sunk into his seat in the

cockpit. With joy on her rumpled blue face, Shelzane returned to the transporter console at the rear of the craft. Riker could see her quandary—helping individuals gave one the feeling of immediate accomplishment, while research and long-term planning might not help at all. But if they hoped to save Helena, they had to rid the entire planet of the bug, not just a few individuals.

A muscular Helenite with black hair and sharp tusks materialized on the transporter pad. He staggered off, and Shelzane rushed to help him into a seat. For the first time, Riker felt as if he recognized a patient's species, or at least part of it. The man had the bulk and unpleasant visage of a Nausicaan.

"Can you help us?" asked Riker. "Where in the city are the doctors? I mean, where are people going for medical care?"

The part-Nausicaan looked up at him, and the brute actually seemed to smile. "Glad to help. The spaceport and the arena are supposed to be emergency hospitals. But I wouldn't go there—no one ever leaves."

"Where are they doing research?" asked Riker.

The patient shrugged his broad, furry shoulders. "I suppose, IGI."

"IGI?"

"The Institute for Genetic Improvement." He shook his woolly head. "I forget, you're strangers here. Some species do not breed naturally with others, and medical intervention is needed to produce a child. In vitro fertilization, cloning, genetic transplants—whatever is needed—they've done it. There are IGI clinics all over the planet."

Riker turned to his readouts. "Could you show me on a map of Padulla?"

The hulking citizen rose to his feet and moved slowly

toward the hatch. "I don't need to—you will see the giant green complex in the center of the city. It's the tallest and biggest. But I've got to warn you—"

"What?"

The Helenite stopped, looking undecided about spreading unpleasant news. "I heard they closed their doors—not letting anyone in or out. Check for yourself."

"We will, thanks." Riker made a note in his log and muttered to himself, "Institute for Genetic Improvement."

He heard a thud, and he turned to see another patient stagger off the transporter pad. Shelzane caught her—a sleek woman with tawny skin and downy white fur on her forehead and neck. While the ensign attended to her, Riker turned reluctantly to his preflight checklist.

As soon as Shelzane escorted her last patient off the shuttlecraft, Riker told her to clear the area. He felt guilty about leaving the medical staff alone, but they knew this was no paid vacation. They could request help from either the shuttle or the *Spartacus,* he told himself.

Ensign Shelzane jumped in the hatch and closed it after her; the Benzite looked energized by the day's work. "Thanks for waiting, Lieutenant. I told them we'd be back soon—there are so many who need help."

"We can help more of them by finding the origins of the infection," he reminded her. "Did you hear anything about how it started?"

"No," she admitted. "I talked to a few people, but they don't know what happened to them. They're still in shock."

"Okay. Prepare for takeoff."

As soon as the area was clear of pedestrians, Riker fired thrusters, and the shuttlecraft rose swiftly from the bluff. It swerved over the ocean and the crashing waves far below and quickly reached an altitude of three thousand meters, where Riker left it. From the outskirts to the center of the city was a short jump in a shuttlecraft, and he wanted to get a good look at everything along the way.

The rolling countryside was startling in its lush growth and natural beauty. The Helenites obviously enjoyed an unhurried but civilized life, with time to walk rather than ride. The only thing out of place was a thin line of sick people wending their way along a footpath to the new clinic. *How had they found out about the medical team so quickly?* wondered Riker. *Maybe hope is also contagious.*

The shuttlecraft flew over a sparkling bay, filled with what looked like seaplanes and small sailing ships, bobbing peacefully in the surf. All that was missing were people. Riker tried to imagine this city a month ago, before tragedy crept up on it. Padulla must have been a bustling paradise, with a populace so confident in their future that they could exchange the Federation for Cardassian rulers. Now their ambitions and dreams were grounded, just like the seaplanes bobbing below him.

The shuttle flew over a rust-colored beach and a picturesque boardwalk lined with quaint two-story buildings. There were actually a few people milling about on the boardwalk, haunting deserted cafés, watching the afternoon sun glitter on the bay. A few pedestrians waved at the shuttlecraft as it passed over, apparently happy to make contact with the visitors. Despite the fact that the handful of people on the boardwalk could plainly see each other, they didn't interact. They obviously preferred their solitude.

The city was large but not oversized, with broad, tree-lined boulevards, ample green belts, and tasteful buildings that didn't dwarf the civic planning. But without any people, it looked like a model of a city, like something on an architect's desk. Riker glanced at Shelzane and could see the Benzite was saddened by the sight of empty streets below them.

"What do they do with the bodies?" she asked softly.

"They may vaporize them with phasers," suggested Riker. "Burn them . . . I don't know." He was about to suggest she help him look for a big green building, when the landmark appeared on the horizon, shaped like a symmetrical tree.

When he flew closer, Riker could see that the jade-green building was actually a massive pyramid built in the Mayan style. It was the central keep of an oval fortress with high, curving walls and billowing battlements. The entrances were minimal—one north, one south, at the tips of the oval. Inside the walls were eight smaller square buildings with the pyramid holding down the center. The sharp angles of the pyramid, and the oval, rounded walls made an odd juxtaposition.

While he circled the complex, looking for somewhere to land, Riker watched for movement within the walls. He spotted none—it seemed to be as deserted as everyplace else. The few romantics on the boardwalk were keeping a lonely vigil for the rest of the city.

There was no landing pad or strip inside the walls, and the spacings between the buildings were just small enough to keep him from landing on the grounds. Outside the northern wall was a landing pad with the wreckage of some kind of vehicle on it. A path led to an archway in the wall and one of the two obvious gates.

As Riker circled, he pressed the comm panel and broadcast on all local frequencies, "Shuttle to Institute of Genetic

Improvement. We're a private medical team, here to help you fight this disease. Please respond."

They listened, but there was no response, as Riker circled lower. The shuttlecraft neared the tip of the pyramid when Shelzane suddenly shouted, "Raise shields!"

Riker did so a moment before a beamed weapon shot from the tip of the pyramid and wracked the shuttlecraft. He slammed on the thrusters and zoomed away before the pyramid got off another shot.

"Whew!" He whistled. "Thanks."

"No damage," said Shelzane, still watching her instruments. "We were scanned, then I caught an energy surge. I thought it might be prudent to activate shields—"

"And save our lives. Quick thinking. So there must be someone in there who wants to keep us out."

The Benzite shook her head. "It could be automated. Our drop in altitude may have tripped the scanners, and the scanners tripped the weapon. I'm not reading any lifesigns, but there is a lot of shielding."

"Then let's land outside." Riker banked toward the landing pad outside the northern gate. As he zoomed over, he noticed that the wreckage on the pad appeared to be fairly recent but already scavenged, some of it placed in neat piles. The debris was scattered badly enough to make landing difficult, so Riker looked elsewhere.

He picked a nearby park and landed in a gently rolling meadow of wildflowers and playground equipment. He gazed out the window at the empty swings and slides; although no one was present, he swore he could hear the cries, shrieks, and laughter of the absent children.

"Suit up," he told Shelzane.

"We've already been exposed," she pointed out.

"Yes, I know, but I want anyone who sees us to know

we're outsiders." Riker worked his controls. "I'll put on security and enable remote transporter control."

Assisting each other, they put on their environmental suits and armed themselves with phasers. Before the attack, Riker might not have considered a phaser necessary; now he adjusted his weapon from low to medium stun. Despite the apparent desertion of the central city, *something* had given them an unfriendly welcome. He wasn't convinced there was nobody home inside the enigmatic IGI fortress.

As soon as he stepped out of the hatch into the field of wildflowers, Riker was sorry that he couldn't enjoy the late afternoon breeze. He could feel the sun warming the silken fabric of the suit that covered every centimeter of his body, and he wished he could take it off. With a sigh, Riker motioned to Shelzane, and she followed him toward the wreckage on the landing pad.

He didn't step directly on the platform. He prefered to walk around the debris. Maybe he was being overly cautious, but Riker knew that a wrecked spaceship could leave numerous toxins and dangerous substances. He could see exposed fuel tanks and no indication whether they were full or empty. Despite his protective suit, he felt oddly vulnerable in this ghost town, and he agreed with Chakotay—*take no risks that don't have to be taken.*

As Riker passed the wreckage, he mused whether the ship had gotten shot down by the pyramid, or whether they had simply made a poor landing. The debris had been picked through too much to tell him anything.

He saw Shelzane checking the wreckage with her tricorder, and she shook her head. "No lifesigns," her voice boomed in his hood.

"Let's try knocking." Riker motioned to the gate in the

circular wall, then took the lead. They moved cautiously down a well-manicured footpath and approached a rectangular archway at the elongated tip of the oval-shaped fortress. The door itself was metal, windowless, and solid, although the wall appeared to be made of a jadelike stone. Riker could see no mechanism that would open the door, except for a small slit for card entry at the side of the door.

In frustration, he knocked, although he doubted whether his gloved knuckles would make any noise whatsoever on the smooth metal. There were no signs or markings, no indication that this complex had once been a vibrant center of commerce and health care. Judging by the variety of hybrids on Helena, the Institute for Genetic Improvement must have been busy night and day.

Shelzane's eyes stayed riveted upon her tricorder, so she didn't see Riker remove his hood. "Hello!" he shouted as loudly as he could. "Is anyone there?"

The breeze whistled ominously through the turrets of the fortress, making it sound like banshees wailing for the dead. But no living voice answered them.

Shelzane shook her head. "Sir, it's highly unlikely that—" She stopped suddenly and stared at her tricorder. "Ten life-signs approaching rapidly on foot."

"From the complex?" asked Riker, looking at the door.

"No, sir. From the southeast . . . outside the wall."

Reacting quickly, Riker put his headgear back on and stepped away from the gate. He wanted to get a better view of the wall to the southwest, but he didn't like the fact that they were exposed, out in the open. "Start dropping back to the shuttlecraft," he ordered Shelzane.

"Yes, sir."

They scurried down the path, keeping in a crouch, but

they didn't move quickly enough. As they reached the landing pad, a squad of infantry jogged around the corner of the wall and dropped into firing position on knees and bellies. A few of them arranged mortars and other equipment.

"Down!" shouted Riker. He and Shelzane dove into the dirt just as the squad opened fire. Their deadly beams raked the brush and twisted metal on the landing pad, causing leaves, twigs, and molten metal to pelt Riker and Shelzane. As he cowered in the dirt, Riker realized that phasers set to stun were not going to do the job.

He squeezed the combadge in his glove. "Riker to shuttlecraft. Two to beam back. Energize now."

When nothing happened, he stared at Shelzane, and she shook her head. She mouthed something, but he couldn't hear her. Since wireless communications had broken down, and Riker didn't like the poor visibility, he ripped his hood off. Then he set his phaser to full.

"Surrender yourselves!" shouted a voice.

Riker looked at Shelzane, who pulled her hood off and pointed to the attackers. "A dampening field."

He motioned to her to keep moving, all the way back to the shuttlecraft. Scurrying on her hands and knees like a lizard, the Benzite darted from one clump of brush and debris to another.

"Surrender? By whose authority?" he shouted back.

"By authority of the Cardassian Union!"

*Cardassians!* Riker lifted his head from the dirt to peer at the gray-clad soldiers. They were a well-trained unit. They broke from kneeling positions and scattered to cover, moving ever closer to him. Riker glanced around but could see no support ships, then he remembered that the Cardassians had a garrison on Helena.

"We're just a medical relief team!" he called out.

Riker heard a loud whooshing sound, followed by a tremendous concussion that shook the ground like an earthquake. He covered his head as dirt and flaming debris rained down on him, scorching his environmental suit.

"Surrender!" shouted the hidden Cardassian. "Or prepare to die!"

# Chapter Seven

SURROUNDED BY A PATROL of well-armed Cardassians, cut off from the shuttlecraft, unsure what had happened to his co-pilot, Riker needed a big diversion. He aimed his phaser at one of the exposed fuel tanks and fired a searing blast. The tank ruptured in a fireball that ballooned high into the dusky sky. Riker was driven to the ground, as more flaming debris rained down.

*A dampening field.* He recalled the equipment the Cardassians had set up the moment they charged into view, just before they opened fire. While the wreckage on the landing pad continued to burn like a bonfire, Riker scurried forward and found a vantage point atop a decorative mound. Searching for the place where the Cardassians had rounded the wall, he quickly spotted two metal boxes on tripods.

Without time to think, Riker aimed his phaser and

opened fire. Despite the beams whistling past his head, he didn't finish firing until he had completely destroyed the two portable dampening boxes. Then he rolled down the hill and cowered in the dirt from a barrage of phasers and concussion mortars, which turned the ground into quivering jelly. He began to sink into quicksand.

Desperately he tapped his combadge. "Riker to shuttle, beam me up now!"

As a phaser beam melted a chunk of his environmental boot, Riker tried to float atop the liquified soil, but he only succeeded in burying himself deeper. The withering fire never stopped, and he was sure death was near . . . until he felt a tingle along his spine. The lieutenant curled into a fetal position until he was certain that he had transported from the fire zone.

Dripping mud, Riker rolled off the transporter pad into the cabin of the shuttlecraft, then he dashed to the transporter controls. Ripping off a glove, he set to work retrieving Shelzane. An explosion sundered the ground just outside the craft, and Riker staggered. His fingers pounded the console as they worked.

With a surprised but grateful look in her eyes, the Benzite tumbled off the transporter pad three seconds later. Riker didn't wait to greet her—he hurried to the cockpit. Even before he got into his seat, he had punched up the shields and ignited the thrusters. He sunk deep into his chair at the same moment that the shuttle left the ground.

Their shields took a direct hit, and the shuttle rocked— but Riker maintained control as he zoomed into the darkening sky. The jade pyramid was lit up like an amusement park by the explosions and light beams hurled at them. With Riker on the conn, the shuttlecraft weaved back and forth through the barrage, unscathed.

Shelzane staggered into the seat next to him. Her environmental suit was scorched and ripped like his, but unlike him she had a dribble of blood on her hip. He recognized that purple color from her previous head wound.

"You were hit?" he asked with concern.

She shrugged, but her blue tendrils quivered for a second. "It's just a scratch—from a rock, not a phaser."

"Let's go back to camp and have the docs look at it." Riker gave her a sympathetic smile.

"We haven't really found out much," said Shelzane with a grimace.

"And we won't until we figure out a way to get into that IGI complex." After making sure they had swung well wide of the pyramid, Riker set course for the clinic. He mused aloud, "Do the Cardassians have control of that place? Or were they just in the neighborhood?"

The Benzite shook her head. "We don't know. With their dampening equipment, they could stay hidden from our sensors. Or they could transport in."

"Maybe later tonight we'll pay them another visit," said Riker with determination.

A huge green pyramid with boxy angles and long staircases commanded the center of the city below them. It glistened in the midday sun like a jewel. B'Elanna Torres had difficulty taking her eyes off the breathtaking landmark. But she had to watch her instruments as Chakotay brought the *Spartacus* down for a rare landing. Following Echo's advice, they had decided to make an impressive landing rather than just transporting down.

Chakotay had agreed to this only because the *Singha* had returned with more medical supplies, scrounged from a dozen Maquis hideouts. The *Singha* was taking their place in orbit, ready to respond to an emergency or fend off a Cardassian attack.

Torres cycled through her checklists as they prepared to land in a fallow field about two kilometers outside of town. She looked out the window to see the quaint streets of Astar swarming with people during the midday break. At least all of them would get a good look at the novelty known as the Maquis.

"The Cardassians destroyed all of our starships," said Echo softly. "So your arrival will be unexpected." The Helenite was seated at the auxilary console in the rear of the cramped bridge.

"B'Elanna, let them know who we are," ordered Chakotay. "But let's keep our shields up."

The Maquis engineer nodded and opened the local frequencies. "To the people of Dalgren," she announced, "this is the Maquis vessel *Spartacus*. We are here to offer medical assistance. Repeat, we are here to help you during your medical emergency. We will land in a field two kilometers northwest of—"

"Don't land!" a voice broke in. "Traffic between Padulla and Dalgren is not permitted."

"We haven't been on Padulla," she snapped back. "We can inoculate your citizens and help you beat this plague."

"We have no plague on Dalgren!" insisted the voice from the ground. "And we don't wish to anger the Cardassians. Maquis vessel, we urge you to turn back!"

Chakotay slid a finger under his throat in the universal sign to cut them off. Torres did so gladly. "Nice, friendly people," she muttered.

Echo looked pained. "They *are* nice people, normally. But they're afraid. They must have seen reports from Padulla."

"They can't hide forever," said Torres. "The disease is airborne, so they'll be exposed to it, anyway."

"Nobody thinks like that," said Echo with a wan smile. "This is the kind of thing that happens to somebody else . . . someplace else."

"So far," added Torres.

Chakotay heaved his broad shoulders and edged the craft into a gradual landing approach. "They haven't fired at us, so I think I'll land. Remember, B'Elanna, you do the talking. You and Tuvok will be the ones who stay and make the arrangements. We need to exchange information, and research any cases they've had."

"What about my son and me?" asked Echo.

"We'd like you to stay on board and advise us. We have to find out the situation on the other continents as well. But we'll beam you directly to your home whenever you wish."

Echo's shriveled brow grew more wrinkled as she came to a decision. "You can send my son to his aunt's place. I'll stay with you—I think you'll need my help."

"Good." Chakotay turned to Torres. "How are we fixed?"

She studied her readouts but found nothing abnormal. "All systems are green."

"Stand by for landing." The attack craft, which seemed small in space but gigantic as it drew close to the ground, dropped into its final approach. Chakotay fired thrusters and set her down in the barren field.

Torres braced for impact, but the landing was surprisingly gentle. The *Spartacus* tilted on her landing legs as she settled into the furrows, but the aged ship held together.

Chakotay smiled at her. "You can let your breath out now."

"Nice landing. That's not what I'm worried about." She looked pointedly at him. "What if they won't listen to me?"

"Just give them a little of that famous B'Elanna Torres charm," replied Chakotay.

"No," interjected Echo. "*Command* them. They'll listen to you."

The captain tapped his comm panel. "Tuvok, meet Torres at the transporter. We'll wait here until you signal that it's safe to leave."

"Yes, sir," replied the Vulcan.

"Good luck," the captain said to Torres.

"If I had any luck, would I be a Maquis?" With a scowl, B'Elanna rose to her feet and strode off the bridge.

Twenty seconds later, she entered the cargo bay, which had been turned into a flying laboratory. A handful of researchers looked on as she crossed to the transporter platform, where Tuvok waited. She nodded to the Vulcan, who handed her a combadge and a holstered phaser pistol. As she added these accessories to her plain brown uniform, Torres glanced again at the researchers and doctors. They looked scared. They had trained all their lives for this battle, but they had never been on the front before. The fight would be until the bitter end, because this enemy took no prisoners.

B'Elanna tossed her short brown hair, prepared to stride out there without an environmental suit. She told herself that she had been inoculated with the best drugs Starfleet had to offer, and the biofilter would remove the multiprions whenever she transported back. But no one could be calm about facing death so squarely.

"Ready?" asked Tuvok.

Torres nodded and stepped upon the transporter platform, her hand resting on the butt of her phaser pistol. Opening and closing the hatch on this old ship was a pain, so they had decided to transport outside the ship. "Energize," she told the operator.

A moment later, she and Tuvok materialized on the other side of the hull, a few meters beyond the *Spartacus*. There was nothing around them but rich, loamy soil piled in rows, awaiting seed. About ten meters away, a spring gurgled in the center of an old artesian well, and an orchard of venerable fruit trees rose beyond the well. In the distance, Torres saw a cloud of dust on the dirt road, and she pointed it out to Tuvok.

The Vulcan checked his tricorder and nodded sagely. "There are three hovercraft headed toward us. Eighteen people, total."

"Are they armed?"

"There are no unusual energy readings. They may have small arms."

She tapped her combadge. "Torres to transporter room. Stand by for emergency beaming."

"Yes, sir," answered the Bolian on duty.

Torres stood her ground as the small craft sped toward them. When they came within range of her sharp eyesight, she could see the fear and anger on their distinctive faces. These Helenites looked wild, almost fierce, in their colorful, billowing clothes, unfurled ribbons, and windblown hair. They were all hybrids she had never seen before, because they had never existed before; and they existed nowhere else outside of Helena.

The three hovercraft stopped at a respectful distance, and six riders in each jumped out and started forward. The garishly garbed welcoming committee didn't appear to be armed, but they did look angry and upset—and uncomfortable with both emotions. As they got closer to the stoic Vulcan and the scowling half-Klingon, their fierce expressions softened, and some of them gawked openly at Torres. Most of them fell back to talk in hushed whispers, and only a handful of them kept coming.

The one in the lead was a tall, dark-haired humanoid with an olive-green complexion and fine golden hair growing down his neck into his gaudy tunic, which had puffed sleeves and golden braid. His age or ancestry would be difficult to guess, but from the way the others fell back and let him approach alone, she assumed he was the one to deal with.

"Hello!" she said, trying to muster some of her allegedly famous charm. "I'm B'Elanna Torres, chief engineer of this vessel."

He stopped and bowed respectfully. "I am Klain, the prefect of Astar, a Royal Son of the Dawn Cluster. I beg your pardon, but we are not accepting visitors at the moment. We ask you to leave."

"We're like the plague," countered Torres, crossing her arms. "You're going to get us whether you want us or not. You can't just cut yourselves off from the rest of Helena and hope it doesn't happen to you. Help us study this disease and find the transmission vectors."

"How do we know *you* aren't carrying the disease?" asked Klain suspiciously.

"We just arrived. We've got tests, inoculations, and Starfleet records about this disease. Our ship has a laboratory and a clinic." B'Elanna shook her head, growing impatient with this begging. "Listen, we just want to combine forces—if we find that we have to quarantine Padulla or someplace else, we will. Just work with us."

Klain smiled and held out his hands. "Let us show you around and prove to you that we don't have this terrible malady on Dalgren."

"Not a single case?" she asked, incredulous.

He shrugged. "Not that I've seen. Granted, I'm not a doctor. Are you?"

"I've said, I'm a ship's engineer. But we have doctors on board—let them examine a few of you. We'll include an inoculation and a trip through our transporter's biofilter, which will take out the fully developed multiprions."

Klain bowed to her, but there was an amused smirk beneath his smile. "As you wish. Lanto! Harkeer!"

Torres watched curiously as two Helenites ran forward to do his bidding. "I've a favor to ask. Would you two go aboard this ship and allow this Maquis medical team to examine you?"

One of them, a tall woman with long, apelike arms, grimaced with alarm at the idea. "How do we know we can trust them?"

"We have their guests here with us," explained Klain, motioning to B'Elanna and Tuvok. "I'm sure there's no danger."

While this conversation was going on, Torres caught sight of another colorfully garbed Helenite training a tricorder on her. When he saw her looking at him, he folded the device shut and melted into the crowd that was gathering.

She tapped her combadge. "Torres to bridge. We're going to take a tour of the city, and we have two locals to beam aboard for tests. They're about two meters in front of me."

"We're locked on," replied Chakotay's voice. "As soon as we get them, we'll head back into orbit. You're doing great—maybe we'll make you an ambassador."

"I'm holding out for admiral," muttered Torres. "Team out."

She and Tuvok stepped away from the *Spartacus* and motioned the others back as well. Still looking frightened, the two sacrificial Helenites clutched hands as they waited to be transported aboard the strange ship. Judging by the welcome given to the Maquis, Torres guessed that the Helenites had already gotten a good dose of Cardassian threats and propaganda. Or maybe they were just cautious people by nature, despite their flamboyant appearance.

When the two finally dematerialized and the *Spartacus* lifted off into the lustrous blue sky, the Dalgrens seemed to relax for the first time. Torres saw Klain talking to the man with the tricorder, and she hoped they had gotten a clean bill of health. For people who didn't believe the plague could touch them, they sure took a lot of precautions.

She glanced at Tuvok, who raised a noncommittal eyebrow. Torres wanted to head back to the ship and keep moving, letting these ingrates fend for themselves. But they had to confront this disease right here, right now, or they might have to chase it over every centimeter of the Demilitarized Zone for years to come.

Prefect Klain walked toward her and held out his arm like a gentleman. His black hair and olive skin glistened with a healthy sheen, and he looked as strong as a Klingon. With a sigh, she took his brawny arm, but only so as not to offend him. Several other Helenites smiled and nodded with satisfaction, as if some event had transpired of which she was not aware.

"Have you ever been to Helena before?" he asked as he led her toward a hovercraft. Tuvok followed closely behind them.

"No," answered Torres. "Why would I?"

"The way you look. Excuse me, but you are half-Klingon, aren't you?"

She nodded. "And half-human."

Klain's dark green eyes twinkled with admiration. "Half-human and half-Klingon. I've seen computer simulations, but never the real thing! And you were conceived naturally?"

Torres bristled. "Well, I wasn't there, but that's what they tell me."

"Remarkable! Obviously, they sent you to Helena because of your unique lineage?"

"No, I'm here by chance. The Maquis doesn't have the luxury of picking and choosing who they send places."

She stopped at the door to the hovercraft, expecting Klain to open it, which he quickly did. If they wanted to treat her like royalty, she would oblige. Torres slipped into the open vehicle ahead of him, and Tuvok followed, keeping a close eye on their hosts. They sat in the back row of seats, allowing a driver and two more passengers to climb into the front. The other locals crammed into the remaining hovercraft as best they could. All three vehicles lifted off the ground at the same time, as if linked, then the caravan glided smoothly down the rough dirt road.

For the first time, Klain turned to Tuvok. "And you, sir, are a full-blooded Vulcan?"

"I am."

"I myself am Antosian/Betazoid on my dam's side, Deltan/Orion on my sire's side. Here we pride uniqueness—the more unique, the better."

He turned to gaze at Torres with unabashed adoration. "You, B'Elanna Torres, are special indeed."

"Aren't there any full-blooded species who live here?" she asked irritably.

"Unibloods, as we call them. Of course, there are." The big man looked wistful for a moment as the hovercraft cruised slowly between rows and rows of flowering vines. The smell of ripe fruit was redolent on the tropical breeze. "Helena wasn't always like it is now—isolated—with all this strife and uncertainty. We used to have many visitors, great commerce, spaceports in every city. A lot of unibloods came here to help us with our breeding programs, and just decided to stay."

"So you are saying that the majority of Helenites are genetically mixed," concluded Tuvok, "while unibloods are a minority, mostly newly arrived immigrants."

"That's right," agreed Klain. "If you stay here long enough, your children will undoubtedly be unique."

"Why is that?" asked Tuvok.

Klain smiled. "You've got to understand where our ancestors came from. They were persecuted all over the galaxy for being of mixed blood. Mixers, they were called in some places. Hundreds of years ago, our ancestors banded together to form a colony that would always be a refuge for persecuted mixbloods, but they did much more than that—they established the Cult of Uniqueness. It became our creed to combine species in as many permutations as possible. And some that weren't possible."

"You employ artificial means of procreation," said Tuvok.

Klain stuck his chin out defensively. "Only when necessary. Most Helenites don't have families and children in the accepted sense. We have clusters, which are communal dwellings . . . a type of clubhouse. For the most part, adults tend to raise their children alone, and the absent parent or parents are regarded as donors.

"We select the genetic traits of our children very carefully, weighing what kind of life we want for them, how much medical intrusion we're willing to allow. And, of course, how attracted we are to the donor." With a glance at B'Elanna, his defensiveness faded. "To be granted such blessings naturally, as you have been, is a great gift."

No matter how attractive the messenger, the sentiments were still disturbing. Maybe it was the Klingon in her, but

Torres found the idea of total dependence on genetic engineering to be unnatural. She switched her gaze to the buildings that had come into view: tidy two-story houses with intricate metal fences and spacious balconies. Helenites rushed onto those balconies to watch the caravan of hovercraft as it entered the city. No one waved or shouted, but they didn't throw bricks either. Torres felt like the centerpiece of an impromptu parade before a respectful but fearful audience—the leader of a conquering army.

They passed an open-air market, and the hovercraft had to slow down to accommodate all the pedestrians. It seemed almost like a holiday, with so many gaily festooned Helenites strolling under the cheerful pennants and striped canopies. The goods in the marketplace were bountiful, ranging from fresh fruits and roasted vegetables to utensils, musical instruments, and more gaudy clothing. At first, Torres tried to pick out the different species in the faces and bodies she saw, but the Helenites were such a hodgepodge of different traits that it became impossible. It was easier to consider them all one race that came in infinite varieties.

As they pulled away from the market, she saw a full-blooded Ferengi, who came charging after them in pursuit. But their hovercraft moved more swiftly than a Ferengi on foot, and they skittered around a corner and were gone.

"Where are we going?" asked Torres.

"The Institute for Genetic Improvement," answered Klain, straightening the magenta cuffs on his billowy shirt. "Then to the Dawn Cluster, my home. But I want you to note that the people of Astar do not seem sick, or in a panic. Yes, we have protected our borders from the terrible tragedy on Padulla, but what would you expect from us? You are looking for transmission vectors, and we have sealed off the obvious one."

Torres gazed at the opulent city all around her, with its chic shops, grand commerce buildings, blooming parks, and contented populace. She did find it hard to believe that they were on the verge of annihilation. "You must have some sick people," she pointed out

"Yes," the prefect assured her. "We are going to IGI now to interview the scientists and the few patients we have. The finest minds on the planet are found at IGI."

He reached forward with an olive hand that was ringed on the wrist with fine blond hair, and he brushed her wrist. "I would consider it a great honor if you would have supper with us at the Dawn Cluster."

"Yes, Tuvok and I will eat with you."

Klain bowed his head apologetically. "We'll make other arrangements for Mr. Tuvok to dine with fellow unibloods at the Velvet Cluster."

Torres glowered at him. "Are you telling me that Tuvok can't eat at this fancy club of yours?"

"He can't even go in the building," said Klain.

While Torres sputtered, unable to find the exact words to rip this popinjay up one side and down the other, Tuvok held up his hand and declared, "I would prefer to eat with the Velvet Cluster. We are on a fact-finding mission, and it would be wise to interview the uniblood community. Perhaps they are not as immune to the disease as the hybrids."

Klain smiled gratefully. "I think Tuvok understands. The Velvet Cluster is every bit as grand as the Dawn Cluster. Ah, here we are."

Torres looked up to see them approaching a gigantic green wall. Behind the green wall loomed the pyramid she had seen earlier, looking like a mountain with intricate steps carved into its gleaming sides. The three hovercraft made a small circle and came to a stop, sinking softly to the ground.

Klain bounded from the hovercraft and ran to the other two vehicles. As they conversed, Torres and Tuvok sat patiently, their eyes moving between their hosts and the incredible structure looming before them.

"They're bigots," Torres whispered to the Vulcan.

He shrugged. "Perhaps. But every culture has a social order, even if it is not as pronounced as this one. It is not unusual for a persecuted group to duplicate that persecution in another form. Otherwise, the Helenites seem to be prosperous and well adjusted."

"At least this place hasn't been devastated by the plague," said Torres with relief. "We're not too late."

Klain returned to their hovercraft, while the other two vehicles lifted off the ground and glided away. "I told them you weren't a security risk," he explained. "That's correct, isn't it?"

"If we were looking out for ourselves," answered Torres, "we wouldn't be here."

The prefect nodded in agreement. "Yes, I suppose, we haven't been fair to you . . . or to our neighbors. But we've fought so hard to keep our home, and our way of life. Our ancestors built this colony from nothing—in the farthest corner of Federation space. The early years were very hard, and our founders suffered greatly—I'd like to show you our histories sometime. We put up with the Federation, we put up with the Cardassians, and now the Maquis—but one thing is certain, we're going to keep our homeworld."

"But you would sacrifice your citizens on the other continents?" observed Tuvok.

"They have the same technical capablities we have," countered Klain. "If they can't cure it, neither can we! And you forget—the Cardassians destroyed all of our long-range vessels. The only way to get across the ocean now is by sea-glider, and that's not the way to move supplies and sick people. We have no way to get off the planet, no way to get help—"

"Until we came," said B'Elanna.

"All right," he conceded, "you came. And how long will you stay here? My guess is that you'll leave the moment more Cardassian ships show up, which could be any minute."

"Then we'd better hurry," said Torres, striding past Klain toward an archway in the green wall. Tuvok walked after her, leaving the Helenites to gape at the audacity of their guests.

Leaving his three comrades with the remaining hovercraft, Klain followed them to the gate. In the archway was a heavy metal door which didn't suit the exquisite green stone of the wall. Beside the door, Torres noticed what looked like a card slot, but their host paid no attention to it.

"Just stand here," he explained. "We'll be recognized."

Sure enough, the door opened, and Klain led the way inside. The walkway sloped downward, with handrails on either side. Torres realized they were headed underground, into a network of tunnels. The lighting came from luminescent strips embedded in the walls, ceiling, and floor of the jade corridor. Their footsteps echoed plain against the dull stone as they descended.

In due time, they came to a shiny metal turbolift, which opened invitingly at their approach. They stepped inside the well-appointed chamber and, following Klain's lead, stood quietly. After a jarring ride that made Torres dizzy, the doors opened, and they found themselves in a sumptuous office, furnished with mementos, plaques, and awards.

There were so many chairs arrayed against the walls that Torres decided this was a waiting room, with no one waiting.

A chime sounded, and a small bookcase in the corner spun around. A little man wearing a white laboratory coat stepped off the platform and gave them a crinkled smile. From the riot of spots and bumps on his face, it was impossible to tell what species his ancestors might have been, but it was certain that he was old. White hair sprouted in unruly tufts from his head, eyebrows, and chin, only adding to his gnomelike appearance.

"Hello! Hello!" he said, striding forward. "I am Dr. Gammet. Welcome to IGI." Although he tried to include all of them in his conversation, his pink eyes drifted toward B'Elanna Torres. "Yes, yes . . . remarkable."

"Dr. Gammet," said Klain warmly. "I'm so glad you could see us personally. This is B'Elanna Torres and Tuvok from the Maquis vessel."

"Has their ship left the ground?" asked Gammet.

"Yes, it's back in orbit."

"Good, good," said the little man with extreme relief. He turned apologetically to B'Elanna. "We still worry about the Cardassians more than anything else, and we don't want to give them any excuse to punish us. Although it may not seem like it, I'm glad you're here."

"You people are in denial about this plague," said Torres. "You can't hide from it and hope it goes away."

"I told them we didn't have any cases," insisted Klain.

Gammet scratched his wiry goatee. "I'm not sure of that anymore. It's possible that we could have had some plague cases and not recognized them. People could have died in the countryside without our knowing it. We need to cooperate with these people to find out."

Torres took a isolinear chip from her breast pocket. "I've got all the Starfleet data on the previous outbreaks."

He took the chip and shrugged. "I've seen the data, including some Cardassian files you could never obtain. I didn't tell Klain, but we have samples of the prions, smuggled out of Padulla before the quarantine. We were studying the disease, but it moved too quickly for us to save Padulla."

"Then you know this is serious," said Torres.

The doctor nodded somberly as he paced the quiet library. His shuffling footsteps were the only sound, except for the far-off drip of a faucet.

"It's more serious than you think," he began. "Much more serious. This strain is just as virulent as previous strains—but even more contagious. My theory is that it's a chimera, a genetically engineered combination of two different organisms. In this case, it would be the original virus combined with a less deadly disease that is easy to contract. So we have a disease that was already deadly, only now it's more contagious than ever."

"Who engineered it?" asked Klain, shock spreading across his handsome face.

Dr. Gammet shook his shaggy white mane. "That's unknown. We don't even know what the second organism is, and I've got people in this building who disagree with me—they think it evolved naturally. We've just started looking at this thing, and it could take months, or years, to crack it. And we may not have that much time—either from the disease or the Cardassians."

The little gnome looked into B'Elanna's eyes. "And no one is going to allow us to leave the planet, are they?"

She cleared her throat and returned his frank gaze. "No, we have to fight this battle right here, right now. Win or lose."

"Aren't there drugs that can delay the onset?" asked Klain hopefully.

"Yes, but there is no cure," stressed Dr. Gammet, his pace turning into a nervous jog. "Only by tracking it back to its origins can we hope to snuff it out. Now that we've got a couple of Maquis ships and the means to move quickly around the planet, let's use them."

"I'll get you together with our doctors." B'Elanna tapped her combadge, but nothing happened.

Gammet smiled slyly. "That won't work in here, my dear. No, no. I would suggest that we have as little contact with your ship as possible, in case the Cardassians show up again. In fact, there's a garrison stationed west of here in Tipoli, and they keep a close eye on us.

"So we'll exchange records and personnel as needed, while you two stay with us to coordinate the research. Your ships will do the fieldwork—as they're already doing on Padulla. But direct contact with your ship should be kept to a minimum. Also, it might help if you two didn't go around openly proclaiming your identity as Maquis. Just say you're Helenites."

"With *these* clothes?" asked B'Elanna, pointing to her drab uniform.

"Yes, yes, we'll do something about that." Gammet gave Tuvok a crinkly smile. "You, dear boy, could make a fortune while you're here—in donor fees. Wouldn't require much work on your part—we can induce *Pon farr.*"

While it was not possible to embarrass a Vulcan, Tuvok did manage to look offended. "That is the most unappealing job offer I have ever received."

The little man shrugged. "Not to fear, it is entirely your decision. Romulans are so similar to Vulcans that we've learned to use them almost exclusively. But never mind about that. Are we agreed on how to proceed?"

B'Elanna could feel the leadership of this mission slipping away from her, flowing toward the charismatic little doctor. Then again, they needed help desperately. And he was right, if the Cardassians showed up in force, all bets were off. It was a good idea to make the Helenites self-sufficient, as eliminating this disease was going to be a long, hard job, even if they were successful in containing the outbreak.

She looked at Tuvok, and the Vulcan raised an eyebrow, awaiting her decision.

"All right," she said. "We'll stay with you and coordinate."

Dr. Gammet clapped his gnarled hands. "Excellent! Excellent! I feel very confident that we can fight this chimera. Our people have a lot of natural resistance built into their genetic makeup."

"Do you have biological warfare?" asked Torres.

"No!" squeaked the little man, looking horrified at the idea. "We've never had war of any kind, biological or otherwise. The Cardassians could have wiped us out anytime they felt like it, with conventional weapons. There's no reason they should introduce a disease—or that anyone else should."

Torres nodded, more troubled than relieved by that thought. As she had asked Riker days ago: *Why here? Why now?*

# Chapter Eight

A LOUD, WRACKING COUGH sundered the silence of the examination tent, and a thin, naked man shook uncontrollably on the metal table. He looked old and used-up, although that may have been a result of the disease. For all Riker knew, he could have been a young man in the prime of life. This disease attacked every organ at once, bringing on instant aging.

Two medical workers in white gowns and hoods leaned over the old man, conversing silently inside their headgear. Riker stood nearby, waiting to see if the patient had to be transported to the shuttlecraft. Finally one of the doctors turned to him and shook his encased head.

"He's too far gone," said a disembodied voice in Riker's hood.

The lieutenant didn't need any further explanation. He

had seen plenty of patients like this one in the last few hours. Although the multiprions that caused the disease could be removed from their bodies by the transporter biofilter, their weakened bodies could not be repaired. Too many other opportunistic diseases had taken over; too many organs were failing; too many healthier people needed attention.

Unable to watch any longer, Riker waved to the doctors. "I have to check something." They waved back and grabbed hypos that would alleviate the man's suffering but not prolong his life.

Feeling constricted inside his hood, Riker stepped out of the examination room into a primordial night. The sky above was sugared with stars, and the dead city cast a boxy silhouette in the distance. The clinic's lights were the only lights between their encampment and the stars.

A clutch of Helenites waited nearby, staring at him. After a moment, he recognized them as the people who had carried the old man in. Their gaily striped and billowy clothes were soiled and tattered, making them look like an impoverished theater company. From their concerned yet hopeful faces, he knew they wanted some reassurance, but he couldn't give them any. It wasn't even his place to talk to them, but Riker knew that if he didn't, no one else would. He removed his headgear and walked toward the people.

"Will the prefect be all right?" asked a female who might have been attractive before worry and tragedy carved themselves into her mahogany face.

Riker looked frankly into eyes that were perfectly round. "I'm sorry, but the doctors say he won't recover."

A man with puckered magenta skin pushed his way through the group to confront the lieutenant. "But the transporter—we saw others being cured!"

"Others who were infected but not that sick," explained Riker. "We have to catch it within forty-eight hours. I'm sorry."

He started to walk away, but the man, who was good-sized, grabbed Riker's shoulder and whirled him around. "That's our *prefect* you're talking about—the chief of the Star Cluster! You have to save him!"

Riker tried to remain calm as he pried the Helenite's fingers off his shoulder. He also tried to ignore the way the man had spit into his face. "We're medical workers, not miracle workers. We're trying to save as many as we can, while we make the others comfortable."

"You'll save him!" shouted the man. "Or I'll tell the Cardassians you're here!"

Riker glanced worriedly into the night sky. "I'm pretty sure they already know we're here. I met a few of them in town, around the IGI building. What are they doing there?"

"You're evading my question!" sputtered the man.

"No, I'm trying to help people in this place . . . and getting shot at, threatened, and exposed to plague for my trouble!"

When the man wouldn't calm down, two of his friends grabbed him in an emotional hug. "Don't make it worse, Jakon," begged a woman. "We knew he was very sick. Let him go."

"They are only trying to help," insisted another friend. "Let's get in line for inoculations."

With lingering anger and denial, the magenta man glared at Riker. The lieutenant knew he should show more sympathy, but death was all around, breathing down their necks, and he wanted to survive. "What are the Cardassians doing around the IGI complex?" he asked again.

The man looked past him, grief finally taking the place

of anger, but a pointy-eared lad stepped forward. "They're shooting down any ships that can leave the planet. Those have been their orders for a while."

"And what about IGI? A weapon in that pyramid tried to shoot *us* down."

"That's their regular security," said the boy, sounding proud. "It's to protect trade secrets from their smaller competitors."

"Some secrets," muttered Riker. "Thank you. Once again, I'm sorry."

He hurried off before he could get involved in more grief, sickness, and death. With the *Spartacus* and *Singha* in orbit, Riker wasn't that concerned about an attack from space, but he didn't like squads of Cardassians popping up here and there. If that crack patrol ever decided to attack the clinic, they could wipe them out in less than a minute. It was doubtful the ships in orbit could respond quickly enough to help.

He crossed the flower garden to the shuttlecraft, which was parked on a grassy hillside overlooking the ocean. The hatch was open, and a feeble yellow light spilled into the darkness. In the gloom, the shuttle looked like a panel wagon belonging to a couple of traveling peddlers. It was too dark to see the ocean, but the waves crashed soothingly to the shore; the monotonous sound gave a false impression that all was well.

He stepped into the shuttlecraft, about to blurt orders, when he saw Shelzane sprawled like a limp starfish in the pilot's seat, fast asleep. She looked so peaceful, he didn't want to wake her up, but they were endangering the clinic by being here.

"Ensign!" he snapped, dropping into the seat beside her. "Prepare for takeoff."

Shelzane bolted upright, blinking her blue, hairless eye lids. "I'm sorry, sir, I don't know what happened—"

"I know what happened—you got tired. But don't worry about that. We've got to get out of here. Can you take over the checklist?"

"Yes, sir." The Benzite's hands dropped onto the board, and she was instantly at work

Riker tapped the comm panel. "Shuttle to *Spartacus.*"

"We hear you," replied Chakotay.

"We're assuming orbit, because I'm worried that the shuttlecraft is endangering the clinic. The Cardassians on the ground are out to get every ship that can leave the planet."

"Understood," said the captain. "But the situation may change quickly, because we're out of contact with Torres and Tuvok on the other continent. We've got no reason to believe they're in danger, but they're not responding to hails."

Riker frowned. "Is there anything I can do to help?"

"No," muttered Chakotay. "They went into a building where there may be shielding. And sometimes those surplus combadges can fail without warning. Let's give them a little longer."

"Okay. After we get in orbit, I'd like permission to beam down to the planet to scout Cardassians and a medical facility."

"Is this important?"

"I think it is. We've got to get records and find out how this thing started. The problem is, Padulla is a ghost town— everything is boarded up. The only ones out and about are Cardassians. How have they avoided the plague? I'd like to know."

"Okay, but keep in touch."

"You've got to take over the transport duties for the clinic," said Riker.

"We just entered synchronous orbit, and the transporter is going full time, no waiting."

"Okay, see you up there. Shuttle out."

Riker punched up the launch sequence, as Shelzane gazed at him with concern. "We're going back to that place?"

"Yes, but we're not going to march right up and knock. Let's launch, and we'll discuss it on our way."

Lieutenant Riker and Ensign Shelzane beamed into what they thought was an empty administration building near the IGI complex. When they shined their lanterns around the dark workroom, Riker was glad he had insisted they wear environmental suits. They were surrounded by hundreds of shrill rodents, interrupted in the middle of dining on two dismembered corpses.

When the rodents advanced, teeth bared, Riker raked the front row with phaser fire; they fell back, squealing. The line of charred rodents pointed the way to a second door, and Riker jogged in that direction, keeping the light in front of him and Shelzane.

The door was automatic and should have opened at their approach, but the power was off. He trained his lantern back on the rats, several of whom were bravely sniffing their footprints, trying to decide if these intruders were a danger or more food. "If they get close, shoot at them," he ordered Shelzane.

"Yes, sir," replied the Benzite with a tremble in her voice.

Riker stepped back and surveyed the area around the door, finding an access panel that might control the mechanism. Since Helenite technology was based on Federation technology, Riker had no trouble opening the panel and determining which circuits he needed to disable to allow it to open manually. He didn't have much hope of restoring electrical power to the building, but he wanted to be able to open a door without blasting through it.

A flash of light caught his attention, and he whirled around to see Shelzane firing at a wave of scurrying rats. "Keep them at bay!" he ordered her.

Riker wormed his gloved fingers into the crack between the two halves of the door. Using every muscle in his upper body, he pried the door open, as Shelzane backed into him. She fired continuously at the rodents, but a sea of fur undulated across the floor, caught in the wavering light of their lanterns.

"Get out!" Riker straightened his arm, forming an archway and holding the door open for the Benzite. When she didn't move fast enough, he grabbed her and shoved her through the door. With a final glance at the frenzied rats, Riker turned the light away and plunged the room back into darkness. With his hold on the door weakening, he squeezed through and let it snap shut behind him.

They found themselves in a deserted corridor, which was fine with Riker, since he wanted to search for the best observation post. He picked a direction and started walking. Shelzane shuffled behind him, keeping an eye on their rear. With no lights except for their portable lanterns, it almost seemed as if they were exploring a mine.

Midway down the hall, they came upon a door that bore the universal pictograph for stairs. Riker gave it a push and found that it wasn't locked or automatic. He held the door open and motioned Shelzane ahead of him, while he took a last look down the length of the bleak hallway.

Once in the stairwell, Riker decided that they might as well stake out the highest ground. He pointed up the stairs, then took the lead. Upon reaching the top landing, he was confronted by another automatic door. While Shelzane held the light for him, he opened the access panel and disabled the circuitry, allowing him and Shelzane to push the door open.

When they stepped onto the flat roof, they were unprepared for the sight that greeted them. Helena's double moons had just risen, casting an eerie blue light upon the dark cityscape. With their intricate wrought-iron balconies, sharp angles, and terraces, the buildings looked like giant mausoleums.

Riker turned off his lantern and motioned to Shelzane to do the same. Then they crouched down and took a good look at their surroundings. Arrayed along the roof were a few communication dishes and antennas, plus some environmental equipment, but little else of interest. Moonlight bathed the pyramid, making it look ebony instead of green.

The two of them dashed to the edge of the roof and peered over a wrought-iron railing at the street below. From a height of about six stories, they had an excellent view over the wall into the IGI complex, where they could now see smaller buildings in addition to the pyramid. They also had a commanding view of the street in two directions. The only disadvantage of having a post on the roof was that they would be visible by air surveillance. But thus far, they hadn't seen any Cardassian aircraft, and Riker didn't think they would have to worry until morning.

He got into a comfortable yet effective reclining position, then removed his hood. After a moment, Shelzane did the same. "What are we looking for?" she asked.

"To see if anybody is in that place. If there's someone

home, we have to attract their attention without alerting the Cardassians. Let's just be ready to gather information . . . and move fast if we get the chance."

As the two of them watched the massive pyramid and deserted street, time hung suspended over them like the glittering moons. It seemed as if they were the only people in the universe, keeping a vigil for a long-dead traveler who would never return home. Even though the buildings were standing, and the infrastructure of the society remained in place, this city was dead. Riker wondered if the survivors in Padulla could be relocated somewhere else on the planet, allowing them to start over.

Shelzane tapped Riker on the leg, jarring him out of his reverie, and she pointed to the west end of the street. He peered in that direction but could see very little in the shadows. So he took a small scope from his pack and adjusted it to his eye.

Immediately he spotted a squad of Cardassians strolling down the street, probably the same ones who had attacked them on their last visit. From their movements, it was clear they thought they owned the neighborhood and had nothing to fear. Riker still wondered if they were connected with the IGI complex—or had just discovered a good place to trap unsuspecting shuttlecraft.

*Maybe I can find out.*

As the patrol drew closer, unaware of the watchers on the roof, Riker turned to Shelzane and whispered, "Remember that payload we talked about beaming into the complex?"

The Benzite nodded. They had discussed transporting themselves directly behind the walls, then had decided to send an inanimate load first. After collecting a few objects to send down, they had finally decided to scrap that plan until they were more desperate.

Riker went on, "I want you to return to the shuttle and beam the package into the complex. Put it on the other side of the wall, where that shrub is. See it? The Cardassians should pass by there in about a minute, but wait for my signal."

"Yes, sir." Shelzane looked for the shrub and checked the coordinates on her tricorder. Then she pressed her combadge. "Shelzane to shuttle. One to transport—now."

With a twinge of dread, Riker watched his cohort vanish into the night like a swirl of dust caught in the moonlight. He had really come to rely on Shelzane, and he didn't like being without her, even for a few seconds.

Creeping along the lip of the roof, Riker peered through the wrought-iron lattice. He could see the unsuspecting patrol, strolling the street with a swagger typical of conquering soldiers. This time, they were wearing some sort of gas masks, although no protective clothing—just their regular gray uniforms. He appreciated the way they skirted close to the green wall in order to avoid a clump of debris in the street.

When they were only a few steps from the shrub on the wall, Riker tapped his combadge. "Energize now."

Gazing down at the complex from above, he saw a blue ripple race along the interior of the wall, as if a force field had rejected an attack. The blue anomaly moved outward in concentric circles, like a ripple in a pool, flowing over the walls and encompassing the unsuspecting soldiers. They screamed in agony, and half-a-dozen of them collapsed to the pavement. The others staggered, although some recovered quickly and aimed their weapons at the wall, which had seemingly attacked them for no reason.

The Cardassians cut loose with a withering blaze of fire, which only carved a minor dent in the impervious green stone. Nevertheless, the defenses of the complex reacted as if a full-scale attack was in progress. A red beam shot from the tip of the pyramid and melted a screaming Cardassian. Now the rest of them stopped firing and beat a hasty retreat, dragging three of their comrades with them.

Riker heard a snort and he turned to see Shelzane watching the curious spectacle. Subconsciously, she rubbed her injured hip.

"Did the package get through intact?" he asked.

"I don't know. The transmitter stopped working, and heavy-duty shields blocked our sensors. We had an isolinear chip in there with all of our data, so maybe they'll take notice."

Riker nodded with satisfaction and turned his attention to the stunned Cardassians. One of them crawled away, but two of them lay completely still, as still as death. They had been the closest ones to the wall, and Riker had a feeling they were not going to get up.

He whispered to Shelzane, "Whoever is in that complex, they're not allied with the Cardassians."

Shelzane started to reply, but a howling noise interrupted her. Screaming out of the night came a missile that slammed into the green wall, exploding with a thunderous concussion that shook the whole street. Shelzane and Riker were hurled away from the edge of the roof into a thicket of antennas. Green hail rained down upon them, and it took Riker a moment to realize that the gemlike pellets were melted bits of the wall.

He crawled to the edge of the roof and peered into the acrid smoke and swirling embers. He was amazed to see a gaping hole in the wall, with sparks glittering around its edges.

Movement caught Riker's eye, and he looked up. From the top of the pyramid, the deadly red beam raked a building farther up the street. Riker was curious about the target, but he couldn't stick around long enough to study it. The heat from the pyramid's weapon was scorching, turning the air into an inferno. He rolled away from the edge of the roof, yanking his headgear back on.

Scrambling to his knees, he spotted Shelzane crouched by the door to the stairwell. He dashed toward her, and the two of them tackled the door; with their adrenaline pumping, they pushed it open in seconds. Just as a monstrous explosion shook their building, they ducked into the cover of the stairwell.

After scurrying down a flight of stairs, Shelzane and Riker finally took a moment to catch their breath and slump against the narrow walls of the enclosure. "I guess they don't like each other," observed Shelzane, panting.

"This would be a good time to get into that complex," breathed Riker. He flinched from another blast that sounded altogether too close, as bits of plaster and dust fluttered down on them.

"Whatever we do next," rasped Shelzane, "I say we get out of here."

"Agreed." He tapped his combadge. "Riker to shuttle—two to beam up. Now!"

They dematerialized just as an explosion ripped off part of the roof, causing beams and debris to cascade down the empty stairwell.

Back on the shuttlecraft, safely in orbit, Riker didn't take time to congratulate himself. He charged to a console and scanned the breach in the wall, while Shelzane slumped into the closest seat.

"That hole goes all the way through," said Riker, "and there's no force field. We could beam right inside—onto a walkway."

"The shooting?" asked the Benzite.

"Has stopped for the moment—both sides are quiet. I'll go by myself if you don't want to go." He checked the other readouts.

"I'll go," said Shelzane, rising wearily to her feet. She pulled the hood back over her head and checked her suit. "We have to find out what's in there."

After making sure that the shuttle's orbit was stable and her status was good, Riker punched in commands and motioned his co-pilot back onto the transporter pad. "Phasers on full."

"On full," she agreed, drawing and checking her weapon. With the lieutenant deftly handling the controls, the Benzite faded into a glittering shimmer. He jumped onto the platform after her, leveled his phaser, and vanished.

The two strangers materialized inside a gloomy walkway that sloped downward. It would have been well lit in daytime, thanks to a ragged hole in the wall about six meters behind them. Riker pushed Shelzane along, because there was a lot of moonlight spilling through that crevice.

As they descended into the walkway, Riker felt a handrail at his side, and he grabbed it. There were enough green pebbles and debris to make walking treacherous. He turned on his lantern and played the yellow beam upon the glistening walls of the corridor. The entire thing was made of the same green material as the exterior. Riker knew he could learn more from a tricorder reading, but he didn't want to take his eyes off his surroundings.

"Ahead," said Shelzane. She pointed her lantern beam straight down the corridor until it glinted off shiny metal. "It may be a door."

He nodded, motioning her to go on. If they both had to

return fire, it would be better to have the shorter person in the lead. Suddenly, strips of light glimmered in the floor and ceiling of the corridor, causing the visitors to drop into a crouch.

"They're only lights," Riker said with relief, rising to his feet.

He felt a slight tremble, and he looked back in the direction they had come from. At the far end of the corridor, the green jade appeared to be moving—sliding—and he wondered if it was a trick of the light. Looking closer, he realized that the walls of the corridor were slowly oozing toward the breach, as if they were trying to heal it. He couldn't take time to watch this phenomenon, because Shelzane was already moving toward the gleaming door.

Riker shuffled after her, his booted feet making hissing sounds on the smooth green stone. When they reached the door, it slid open at their approach, revealing a small, conical enclosure within.

Shelzane fumbled for her tricorder, but Riker touched her arm. "It looks like a turbolift."

She looked up and nodded nervously. This time, Riker led the way inside, and Shelzane followed, keeping a watch on their rear. There were no buttons to push, no controls to operate. The doors whooshed shut, and the lift moved so quickly that Riker felt a heave in his stomach and slight disorientation.

The doors opened a moment later, revealing what appeared to be a cluttered waiting room. Diplomas, plaques, citations, and letters hung on every spare centimeter of the walls, while jumbled bookshelves filled the rest. The furniture looked old and comfortable, as if this were a good place to read a paper, have a discussion, or take a nap. By the turbolift was an umbrella stand with two polka-dot umbrellas stuck in it.

Riker stepped gingerly into the room, surveying the walls for other entrances and finding none. Shelzane slowly followed him into the room, her phaser leveled for action. They hardly noticed when the turbolift doors slid shut behind them.

Suddenly one of the short bookcases began to revolve, revealing a small man in a white laboratory coat. His face was a remarkable road map of the most startling traits of half-a-dozen different species, and his broad smile was equally universal. He wore no protective clothing, and his white hair bristled energetically as he strode across the room toward them.

"Welcome! Welcome!" he called, clapping his hands together. "Your perseverance has paid off. I thought we wouldn't be having any more customers for a while, but here you are!"

"We're not customers," said Riker through his speaker. "There's a plague going on out there."

"Let me show you our plans," said the little man. He crossed to a bookshelf and took out a large photo album. "According to our scans, the sire will be uniblood human, and the dam will be uniblood Benzite. Your child will be quite unique, but some intervention will be called for at the fertilization stage. We'll also have to perform lung surgery in the womb, if you want an oxygen-breathing child."

Riker pulled off his hood, thinking the old man couldn't hear him properly. "We're here because of the plague—not to have a child."

The old doctor frowned with disappointment. "You've changed your minds then. That's too bad. It's a big step, I know, but IGI will always be here for you when you're ready."

"Don't you know anything about the outbreak up there?" snapped Riker, losing his patience.

"You're wasting your breath," interjected Shelzane. He glanced over to see the Benzite intently studying her tricorder. "He's a hologram."

Riker peered closely at the little doctor, who gave him a crinkly smile in return. "I haven't had much experience with holograms," said the lieutenant. "I guess this one has been programmed to deal with prospective parents. Are there any *real* people in this building?"

She shook her head. "I can't tell. The shielding is very thick—I can't see anything beyond these walls. I doubt if our combadges would work."

Riker tapped his badge immediately. "Riker to shuttle." There was no response. "Riker to *Spartacus*." The only sound was the bubbling of a small aquarium on a corner table.

The gnomelike doctor chuckled warmly. "If the expense is a problem, let me tell you about our installment plans. Or perhaps you qualify for financial assistance. Let me check."

"We want to see where the procedures take place," demanded Riker. "We want the grand tour."

"Right this way!" chirped the kindly doctor. He started for the turbolift, then stopped and shook a finger at himself. "Sorry, sorry, I keep forgetting. You'll have to remove your weapons. Regulations, you know."

With a scowl, Riker holstered his weapon, and so did Shelzane.

"No, I mean, leave them here." He held out a spotted, white-furred hand. "I'll put them in my drawer—they'll be safe."

Riker's hand hesitated on the butt of his weapon. It seemed unwise to hand it over at this point. "Maybe we'll just be leaving," he said, edging toward the lift. "Just tell us how to get out safely."

The congenial gnome clapped his hands with joy. "The decision is in! You have been accepted as patients on a full scholarship basis. Your pregnancy is completely free!"

"We'll be going now," insisted Riker.

"But it's time for your anesthesia."

Something sharp pierced Riker in the center of his back. He struggled to reach it, but he couldn't in the bulky suit. An instant feeling of well-being spread over him, and he stopped struggling, using all of his facilities just to stand on his feet. Swaying back and forth like a drunkard, he tried to remember why he had come in here.

Riker caught sight of some movement in the room, and he turned very slowly—in time to see Shelzane pitch forward onto the carpet. For the first time he realized that something was wrong.

A throaty chuckle emanated from behind the revolving bookshelf, and he tried to focus his eyes in that direction. A figure in a black environmental suit stepped into the waiting room, trained a phaser rifle on him, and pulled the trigger.

All feeling in Riker's body disappeared, and his head rolled into a black pit.

# *Chapter Nine*

B'ELANNA TORRES LOOKED DOWN at the patient, who showed the strong reptilian traits reminiscent of a Saurian, although in a more muscular body. Through the gauze of a protective canopy, the patient nodded weakly at her, Tuvok, Dr. Gammet, and Prefect Klain. Torres looked around the intensive care unit, impressed with the efficiency and quality of IGI's infirmary. Their tour had been extensive, and they hadn't even seen the obstetrics ward, the biggest wing of the complex.

"This patient is our best in-house possibility for a case of the plague," whispered Gammet softly. "We've had other possible cases, but all of them have recovered. I gather that's not the typical profile. What do you think, Mr. Tuvok?"

The Vulcan studied a large padd containing the man's medical records. "At a glance, it would appear this man has a respiratory infection, not the plague. I would like to have our doctors look at this data, as well as the patient. Can we contact our ship and beam him up?"

The little man sighed, as if this would be possible but inadvisable. "I suppose we'll have to risk it. Why don't you take time right now to go back to the surface, where you can use your communicators."

"How far underground are we?" asked Torres, beginning to dislike this arrangement.

He shrugged cheerfully. "A hundred meters or so, that's all."

"I don't think being cut off from our ship is going to work," she declared. "If this is your only facility, we'll have to move most of the work to the *Spartacus.*"

"Excuse me," said Klain. "What about the two healthy people you took earlier?"

"That's another good reason to get in contact with our ship." Torres began to pace the ICU, growing impatient with the time this was taking. The tour had been a good idea, but it still felt as if they were in diplomatic mode, when they needed to be on the offensive.

"Prefect Klain can take you to the surface," said the old doctor reassuringly. "I'll get this patient up there, and we can make all the arrangements we need. I know you understand the need for us to distance ourselves from you, but I also realize the necessity for *some* contact. I do."

"See you later, Doctor," said Torres. "Thanks for all your help."

The diminutive fellow gave her a crinkly smile and waved both hands. Klain patiently herded them away from the intensive care unit.

The prefect looked relieved to get this unpleasantness behind them, and he asked conversationally, "Don't you think it's possible that the disease has bypassed Dalgren? We're a long distance from anywhere."

"I don't know what's possible," admitted Torres, "but if you had seen conditions on Padulla—"

"Helena has awfully big oceans," Klain reminded her. "They give our planet much of its character, and they protect us. You'll grow to love them."

"You sound like we're going to be here for a long time," she grumbled. They paused to let the door open, and the air rushed outward into the corridor; the facility used uneven air pressure to keep contaminants out of patient areas.

"I don't know how long it will take to stamp out this terrible disease," said Klain. "But I know that you can't be a Maquis for the rest of your life, B'Elanna. You'll have to look for peace eventually, and no place would suit you better than Helena. Here you would be worshipped, part of the social elite. You could be whatever you wanted to be."

She scowled. "I'm a ship's engineer, and you don't have any ships."

"Not now, but we're a resilient people. We'll build up our merchant fleet again. You can help us." Klain glanced at Tuvok as they stepped into the jade-green corridor. "In fact, I would say that *all* of the Maquis could blend into our society with ease. You have skills we need to rebuild, and we would welcome you with open arms. Where else can you go? None of you can ever return to the Federation, and most of your homes in the DMZ are gone."

"Your arguments have merit," conceded Tuvok as their footsteps echoed dully in the featureless corridor. "The Maquis do not have a plan to return to civilian life. They lack long-range planning skills."

"Not everyone thinks like a Vulcan," Torres grumbled.

Klain pounded his fist into his palm. "I'm going to bring

it up at the next Grand Cluster—sanctuary for any Maquis who wishes to settle here! After you help us save our home, it can become *your* home."

The prefect smiled warmly at Torres, but she was still thinking about what Tuvok had said. "Do you really think we should start planning to get out?"

The Vulcan looked pointedly at her. "Service in the Maquis can only end one of three ways: retirement, imprisonment, or death. I would prefer to see my comrades in retirement than in either of the other circumstances."

"That's very considerate of you," replied Torres dryly.

As usual, she couldn't fault Tuvok's logic—they *should* have an exit strategy from this insane life. *But peace? Retirement? A return to civilian routine?* After the last few months, these notions sounded like pipe dreams. Torres wondered what had brought on Tuvok's sudden concern for the future. The proximity of so much death, she decided, could give anyone a pervading sense of mortality.

The trio finally reached the turbolift at the end of the corridor, and the doors whooshed open at their approach. Klain motioned to his visitors to enter first, then he followed them into the gleaming metal chamber. The doors breezed shut.

Again, an odd feeling of dizziness and disorientation came over B'Elanna, but it was gone a moment later. They stepped into a corridor that sloped upward and was lit with luminescent strips embedded in the green stone. She led the way, eager to get out of the underground complex. There was no reason for the IGI facility to seem so claustrophobic, especially for a person who lived and worked on a small scout ship, but Torres nearly ran for the exit.

The outer door opened as she jogged toward it, and she dashed into the warm, afternoon sunshine. Their hovercraft was parked right where they had left it, and the crowd of onlookers had shrunk but had not entirely disappeared. She tapped her combadge and growled, "Torres to *Spartacus*."

"B'Elanna!" answered the relieved voice of Captain Chakotay. "Are you all right? You've been out of contact for almost an hour."

"I'm sorry about that, but their medical facility is underground, and we had to take a tour." She proceeded to fill him in on everything that had happened to them, including the fact that the bug might be a chimera.

"I'll get our researchers on that," promised Chakotay. "The two people from Dalgren that we examined are healthy, although one of them has one of the prions in his system."

"We've got a sick person we'd like to beam up," said Torres, "along with some records. Also, we'd like to get a couple of doctors down here to go over their files. They claim that Dalgren hasn't had any cases of the disease."

"Let's hope they're right. Maybe this won't be as bad as it looks—a smaller continent to the north appears to be clean, so far."

"One other thing, Chakotay." Torres chose her words carefully. "When this is all over, we may want to lay low for a while. The prefect of Dalgren wants to offer sanctuary to members of the Maquis who would like to stay here and blend in with the populace."

There was no immediate response from Chakotay. "Captain?" she asked.

"I heard you. There are days when that offer would sound pretty good. Ask me again when it's all over. Right now, we've got work to do."

After making arrangements that would keep the transporters and medical teams busy for hours, Chakotay leaned back in his seat on the bridge of the *Spartacus*. He gazed at the watery blue sphere shimmering in the sun and wondered what it would be like to live down there. It had to be better than dodging Cardassian and Federation warships, and hiding out in the Badlands.

With a sigh, he glanced at Seska on the ops console. "Any word from Riker?"

"No," answered the Bajoran.

"Try them again," he ordered. "I'd be a lot happier if we could just maintain contact with all of our away teams."

Seska worked her console for a moment, then shook her head. "Riker isn't responding, and their shuttlecraft is still unmanned."

Chakotay scowled and balled his hand into a fist. "Let's send a pilot to that shuttlecraft, just in case the entire Cardassian fleet shows up."

"Danken is coming on duty in five minutes. We could send her."

"See to it personally that she gets there," he ordered. "Tell her to stand by the comm channels and stay on alert."

"Yes, sir." Seska jumped to her feet and strode off the bridge, leaving Chakotay alone to contemplate the enormity of their mission.

Their first day had gone almost too well, considering the obstacles. Chakotay wasn't a pessimistic man, but he had a strong belief in fate. Something terrible and unforeseen was about to happen—he could feel it. But he wouldn't worry about it. Destiny had drawn them all to this forgotten corner of the galaxy, and maybe this would be the place where their quixotic pursuit came to an end, one way or another.

Legate Tarkon sunk into his chair, a scowl darkening his bony, gray visage. Like everyone else in the conference room, he cowered from the tirade of Legate Grandok, who pounded the table with a beefy fist as he ranted. The object of his wrath was Gul Demadak, who stood watching his old friend, hoping Tarkon would defend him, or at least save his dignity.

*No, it's not to be,* thought Demadak. He was to suffer this ignominy alone, with Tarkon letting him twist in the wind.

"I cannot believe you let this condition fester as you have!" thundered Grandok, chief of the Detapa Council. "That planet endangers our very existence, and then to let Maquis run wild on it . . . is inexcusable!"

There were grumbles around the room as the other members of the council agreed with their leader. So Demadak let his eyes wander out the large window to the glorious view of the Stokorin Shipyards, high in orbit over the amber clouds of Cardassia Prime. He envied the builders floating in the skeletal frame of a future starship at the next dock. Those menial workers could see the result of their work at the end of the day, while he had to think strategically—decades and centuries down the road. And in this matter, he had kept his own council, so even his friends couldn't speak for him.

"Am I allowed to defend myself?" he finally asked. "Or is it a given that you're going to destroy Helena and be done with it?"

That gasbag Grandok apparently needed to take a breath, because he just waved at Demadak to speak. The military commander appealed to Tarkon and his other allies. "First of all, you act like Helena is in Cardassian space. Technically it is, but it's also in the Demilitarized Zone. We are prohibited by treaty from sending warships in there."

To derisive laughter, Demadak nodded his head. "Yes, I

know we often break that rule. However, the Federation *does* monitor us—as we monitor them—so we're very careful. Sending enough ships to fight off the Maquis and kill everything on a planet is bound to bring them running. You've got to ask yourselves—should we start a war with the Federation over this threat? Before we're ready? I think not."

The laughter faded, and they were finally listening to him. "As for the Maquis, we have a spy on their lead ship. We have a garrison of two hundred mobile infantry on the planet—we know exactly what the Maquis are doing. Like the do-gooders they come from, they're committed to fighting the disease and ending the outbreak. That's a job that needs to be done, and we don't really have the stomach for it. According to our reports, they're maintaining the quarantine, keeping the Helenites on the planet. Who knows? They might succeed. We can always crush them later."

"That's taking a terrible risk," warned Grandok, glowering darkly at Demadak. "The Maquis are unprincipled scoundrels who can't even be loyal to their former masters. If they get sick, they're just as likely to pull up stakes as remain there, spreading the disease elsewhere. After we all get the Bajoran plague, we won't be able to punish you sufficiently."

There were grumbles of agreement after that remark, and Legate Tarkon rose to his feet, waving down the others. "I believe my friend Demadak is thinking rationally, but we can't be rational where this plague is concerned. We have to be *irrational*. We should muster enough ships in that region to make sure that the quarantine of Helena holds."

The majority barked their agreement to this remark, and Demadak could see the compromise forming. Tarkon hadn't gotten where he was by being a fool.

The legate lifted his chin confidently. "We must be ready

to destroy the Maquis at a moment's notice, if they fail, but not so rashly that we alert Starfleet. If we slowly assemble ships in the region, we'll eventually have enough to scorch the planet into dust and escape before Starfleet can react. A done deed is history, not a threat."

There was polite applause at this remark, and Tarkon looked pointedly at Demadak. "What do you say, old friend?"

The stocky gul knew that he was the military governor and could do as he wished in the DMZ, until they replaced him. Tarkon was right. When people got panicked by a plague—especially *this* plague—they did act irrationally. He could not be sure of holding his post if he failed to seize this compromise, and the compromise would at least buy him time. *I can justify it to myself, but can I justify it to my silent partner?*

Demadak decided to deal with that later. Right now, the entire DMZ was close to slipping from his grip. "I believe that plan is workable," he said with a tight-lipped bow. "I'll begin to assemble ships already in the DMZ, and we'll send another warship through every day, disguised as a merchant ship. We'll use proximity to the Badlands to mask our fleet."

Grandok scowled, not liking the fact that he hadn't gotten credit for the compromise. "I want a list of all the ships in this operation."

Demadak nodded. "That list will be so highly classified that I will entrust it to the keeping of the Obsidian Order."

*That should keep your grubby hands off it,* he thought to himself.

"Demadak is right," declared Tarkon, clasping his old comrade on the shoulder. "Every detail about this operation is highly classified. Breathe of it to no one, not even your closest mistress."

They all laughed, breaking the tension in the conference room. While the others congratulated themselves on their good sense, the legate whispered to the gul, "I saved your scales this time."

"All the same," grumbled Demadak, "I don't like people telling me how to do my job. I won't forget your interference."

He turned and stalked out of the conference room, thinking very little about Tarkon and all the self-important legates and guls. Demadak was only worried about what he would tell his secret benefactor.

*Nothing,* he decided. If they could keep this operation hidden from the Federation, the Maquis, and most of Cardassia, perhaps they could keep it hidden from *him.* With any luck, the experiment would soon be over, and Helena would be nothing but a distant, unpleasant memory.

Tom Riker rolled over on the wide, comfortable bed and pulled an armload of silky covers to his chest. Athough it felt natural to remain asleep in this plush splendor, he suddenly realized that he wasn't supposed to be in a bed. He sat up and blinked at the blankets, his silky pajamas, and a large, tastefully appointed bedroom done mostly in white antiques. Sunshine streamed in though the French doors, as did the gentle sound of the surf pounding against the shore.

Riker scrambled out of bed, stepping onto cool, red, rustic tiles. Atop a white armoire, he found a pile of clean clothes; a pair of calf-length black boots stood on the floor. The clothes appeared to be of traditional Helenite design—blousy shirts with colorful stripes and braids, brocaded pants with gaudy buttons and cuffs. Since he seemed to be alone in the bedroom, he stripped off his elegant pajamas and put on the outlandish clothing, which turned out to be warm, well-made, and comfortable.

"Hello!" he shouted angrily. "What am I doing here?"

There was no response, except for a flurry of footsteps that sounded far off but quickly became louder. A moment later, the white door flew open, and Ensign Shelzane stood there, looking very festive in her Helenite ribbons and braids.

He gaped at her. "What's happened to us?"

"I don't know, sir. I woke up in that bed, the same as you. You were still unconscious, so I just got dressed to have a look around."

Riker strode to the door and gazed over her head at a sunny hallway that seemed to open into a large living room. "Where are we?"

"We seem to be in a beach house. I think that's what you would call this place." The diminutive Benzite stepped aside to allow him to enter the hallway.

Riker rushed from room to room, almost thinking he was in a vacation resort on Pacifica. Every room was light and cheery, with comfortable if not sumptuous furnishings. There were two bedrooms, a bathroom, a recreation room with exercise equipment and vidscreens, a compact but functional kitchen, and a living room; his grandmother would have called it a sitting room.

Charging back into the master bedroom, Riker brushed past Shelzane and crossed to the French doors. He threw them open, stepped outside, and felt the sun-kissed, misty sea breeze strike his face. The sun was so bright that Riker had to shield his eyes, but he could tell that he was standing on a white observation deck that commanded a view of a narrow red beach and a few lichen-covered boulders. Beyond the boulders stretched a lustrous sea that looked like blueberry syrup with cream floating on top of it.

Shelzane stepped onto the deck beside him. "What does it mean?"

"Let's think. The last thing I remember is that we were in that waiting room, talking to the little man—the hologram. Then something shot me in the back—"

Shelzane nodded her head vigorously. "Yes, it felt like a dart. We were probably drugged."

Riker scowled angrily. "Before I passed out, I think I remember seeing somebody else . . . they were laughing."

"Who?"

He shook his head. "Someone in a black environmental suit. But who knows, it could've been an hallucination . . . or another hologram. For all we know, *this* could be a hologram . . . one big holodeck."

Shelzane squinted into the bright sunlight. "Yes, but there must be a thousand places on Helena that actually look like this."

"That's true." Riker spotted some stairs going from the deck to the tiny beach, and he bounded down and leaped into the sand. Running, he circled the beach and jogged to the side of the house. To his surprise, the view was virtually identical in every direction—an endless horizon of shimmering ocean.

Off the front door of the house was a small landing pad and a rickety pier that went about ten meters into a picturesque lagoon. Except for three palm trees, there was nothing else.

They were alone on a tiny tropical island.

Riker heard a shuffling sound, and he turned to see Shelzane walking up behind him. Her step wasn't as energetic as usual, and he saw deep furrows on her smooth, blue brow.

"What's the matter?" he asked. "Your injury bothering you?"

She touched her hip. "No, not too much. I just feel a little weak . . . probably a side effect of the drug."

Riker nodded, gazing from the white beach house to the sparkling blue horizon. "I wish I could enjoy the view more. I don't suppose it would do us any good, but we should search the house for a radio, flares, or anything we could use to signal for help."

"We should," agreed Shelzane. "We'll also need food and water."

They returned to the house and soon found that food and water would be no problem. Fresh water ran freely from the faucets, and the kitchen shelves were stocked with freeze-dried food in metallic bags. It was the kind of food that might be found in survival rations, but there was enough of it to keep them alive for several weeks.

Riker was fascinated by the water pouring from the taps, and he traced a pipe under the kitchen sink into the foundation of the house. Going outside, he found a water shut-off valve at the side of the house, and he probed the sandy ground with a stick to find the underground pipe. More investigation revealed that a large pipe lay submerged in the ocean only a couple of meters under the water. Both he and Shelzane decided that this pipe brought fresh water to the isolated isle.

It seemed like an awful lot of detail for a holodeck simulation, and they reached the grudging consensus that their island paradise was real.

Riker dragged two chairs onto the deck off the master bedroom, and they sat there and watched the morning sun rise higher in the sky. This helped them make a guess as to cardinal points, and Riker drew a compass in the sand with an arrow pointing north.

"Why are we here?" he finally asked. "I can guess how, but not why."

"We must have been spared for some reason," answered

Shelzane. "It would have been easy enough to kill us. If so, we're probably under observation."

Riker looked around at the multihued expanse of sea and sky. "Under observation? But how?"

"By long-range telescopes or scanners," she said, looking up. "Or maybe there's equipment in the dwelling."

Riker jumped to his feet and charged through the French doors into the bedroom. Over the French provincial vanity table was a mirror, and there was another one in the bathroom. In fact, there was a large mirror in every room.

In the second bedroom, he grabbed the floor-length mirror and tried to yank it off the wall. An electric shock jolted through his body, and Riker flopped to the floor, twitching like a fish in the bottom of a boat. Shelzane rushed into the room and wrapped her arms around him, and he could feel her trembling warmth. Despite the shock and disorientation, he soon stopped shaking, and his head began to clear.

A cheerful chuckle emanated from the doorway, and Riker twisted around to see the gnomelike doctor in his white lab coat. He clucked his tongue at them disapprovingly. "Please don't remove any of the furnishings. No, no. We only *rent* this house."

With a snarl, Riker charged toward the doctor, then he stopped himself. "You're not real, are you?"

"Nonsense, I'm Dr. Gammet. Don't get impertinent with me. Yes, yes, you are the subjects of an experiment, but it has to be done, don't you see? If we can get enough data on the disease this way, then we can spare all the Helenites who aren't already infected. We can step back and let you save the planet. You'll be saving millions of lives by your cooperation."

"How do you know we'll contract the disease?" asked Riker.

The little man pointed a spotted finger at Shelzane. "Because she already has it."

Riker felt as if he had been stabbed in the chest, and he turned to look at his co-pilot. Her startled face went through three expressions: shock, anger, and a dawning realization. He remembered her injury, her recent lethargy, and the way she had been sleeping at odd hours.

"But she's been inoculated," protested Riker. "The same as I've been."

The white-haired doctor scratched his goatish beard. "We were wondering about that. But her physiology has obviously been altered—to allow her to function in an oxygen atmosphere without a breathing apparatus. What about it, dear? Did that affect you somehow?"

Shelzane lowered her head, and the Benzite seemed to shrink into her outlandish clothes.

"You don't have to answer him," said Riker.

Her voice quivered as she answered, "They told me that the procedure might depress my immune system—it's a known side effect. I should have listened, but I've always been so healthy."

"Then you got injured," said the little man. "That was an intervention of fate; it introduced the disease directly into your circulatory system."

"But I'm not infected?" muttered Riker, hating himself for asking.

"No, Lieutenant. So far, the various Starfleet precautions are working in your system, but I can't imagine it will take long, considering your constant, unprotected contact with Ensign Shelzane. How long it will take—that is a question of great interest to us. The two of you are almost perfect subjects for this test."

Riker could contain himself no longer, and he charged

the pompous little troll. His entire body passed through the image standing in the doorway, and he crashed into the wall in the corridor.

The doctor reappeared to add, "Please behave normally toward the ensign, just as you would toward any loved one." With a blip, he was gone.

Riker picked himself up from the floor and gazed determinedly at Shelzane. "Listen, we will find a way out of here. All you need to do is go through the transporter biofilter."

"Within forty-eight hours," she said glumly. "It's probably already been twenty-four hours. I'm more concerned about preventing *you* from contracting the disease."

Not knowing what else to do, Riker took a step toward her, and she motioned him back. "No, Lieutenant! You have to protect yourself, even though it's probably too late. I'll be getting sicker and sicker, and you'll have to stay away from me."

"No, I have to get us out of here," vowed Riker. "In time to save you."

Through the open window in the second bedroom, he caught sight of the blue silhouette of the ocean; it seemed as vast as space, stretching into the wavering horizon. Also through the window came the timeless crunch of the surf against their spit of land, wearing it down a few centimeters a year. Time hung heavily on this island, and freedom seemed eons away, in another universe.

It dawned on Riker that *time* was their new enemy.

# Chapter Ten

DR. GAMMET AND DR. KINCAID were grinning, and Tuvok, while not grinning, looked satisfied. The patient lying before them in the clean room enclosure was not sick but possessed two of the prions that caused the plague. If the third were present, they would combine to form the multiprion that brought on the full-scale infection. B'Elanna Torres understood that much.

She had been on the bridge of the *Spartacus*, scanning for Riker and Shelzane, while running computer models for the researchers, when she was summoned to the cargo hold. Starfleet's equipment had meshed nicely with IGI's equipment to produce a state-of-the-art laboratory in a clean room enclosure, and now they had their first success. She could see the excitement among the others, but she wasn't quite sure of the reason.

She gazed through the clear screen at the Helenite lying unconscious on the metal table. "Why is it such a good thing that this woman is almost sick?" she asked Tuvok.

"Because she possesses a prion not previously seen in any of the other Dalgrens we have examined," answered Tuvok. "And her exact movements can be traced. She arrived on Dalgren only three weeks ago, before the quarantine, from a small continent known as Santos. This continent lies east of Padulla, so it may be that the infection is spreading westward."

Torres looked with sympathy at the unconscious woman, thinking she looked mostly Argrathi, with her plump face and high forehead. "So we're off to this other continent?"

"Some of us are going there," answered Dr. Kincaid, a middle-aged woman who seldom smiled but was smiling now. "Dr. Gammet thinks it would be a good idea if you returned to Dalgren with him."

"Why?"

"B'Elanna," said Dr. Gammet with grandfatherly patience, "Prefect Klain was expecting you for dinner, and that was hours ago. It's now the middle of the night. He's been waiting a long time."

"But we've got so much to do—"

"The prefect has complied with all of our requests," said Tuvok. "We should comply with his. This mission has a diplomatic component, and devoting one person to that task is an acceptable use of resources. I would advise you to spend time with the prefect and collect information."

"All right," muttered Torres, tapping her combadge. "Torres to bridge."

"Chakotay here."

"Dr. Gammet wants me to go back to the planet with him

and be diplomatic. I'm sorry, but I couldn't find any sign of Riker and Shelzane."

"IGI on Padulla is probably deserted," interjected Dr. Gammet. "People certainly went home to be with their clusters and familes."

"Did you hear that?" asked Torres.

"Yes, we'll keep looking," Chakotay assured them. "They've got to be down there somewhere. You go ahead and be charming, and try to get some sleep, too."

"Sleep? What's that?" Torres strode onto the transporter platform and motioned to the white-haired doctor to join her. "Dr. Gammet, let's go have dinner."

"I shan't be joining you," he said with a twinkle in his eye. "I'm certain that Prefect Klain won't mind."

Torres nodded to the Bolian on the controls. "Put us down in front of IGI."

A moment later, they materialized on the landing pad in front of the immense green pyramid and its protective walls. It was night, and a foggy chill engulfed Torres and made her shiver. She glanced around, expecting the street to be deserted at this late hour, but several onlookers pressed forward, eager to get a look at her. A hovercraft parked on a side street suddenly rose into the air and cruised toward her.

"Good night, my dear!" called Dr. Gammet, as he bustled off to the entrance of the IGI complex.

A whooshing noise grabbed her attention, and she turned to see the hovercraft settle onto the landing pad. At the controls sat Prefect Klain, beaming at her with his perfect teeth, olive skin, and windblown ebony hair.

"They said I was crazy to wait out here, but I knew you would come back." He tempered his joy with a concerned frown. "How goes the battle?"

She walked over to the hovercraft and climbed inside.

"The researchers seem happy—they've made a connection with Santos as a possible origin point."

"Oh, really? That's good, is it?"

Torres shook her head puzzledly. "I keep wondering, Why Helena? Why now? It's awfully convenient."

"Convenient for whom? Not us."

"For someone who didn't want much interference." Torres shook her head. "Never mind. It will be good to get some food. Where are we going?"

"My home. The Dawn Cluster." He lifted a box off the floor of the hovercraft and handed it to her, smiling sheepishly. "This is a gift, but it's actually not a gift. It's practical. I promised to give you Helenite clothing, but I don't really see you shedding your uniform. If you wear this, you'll pass as one of us—in case we encounter Cardassians."

She lifted the top of the box and was stunned to see what appeared to be a handwoven coat made of blazing magenta, purple, and green threads, woven together in a tapestry depicting island life. It was at once the most artistic and ostentatious piece of clothing she had ever seen.

"Thank you. This isn't really necessary." She couldn't hand it back—the question was whether she would put it on. Wearing the fantastic robe, she would look like a queen from some old human fairy tale.

She had to admit, it was rather chilly on this foggy night. Not a star was visible in the gray sky, and the marine layer hung in the air like a damp mop. Torres shivered, stood up, and put on the coat. The natural fabrics were surprisingly warm, yet lightweight, and the wrap flowed down to her knees like a purple waterfall.

"It's beautiful," she said, realizing that for the first time.

"No, *you* are beautiful," Klain corrected her. "The coat pales in comparison."

B'Elanna sat down, at an unusual loss for words. "What will we have to eat?"

"Anything you wish," answered Klain, working the controls. The hovercraft lifted gracefully off the pad and headed down the street. For some reason, Torres was glad to get away from the imposing pyramid.

"We're mostly vegetarians," Klain continued. "And of course we eat seafood, but we have replicators if you desire *gagh,* or whatever."

Torres bristled. "I don't eat *gagh.*"

"I see." He piloted the open-air craft down a deserted cobblestone street lined by chic shops and quaint dwellings, topped by ornate walls and roomy balconies. Flowers and vines bloomed from a profusion of pots, boxes, and small plots, and their scents mingled and hung in the fog like incense. Some of the blooms were so vibrant that they glowed right through the fog. Torres looked down at her gaudy coat and realized where the inspiration came from.

In due course, they turned down a street lined with more stately homes—mansions surrounded by high walls. On this street, the fog reminded her of pictures of Earth in the nineteenth century—places like London and Paris. It seemed like ambassadors row, with houses that were too impossibly grand for one person.

They stopped in front of an intricate wrought-iron gate, and a servant rushed from an alcove to open the door for her. Even before the hovercraft had settled to the ground, he was holding the door open and bowing halfway to the ground. After Torres stepped down, the footman remained in this obsequious position until Klain had also exited from the craft. She couldn't help but notice that the servant appeared to be a full-blooded Coridan.

"Any instructions, sir?" asked the servant, staring at the ground.

"Go ahead and charge her up, Janos. I won't be going out again tonight."

"Very well, sir."

Torres wanted to ask Janos how he had fallen to this lowly position in life, but she remembered that she was expected to be diplomatic. This had to be the one job in the galaxy for which she was least suited.

Klain placed his palm against a security scanner, and the gate swung open. He smiled warmly at Torres and motioned her to place her hand on the scanner.

"Why should I be scanned?" she asked curiously.

"All guests need to register," he answered blandly.

Torres nodded. "Oh, it makes sure I'm of mixed blood."

"Due to the late hour, you won't see the club at its finest," said Klain, ignoring her comment. "But there should be a few night birds up at this hour, and hopefully we can roust a cook to make us a meal."

"I don't want to put anybody out," she protested, imagining some poor servant being dragged out of bed to tend to her culinary needs.

"Our cooks would fight for the right to serve you," Klain assured her. To B'Elanna, that thought was more frightening than the idea that they would be forced to serve her.

They walked along a rustic stone sidewalk that meandered through a garden bursting with blossoms and flowering vines. The perfume of the flowers was almost overpowering, and it mingled with the unmistakable scent of food—real food—cooking on a real oven.

"Do you see," said Klain with a smile, "they remembered

you were coming. I wouldn't be surprised if the whole house stayed up to greet you."

Looming ahead of them in the fog was the mansion, which had to be four stories tall and a hundred meters wide. The ornate building had giant columns, broad porticos, and balconies on every floor, and it was as large as most government buildings on Earth. The house was certainly big enough to house hundreds of people, not counting servants.

They ascended a wide stone staircase and passed between two massive columns. From the open door came the sounds of laughter and strange music played on a reedy string instrument, like a zither. A doorman bowed politely to them as they entered, and Torres noticed that he was unique, not a uniblood. She recalled what Klain had said about unibloods not even being allowed into the building. They needn't apply even as servants, unless they were content to park hovercraft.

They entered a foyer that was decorated with gaudy velvet furnishings, lamps with stained glass and tassels, and numerous hologram portraits morphing continuously on the walls. From the incredible array of faces on the ever-changing portraits, B'Elanna assumed they were past members of the Dawn Cluster, going back hundreds of years.

Word of their arrival spread quickly through the sumptuous club, and members began to emerge from various dining rooms and bars that opened onto the central foyer. They approached Torres with reverence and joy on their faces, and the music and conversation faded away. B'Elanna wanted to crawl into a shell, or at least a dim engineering room. Instead she was wearing a coat that glittered like the dawn, and dozens of Helenites gathered around her, awe in their eyes.

"Yes, she is as beautiful as we heard!" proclaimed a tall

dowager as she gingerly approached Torres. The older woman held out a clawed hand, and B'Elanna had no idea what her ancestry could be. Still she took the proferred appendage, which seemed to be the expected thing to do. At least the other Helenites murmured and nodded their approval.

"The Dawn Cluster is deeply honored," said the older woman with a respectful bow. The others applauded this statement with gusto.

Klain stood behind her, beaming like a proud father. Torres could not believe all this fuss and attention was for *her,* and she fought the temptation to laugh it off or make a snide comment. She had to be diplomatic, which meant bowing and smiling while several dozen strangers gushed over her.

*We're risking our lives to save you people!* she wanted to yell at them. *But you're hung up on the accidental circumstances of my birth.*

Mercifully, Klain put an arm around her shoulders and shepherded her through the crowd into a plush dining room. Waiters in white uniforms formed a line that led to the best table in the house, one which overlooked a beautiful tile fountain. Torres couldn't get over the feeling that she had stepped into a dream—one that wasn't even hers.

A waiter held her chair for her, and she sat down quickly. At last, the other diners returned to their tables, as if it were proper to resume their merrymaking now that the royalty had been seated.

Klain looked at her, amusement and pride on his handsome face. "You really didn't expect this, did you?"

"Are you kidding?" she whispered. "Most places I go, I get shot at."

Klain looked shocked. "Well, never here. Never on Dalgron or anywhere on Helena. Here, you will always be special—the ideal of uniqueness." He glanced at a server, who was instantly at his side.

"Blood wine?" asked the waiter.

Torres scowled, thinking that the worst thing about being half-Klingon was that she was expected to like Klingon cuisine. "Just water."

"Two waters!" ordered Klain imperiously. "And bring us the fresh fish appetizers."

"As you wish, Prefect," said the waiter, stealing a glance at B'Elanna before he hurried away.

Klain gazed at her and smiled with undisguised pleasure. "I'm certainly glad you came to Dalgren first, and not some other continent. Or else we might have lost you."

Torres scowled. "I'm not something to be won or lost."

"Of course not! I didn't mean that. I only meant that some other continent could have gotten the chance to woo you, and we might have been deprived of your presence."

She shook her head with disbelief. "Don't you even realize that there's a plague devastating half this planet? And you're worried about whether I like it better here or somewhere else!"

"Death and sickness come and go," said Klain, "but a uniqueness like yours has not been seen in centuries. Since your arrival, our morale couldn't be higher—it's as if we have seen perfection."

"Believe me, I am far from perfect."

"Not in our minds," said Klain, reaching across the table and taking her hand. She didn't pull away, only because it seemed cruel to be mean to someone who worshipped her. "We trust in your people and the IGI to neutralize the disease, which means that this day will mainly be remembered for your arrival."

The waiter arrived with two glasses of ice water and a steaming dish full of fresh seafood morsels. Torres had to admit that the smell of real food caused her taste buds to water, and her resistance began to break down a little. Following Klain's example, she speared a morsel with a silver needle and popped it into her mouth. As soon as she tasted the delicacy, expertly cooked in a rich cream sauce, she knew that she wasn't going anywhere for a while—not until her stomach was good and full.

"This could be your life," said Klain, "every single day. You would certainly be elected to the Grand Cluster, but your duties could be light. Or full, as you wish."

Despite her good intentions, B'Elanna laughed out loud. "Are you telling me that, even though I just got here, you would make me a leader?"

"You already are my leader," answered Klain, his black eyes sparkling with sincerity. "I'll gladly spend the rest of my life at your feet, and I won't rest until I convince you to stay."

"Wait a minute. You just *met* me, and you're asking me to *marry* you?"

"Not exactly," answered the prefect. "I'm asking you to have a child with me and join the Dawn Cluster, yes. If you wished to stay with me in a conjugal arrangement, I wouldn't resist, but I don't believe in monogamy."

B'Elanna chuckled as she speared another delicious tidbit. "What if I don't want to have children right now?"

"Oh, you wouldn't actually carry and bear children—that would be beneath you. For that, we would use a vase."

"A vase?"

Klain nodded and looked around the elegant dining room. About a third of the tables were occupied, and all of the diners were surreptitiously watching them. He only had to point to a tall, green-skinned woman with a plume of purple hair for her to stand up and sashay over to their table. Torres didn't know exactly why, but this woman reminded her of the women of easy virtue who followed the Klingon fleets.

"B'Elanna, this is Mila, who works as a vase. The three of us could bond tonight, if you wish. My quarters are large enough."

"I would like that," Mila assured her in a husky voice.

Torres blinked at both of them, realizing that she had just been propositioned for a threesome. Or had she? "Wait a minute. Your idea of a first date is for all three of us to sleep together?"

"The sex isn't really necessary, of course," answered Klain, "but I enjoy interspecies sex. I think I would especially enjoy it with you. Mila, or a vase of your choosing, would carry our baby to fruition. We could raise the child together, or you could be the donor, or I the donor. It wouldn't matter to me, as long as we created a healthy offspring."

He smiled warmly at her. "The physical bonding is just an extra expression of our commitment."

Only hunger and curiosity kept B'Elanna from dashing out the door. "I think I need more food. I'm flattered, but I've got to tell you . . . you move a little fast for me."

"As you point out, we may not have that much time." Klain shrugged and picked up his glass of water. "I could recommend the *ratachouille,* which I understand is a Terran dish."

"I recommend that, too," said Mila, staring vacantly into the crowd of people.

"So you have babies for a living?" asked Torres conversationally.

"Yes, and you fight everybody."

B'Elanna picked up her glass of water. "Well, they're both dirty jobs, but somebody has to do them."

"Excuse me," said Mila, bowing her head. "I'm not myself tonight. Yes, I'm a vase. I've been taking a year off, but I might cut that short for Klain and yourself. Excuse me, I . . . have to be somewhere." The statuesque Helenite dashed from the table and out of the room, into an adjoining café.

Klain looked embarrassed, then regretful. "It hasn't been easy to maintain a standard of courtesy under these circumstances. I suppose you could say we're not coping all that well."

Torres looked around at the gracious dining hall, with its holograms, potted plants, antique lamps, handwoven tablecloths, velvet booths, and plush chairs. Several happy diners smiled back at her, and she had to remind herself that it was the equivalent of two o'clock in the morning. "I think you're coping quite well."

"Do you feel at home?" he asked hopefully.

"No," said B'Elanna with a smile. "But I'm a drifter—I don't feel at home anywhere. One of the ways to my heart is through my stomach, though. So impress me."

In the beach house, Riker stepped back and surveyed the large mirror on the wall of the second bedroom. He had given Shelzane the master bedroom, because it was cheerier, with its big windows and deck. She was sleeping, because they both wanted her to conserve her strength for their escape attempt, whenever it came. Riker tried to tell himself that the inoculations were supposed to delay the worst symptoms, too, but he had seen too much suffering on Padulla. Once the disease took hold, the onslaught was swift and sure.

At least Shelzane was resting and eating. She seemed to enjoy the fish broth, and they had plenty of that in their reserves.

He sighed and looked back at the mirror, which he planned to demolish in order to reach the circuits contained inside. If it was transmitting *out*, maybe there was a way to use the transmitter to signal Chakotay. Riker knew enough not to touch the mirror again, and he didn't want to attack it at close range. That last jolt had almost killed him—but not quite. There was a chance that its defenses were programmed to become even more lethal with repeat attacks.

So Riker stood in a corner of the room with a pile of rocks of various sizes, gathered from the beach and tide pools. Near him was an open window, which was his quickest escape route. It was essential to find out what the mirror was hiding, especially if it was a panel of holodeck controls. Riker picked up a melon-sized rock and hefted it, deciding he had better aim for a corner.

He reared back and threw the rock into the full-length mirror, only his aim was a bit off. It struck more toward the upper center, and the mirror shattered a microsecond before it erupted in a gaseous explosion. Riker dove out the window into a thicket of sand and scraggly bushes just as a wave of heat blistered the windowpanes.

When he lifted his head from the sand, he saw acrid, black smoke billowing from the window, and he heard a shout. "Lieutenant! What happened?"

Riker ran around to the back of the house, where Shelzane was standing on the deck, looking frail and worried. She clutched a blanket around her trembling shoulders, as black smoke wafted over the house, contrasting sharply with the seamless blue sky.

"I was, er . . . inspecting the mirror again," explained Riker.

"By setting the house on fire?"

"Let's see what I did." Riker climbed the stairs to the deck and entered the master bedroom. He stalked across the tile to the bedroom door and felt it with his hand before opening it; there was a bit of heat but not much.

When he opened the door, smoke billowed in, and Riker spent several seconds coughing and rubbing his burning eyes. But a draft blew most of the smoke out the French doors into the crystal sky, and he was able to enter the hallway. Reaching the second bedroom, he glanced cautiously around the edge of the door.

The room lay in ruins—blackened with chunks of glass and some kind of grimy brown residue that covered everything. Nothing was burning. Where the mirror had been fixed on the wall, there was only a rectangular hole, filled with melted residue, shattered glass, and chunks of scorched building material.

"You're not going to be able to tell much from *that*," said a voice behind him. He turned to see Shelzane, keeping her distance.

"No," said Riker glumly. He stepped into the room and kicked at a pile of debris on the floor. "I've never seen a mirror self-destruct."

Shelzane coughed and leaned against the wall. "Do you have a Plan B?"

"Yes," he answered with determination. "We're going to build a raft with a sail."

"From what?"

"Actually, the raft is already built—it's that small pier out front. If we need more stability, we could lash together some of these doors. I'll look for a pole to use as a mast, and you can gather sheets, blankets, curtains—anything we can use for sails."

Shelzane grimaced and shook her head. "You'll be stuck with me . . . in the middle of an ocean. It might take days or weeks to reach a port. I can't go with you, Lieutenant. You have to try to save yourself—while you're still healthy."

"Nonsense," Riker answered with an encouraging smile. "We got into this mess together, and we're going to get out together. If you feel weak, I'll do the work. We also have to pack food and water. I'd better get started."

As he strode down the hall, Shelzane called after him, "Lieutenant Riker!"

"Yes?"

"Thank you." The Benzite couldn't smile, but her green eyes glittered warmly.

"Thank me when I get you back to the ship." Riker kept a smile on his face until he had stepped outside into the warm sunshine, then he frowned grimly. Shelzane's blue skin looked as pale as the sky, and it had begun to peel on her face and arms. He had no idea what that meant, but it couldn't be good.

Riker's frown deepened as he strode toward the small pier. Shelzane was a young ensign, just starting her career, and he'd had no business involving her in this madness. True, she had volunteered—but without his personal problems, maybe *he* wouldn't have agreed to this foolhardy mission. If he hadn't said yes to the Maquis, Shelzane wouldn't be here—it was as simple as that. All those grandiose ideas about helping people and saving lives, and now he couldn't even save himself and his co-pilot.

He would have liked to blame Chakotay and the Maquis, but what were they but a reflection of himself? Were any of them really out to save the DMZ—or just give some meaning to their misguided lives? Thomas Riker gave a derisive laugh as he stood watching the rickety pier float on the creamy water. Once again, he was stranded—soon to be alone. Somehow he always knew he would die alone, at the end of a pier to nowhere.

*You didn't give up before, when you were stranded,* came a voice he hardly recognized.

He started to look around for the hopeful voice, when he realized it was inside of him.

# *Chapter Eleven*

B'ELANNA TORRES GASPED when she sat up in bed and saw the size and opulent luxury of her guest room inside the Dawn Cluster. She had seen it the night before in dim light as she staggered into bed in a food-induced coma. Good food was not on the list of perks for a guerrilla freedom fighter, and she had taken advantage of Klain and the Dawn Cluster. If the prefect had thought he was going to take advantage of her, however, he soon realized it wasn't going to happen.

Seen by the golden light of dawn, the pearl-lustre furnishings and pastel drapes and cushions were tasteful and refined. Intricate montages decorated the walls, made from plants, shells, and found objects that must have been gathered locally. Shiny-red flowers blossomed from two vases, giving the soft colors of the room a vivid contrast. It was certainly the nicest room Torres had ever slept in, which wasn't saying that much, she decided.

She staggered out of bed, still wearing the magnificent coat Klain had given her. Several suits of Helenite clothing lay spread on the vanity table, as if awaiting her approval. A silver tray of fruit, toast, and tea graced a flowing desk. B'Elanna had to ignore these offerings for the moment, as she fumbled under her coat for her combadge.

She finally found it. "Torres to *Spartacus*."

"This is Seska on the bridge," came a friendly voice. "We wondered what had happened to you, but Klain assured us you were okay."

"I was definitely okay," muttered Torres, suppressing a burp that would do any Klingon proud. "I got wined and dined last night, and you ought to see this room they put me in."

"I haven't seen Prefect Klain," added Seska with merriment in her voice, "but I hear he's really something."

"Yeah, yeah, very handsome, and he treats me like a queen. Where's the captain?"

"He's due to wake up in a few minutes. Is it an emergency?"

"No," said Torres, glancing around at her sumptuous surroundings and the pot of steaming tea. "I'm just checking in."

"Chakotay said you should stay on duty there, and help the prefect as best you can. Tuvok is going down to IGI in a few minutes, and Kincaid is on the continent of Santos, tracking down that lead. The clinic in Padulla is busy, but it's tapering off."

"What about Riker and Shelzane?"

"No sign of them," replied Seska. "We're still looking, but there's a growing fear that maybe a Cardassian patrol got them."

Torres scowled. "We know they were going to the IGI on Padulla, right?"

"But it was deserted. Even Dr. Gammet says the workers there were probably sent home. Riker reported Cardassians on foot around IGI in Padulla, but since they've basically left us alone, we don't want to start something on a hunch."

"Those two picked a bad place to disappear," grumbled Torres. "I'll check in later. Out."

As she rifled through the pile of clothing, looking for something at least slightly subdued, Torres heard strains of music come wafting through the open window. At first she thought it was instrumental music from some electronic device, but then she realized it was singing—a choir. A smattering of applause and laughter told her it wasn't a recording but live music.

Torres crossed to the window and peered into the court-yard of the Dawn Cluster. Befitting the name of their lodge, thirty or forty people were gathered around the fountain in the courtyard to greet the dawn. When Torres opened the window to get a better look, several of them caught sight of her. At once, there was a flurry of activity as the chorus formed ranks and came to attention, all staring at her.

Uncomfortable with all the attention, B'Elanna almost ducked out of sight. Then they began singing. Their voices floated upward like an orchestra of horns and strings, an intricate arrangement of soaring harmonies covering half-a-dozen octaves. Passersby gathered in the courtyard to listen, but the concert was directed solely toward B'Elanna in a display of admiration and affection. These people were complete strangers to her, but they seemed to adore her.

*So I'm going to wake up and be serenaded*, she thought. *My duties can't get any more surreal than this*. Despite the beauty of the music and the velvety voices, Torres wanted to blend into the crowd—she didn't want to be the object of a command performance.

She looked for Klain in the crowd and found him lurking off to the side, under a tree. He was dressed in his finest stripes and ruffles. Upon seeing her looking at him, he bowed rather clownishly and motioned toward the choir. *Yes, they are magnificent,* agreed B'Elanna, and she couldn't help but to flash him a smile. At this, the chorus seemed to sing all the louder and lustier.

*These aren't people about to die!* she thought with a pang of fear. *They can't be, not people as vibrant and joyful as these. Surely they are right—the plague must be happening someplace else, to someone else.*

Clutching a computer padd in one hand and a case of isolinear chips in the other, Tuvok materialized on the street outside the IGI building in Astar. The Vulcan looked up at the green pyramid, uncertain as to why such an imposing structure was actually needed. His brief forays into the complex had led him to believe that most of the IGI facility was housed underground, not in the ostentatious pyramid.

In most of their buildings and dwellings, the Helenites showed acceptable restraint and taste, but this complex was grandiose for no apparent reason. Its only functions seemed to be to impress the locals and serve as a landmark, and Tuvok preferred architecture that was more practical. According to Lieutenant Riker's report on Padulla, the pyramid probably contained a defense system with a beamed weapon, but even that seemed unworthy of the massive structure and its impressive shielding.

The loss of Riker and Shelzane was troubling, not only because every person was needed, but because they weren't actually Maquis. The moment he saw them, Tuvok knew it was unwise for regular Starfleet officers to be involved in this mission, but he could think of no other way to get the necessary personnel and supplies. He wished he had been able to protect them better, but he couldn't without risking his cover. More than once, the Vulcan had considered telling Riker that he was an operative for the Federation, and warning him to leave. The opportunity had never come, and now it was too late.

In reality, Tuvok decided, having only two people missing in this entire operation was an accomplishment. Still, that didn't prevent him from regretting the loss of two young officers who didn't deserve this fate.

"Sir! Mr. Vulcan!" called a voice.

Tuvok whirled around to see a Ferengi rushing toward him from a storefront across the street. There could be no mistaking those mammoth ears, uneven teeth, and bald pate—he was a full-blooded Ferengi. As he crossed the street, he looked in every direction, as if worried about being followed. But there were few Helenites on the street at this early hour of the morning, and no one seemed to be paying any attention to them. Instead of approaching Tuvok, he jumped behind a tree trunk and motioned him over. The Vulcan complied.

With his gold-brocaded vest, sashes, jewelry, and bright pantaloons, the Ferengi's apparel rivaled a Helenite's in garishness.

"Thank you . . . thank you for seeing me," he wheezed, out of breath. "I knew you would come back here eventually. My name is Shep. This isn't a very good place to talk—why don't you come with me to the Velvet Cluster? It's not far."

"I have business inside," answered Tuvok, pointing to the pyramid.

"Anything you do in there would be a waste of time. Come with me instead. You'll learn more."

When Tuvok considered this request, he remembered that he had been scheduled to dine at the Velvet Cluster the night before, but hadn't kept his appointment. Information gathering was part of both of his missions—the overt one and the covert one—and their efforts to stem the disease were proceeding as planned. He could spare a few minutes for this Ferengi.

"Very well," answered Tuvok. "I will accompany you."

The nervous Ferengi grabbed his arm and spirited him down a side street. "My name is Shep . . . oh, I already said that. What's yours?"

"Tuvok. Why are you so anxious?"

Shep gave a sour laugh. "Why am I so anxious? Oh, nothing to be anxious about—ship destroyed, profits gone, stuck on a plague-ridden pesthole, surrounded by Cardassians! On top of that, I'm forced to deal with the Maquis, of all people. What's to be anxious about?"

"Your situation is not unusual. Be thankful that you are not on Padulla." The Vulcan continued walking down the narrow street, and the Ferengi had to hurry to keep up with his long strides.

"I'm *grateful*, I really am! Hey, I'm risking my life to see you, and I didn't do it just to complain." Shep looked around the deserted street; the heavy dew of the sea still clung to the lampposts and wrought-iron railings. Choral singing lilted over the rooftops from somewhere in the quiet city, as dawn nudged over the buildings and stole down the streets.

"About a month ago, I brought some laboratory supplies here," whispered the Ferengi. "I didn't know I was going to get *stuck* here because of it."

Tuvok tilted his head and replied softly, "Are you saying that you know who infected this planet?"

The Ferengi smiled, showing a row of crooked teeth; he grabbed Tuvok's arm and steered him toward a row of hedges that ran along the sidewalk. "We Ferengi are businessmen—it would insult our heritage if I were to give you valuable information without getting something in return."

"What do you wish?"

"I wish to get off this blasted planet!" he nearly shouted. "You've got a ship—you could take me!"

"None of us are leaving until this plague is under control."

"Yes, but it's safer up there, isn't it?" The Ferengi pointed into the gray sky. "The transporters cure you, or so I've heard."

"The best I could offer is to take you aboard our ship and let you speak with our captain. It is not a cure, but a trip through our transporter is effective during a certain stage of the disease. You could always be reinfected."

Shep's scrawny shoulders slumped. "So it's hopeless. We're all stuck here . . . for the duration."

Tuvok stopped abruptly and drilled the Ferengi with ebony eyes. "If you know who started this deadly disease, it is your duty to tell us. It could help save the population and the planet, and bring the perpetrators to justice."

"I only dealt with a syndicate," muttered the Ferengi. "Knowing them, I doubt if they even knew who the customer was. The people who removed the cargo were wearing environmental suits—I didn't get a good look at them."

"Then you have no information," said Tuvok curtly.

"I do so," sniffed the Ferengi. "I'll tell you something that none of the Helenites will ever tell you. They're so image-conscious—they always keep up appearances no matter what horrible things are happening under the surface."

Shep took the tall Vulcan's elbow and steered him down the street, their shoes scuffing the quaint cobblestones. "There's a war being waged on this planet, and I don't mean between the Federation and Cardassia, or between the doctors and the plague."

He looked around and stopped, waiting until a small bird fluttered from under a bush and flew away. He breathed heavily and continued, "For centuries, the Institute of Genetic Improvement has controlled the Helenites' reproductive functions, but IGI has gotten too big and greedy. In some places, they put in holographic doctors instead of real ones—things like that. So a few years ago, some wealthy Helenites formed competing companies to do the same work—making hybrids."

Walking once again, the Ferengi continued to glance over his shoulder and around corners. But they seemed to be alone. The air was empty of sounds except for the occasional creak on a balcony. "The competition has been brutal," he whispered, "sometimes resulting in industrial sabotage—if you get my drift."

Tuvok raised an eyebrow. "Are you saying this plague may be the result of industrial sabotage?"

"Well, it has effectively crippled IGI—they're not the monolith they used to be. I'd heard that a few of the smaller companies had gotten together to pull a dirty trick on them. When somebody has a monopoly on reproduction, sometimes competitors will do almost anything to get rid of them.

"If you think about it, the local companies will probably survive this outbreak, but IGI has gotten swamped by plague victims. Most of their facilities are closed, and their operations are shut down. Worse yet, they've had to open their doors to the Maquis and people from outside. Believe me, IGI is the picture of arrogance, and they wouldn't be talking to *you* unless they were desperate."

Tuvok nodded, recognizing an accurate observation. He quickened his pace, a feeling of urgency taking charge of him. "We believe the disease is genetically engineered."

"And who better to do that than genetic engineers?" Shep scowled and kicked a stone in the street. It skittered into the gutter. "I should've gotten off Helena when I had the chance, but they've got the only good restaurants in the DMZ! Even though I'd heard there was a disease on Padulla, I didn't think anything of it. Then *boom!* Without warning, that big Cardassian freighter blasted my ship out of orbit, killing my whole crew. We were told the freighter was a *hospital* ship, for Zek's sake! I'm so glad you shot them down. Luckily for me, I was down here, negotiating a return cargo."

"I am sorry," said Tuvok, abruptly stopping. "I could not enjoy a relaxed meal with this knowledge. I have to act on it."

"But you've got to be my guest at the Velvet Cluster!" insisted Shep. "Later tonight. Please! It would get me more credit. The lodge is right around the corner on Velvet Lane. Just come in and ask for me—Shep."

"I will try to make it," pledged Tuvok with a bow. "You have been most helpful. If the captain wishes to speak with you, I presume you are staying at the Velvet Cluster."

"As long as I can afford to," muttered the Ferengi. "Of course, in these times, who worries about piling up credit?"

"Indeed." Tuvok turned in the other direction.

"And please, bring your captain, too. He's uniblood

human, right? And remember, I gave you something for free. You owe me."

As Tuvok strode briskly down the sidewalk toward IGI, it all began to appear very logical. The outbreak could have been a dirty trick gone awry, or even an accident. He had to verify Shep's information and find out who controlled these smaller genetic companies.

He tapped his combadge. "Tuvok to *Spartacus*."

"Bridge here," came the reply. "This is Seska."

"Is the captain on the bridge?"

He could hear the bristle in Seska's voice as she responded, "No, he's not. Can I help you?"

Tuvok ignored her annoyance and pressed on. "When precisely will he return?"

"Precisely after his flying lesson with Echo Imjim. We think that gliders may be the best way to look for Riker, because the Cardassians don't usually fire on them."

"You're alone on the bridge?"

"Yes, and I kinda like it that way. Want to leave a message?"

"Please hail me when he returns. Tuvok out." He continued walking along the street, but he was suddenly conscious of movement on a roof three stories above him. He whirled around to see something duck into the shadow of a large vent. Tuvok couldn't be sure what he had seen, or if he had seen anything at all. A curtain in a balcony window moved—perhaps that was what had distracted him.

Except for a few lemurlike primates in the rural areas, Tuvok hadn't seen any animals running loose on Helena. He wondered whether a few of those primates sneaked into the city at night, to go through garbage and whatnot. On the other hand, there could be people observing him. The perpetrators of this catastrophe were still at large, according to

Shep. Tuvok walked more briskly, keeping an eye on roofs, balconies, and windows, and his hand didn't stray far from the butt of his phaser pistol.

He tapped his combadge. "Tuvok to Torres."

"Hello, Tuvok," she said, her voice lilting, as if coming off a laugh.

"I am sorry to bother you, but I have some important information to verify, and the captain is unavailable. I would prefer not to investigate alone."

"Give me a few minutes, and I'll be there. Where?"

"The IGI building in Astar."

Chakotay beamed with delight as the sea-glider under his command soared over the endless ocean, which looked like blue enamel rimmed in gold from the morning sun. The sun was so bright that it stung his eyes, and the sky looked as endless as space. Chakotay had flown many crafts in his varied career, but never one so responsive and natural. Gliding with the wind made him feel at one with the elements, and the brush of the wind against the fragile hull was like a gentle drumbeat.

"You're doing very well!" called Echo from the co-pilot seat behind him. "But did you notice that you're off course?"

He glanced at the compass and shook his head. "Sorry. It's hard not to get distracted by the beauty."

"Winds shift," said Echo disapprovingly. "You have to watch them. Don't let the wind ride you—you ride the wind."

"Checking sensors," said Chakotay, doing just that. "I've got a northerly wind pattern at three thousand. Should I take it?"

"Go ahead."

Lining up his wings with the horizon to keep level, Chakotay edged the antigrav lever upward. He knew that powerful and sophisticated gravity suppressors were working in the underbelly of the glider, but to him it felt as though a sudden draft had caught their wings and lifted them upward. Since he usually worked in artificial gravity, trying to avoid the problems of weightlessness, it seemed strange to seek safety in weightlessness. The farther he rose above the ocean, the more his sense of wonderment increased.

He glanced back at his Helenite instructor. "How am I doing now?"

"You're a natural!" shouted Echo. "You've got all the basics down. Of course, the hardest part is landing."

"I've had some experience at that. I could fly around like this all day, but I think we should do something useful while we're up here. Do you feel like taking a short flight over Padulla?"

She laughed at him. "Sure, but it would take us days to get there."

"Not when you have friends." He tapped his combadge. "Chakotay to *Spartacus*."

"Bridge here. Seska on duty."

"Everything under control?"

"Yes, Captain."

"Seska, I want you to lock onto our glider with a tractor beam and carry us over to Padulla. We need to come in near the capital. Let me know when you're ready, because I want to turn off the antigravity and put us at normal weight."

"All right, sir. Give me a moment."

Echo cleared her throat nervously. "Er, Captain . . . remember, the Coastal Watchers are going to want their glider back in one piece!"

"That's my intention," vowed Chakotay. "For my own peace of mind, I've got to look for the missing team. If we see Cardassians encamped around the area where they disappeared . . . we'll assume the worst. We won't take chances. Are you sure they're not going to shoot at us, too?"

"I'm not sure about anything anymore," admitted Echo. "Before, they were only shooting down ships that could leave orbit, not surface craft."

*"Spartacus* to Chakotay," a voice cut in. "We're in range and able to lock onto you with a tractor beam."

He put the lever down to zero, going into free flight at their real weight, which wasn't much. Still, the silver nose cone of the graceful plane started to edge downward.

"Proceed, *Spartacus,*" ordered the captain.

A sudden jolt let them know that the wind no longer controlled their tiny craft. Now it buffeted against them. He tapped his combadge. "Chakotay to Seska! Increase the field to encompass the whole glider."

"Yes, sir. Good thing I started slowly. Compensating—"

When the sea below them began to ripple past like a cascading waterfall, Chakotay sat back and relaxed. It felt as if they were standing still, not moving at all, but he had to look at the sky to keep from becoming disoriented. Like the passengers, the sky appeared to be standing still.

"Ah, this is the way to travel," said Echo, putting her feet up. "Why did I ever bother to go the long way?"

Chakotay looked at the unique Helenite with admiration. "This must be a hard way to make a living, piloting one of these planes across a great ocean."

"I don't hop continents very often," said Echo with a shrug. "Well, maybe more than I want to. If you have a good co-pilot, it's not so bad. That last trip with my son was the hardest of all."

"You risked a lot, including the lives of the people on Dalgren."

Echo frowned, and the furrows in her gray skin deepened. "I know . . . I'm not proud of it. But I wanted to save my son, and I wanted to go home. Those are the things you think about when death is staring you in the face." Chakotay was silent for a moment. He couldn't argue with that.

"Too bad we can't just stay up here," he finally said wistfully. "It's all sunshine and blue sky."

"I always thought I would die on a day like this, plunging into the West Ribbon Ocean," said Echo. "You barely kept me from doing it already. If the plague is about to get me, I think I'll drag myself into a glider and come up here to die."

A voice broke in, "*Spartacus* to Chakotay. We're getting close to Padulla."

Both he and Echo stared into the glittering horizon. "I see it," said his co-pilot, although Chakotay didn't see anything but a blurred ocean.

"Are we close enough?"

"Yes," said Echo. "Why don't I take over?"

He nodded. "Chakotay to *Spartacus,* cut us loose."

"Yes, sir. Happy hunting." With another jolt, they were flying free again, and Chakotay reluctantly took his hands off the controls. Echo knew her way around much better than he did, but it was hard to give up the thrill of flying the sea-glider. He could understand why they were so popular. Not only were they practical transportation, but they kept adventurous, young Helenites at home rather than exploring outer space.

Chakotay checked the sensors, but they were designed to search vertically for wind currents, not horizontally for life-signs. He had navigation and weathercasting tools, but he already knew the weather was delightful, as Echo Imjim flew by dead reckoning. So Chakotay used his eyes to survey the coastline, picking out the carved bays, green bluffs, white cities, and copper beaches from a distance.

Harnessing the wind, Echo masterfully guided the glider into a low approach that took them directly over the nearest cityscape. "We usually get navigation beacons and landing instructions about this time, but no more."

As they swooped over a sparkling bay, which sheltered a few sea-gliders and sailboats, Chakotay felt like a seagull coming home after a long flight. Only this was a home that was too quiet, too idyllic—the noisy flock had moved on. As they flew deeper into the city, the sight of the empty streets, silent buildings, and deserted courtyards gave him a chill. He didn't know this place or its people, but he could feel their restless ghosts walking beneath him.

Chakotay recalled pictures he had seen of the great pueblos of his ancestors on Earth, deserted even when the white man first saw them. In a thousand years, this place would be like one of those old pueblos—no one would know what had happened to its people, only that they were gone forever.

"We're getting close to the IGI pyramid," said Echo. "How close do you want to go?"

"Close enough to get a good look. Make several passes if you have to." Chakotay could see the green pyramid in the distance, looking alien among the traditional town houses and baroque buildings.

He wished he had told Riker to stay away from the place, but so many operations were going on at once that it was hard to anticipate the risks. Riker had been certain there was information to be gathered here, so Chakotay had let him come back, even after they had barely escaped the first time. Now it was probably too late to do anything to help them. No matter how many ways he justified it, he had lost the one member of his crew who could make a big difference in their struggle with the Federation.

"Captain, is this close enough?" asked Echo.

His troubled reverie broken, Chakotay leaned to the left to view the pyramid as they swooped past. "Yes, this is fine." The jadelike pyramid was impressive, but it couldn't overcome the gloomy pall of the deserted city. It was like the biggest tombstone in a dark cemetery.

He checked his compass. "This is the east side. Let's make a pass on all four sides, gradually moving outward."

"Okay, here we go."

In a slow bank, the glider came around to catch an air current that took them by the north side of the oval complex. Chakotay spotted the landing pad outside the north gate, as well as the wreckage mentioned by Riker. A moment later, they overshot the pyramid and had to dip lower to catch a current that took them by the west wall.

On this pass, Chakotay spotted movement on the street adjacent to the complex. Looking closer, he spotted two gray-garbed figures moving equipment into a dilapidated building. Glancing the other way, he thought he saw a hole in the west wall of the complex, but they soared past before he could tell for certain.

"Make another pass," he ordered. "I saw people down there."

"So did I," answered Echo, sounding worried. "They were definitely Cardassians. And I recognized those launchers they've got—they could shoot us out of the sky in a microsecond."

Chakotay scowled. He knew that Echo was right—they shouldn't push their luck with the Cardassians. Riker had pushed his luck, and now Riker was gone. "Is there any chance we could negotiate with them?"

Echo shrugged. "Well, the Federation negotiates with them. We've seen how well that turns out."

"Yeah," muttered Chakotay. "Head back for the open sea, and we'll hitch a ride home."

"Yes, sir!" answered the Helenite with considerable relief. She shoved the antigrav lever upward, and the glider soared high above the pyramid. Chakotay couldn't tell which she was more eager to put behind them: the Cardassians or Padulla itself.

*That's what I have to do with Riker,* he finally told himself, *put him behind me.* As they sped away, Chakotay stole a glance at the dead city and wondered whether any of them would get off this planet alive.

Only a hundred kilometers beyond the southern coast of the continent of Tipoli, Thomas Riker swayed uneasily on the deck of the raft he had strung together from doors and the sturdiest planks he cound find on the small pier. Dusk was blanketing the glistening sea, and he feared launching and sailing into the darkness, but he was anxious to test his new craft, with its single mast and sail.

He glanced back toward the house and could see Shelzane seated by the front door, wrapped in a blanket. It was hard to tell if she was even awake. The Benzite had been watching his progress out of support for his plan, although she hadn't been able to help much. Riker still entertained the thought of taking her with him, but it seemed more unlikely with every passing minute. How long would it take them to sail this raft to land? Days? Weeks? That is, if they were wildly lucky and made it at all.

Riker knew, unless they did something quickly, it would

be too late to save Shelzane. Even if they were rescued or escaped, she would be too sick for the transporter to help her.

"I'm taking her *out!*" he yelled. In the gloomy dusk, he thought he saw Shelzane wave back.

Riker checked his rigging, made from curtain cords, then he cast off from the dock and unfurled his sail, made from the curtain. To his astonishment, the wind grabbed the sturdy curtain and dragged him across a stretch of choppy surf. The planks and doors shuddered under his feet, but the raft held together for the first few meters of its maiden voyage.

Two minutes later, he was about sixty meters offshore, where the water was considerably calmer and deeper. Out here, Riker figured he could make decent speed, and he was filled with a giddy sense of accomplishment. Maybe there really *was* hope for them to escape. They would be slaves of the wind, forced to go where it led them, but that was better than sitting ashore waiting to die.

His joy was cut short by a sudden jolt that nearly pitched him overboard. Riker gazed over the side, thinking he had struck a sandbar. When he realized there were dark shapes—huge shapes—moving just under the surface of the water, he got down on his hands and knees for better balance.

Not a moment too soon, as his fragile raft was jarred again, and two planks of wood shattered. This time, he got a glimpse of an elephantine trunk and a spiny fin attached to a huge black form that slid across the water like an oil slick. Maybe these marine creatures were just being playful, he hoped, although this kind of play could have him swimming back to shore.

Suddenly one of the creatures rose out of the water and tried to board his raft, smashing it in half and nearly swamping Riker. He clung to the mast to keep from plunging into the cool, salty brine, and this time he got a close look at the monster before it eased back into the water. It was shaped like a lumbering manatee, but it had a mouth like a lamprey, with rows of jewel-like teeth glittering in its round, sucker-shaped mouth. The giant leech slid back into the water with a final grin, as if to say that dinner looked delicious.

Water sloshed over the sides of the raft, and the creatures began to swim in a frenzy.

# *Chapter Twelve*

WITHOUT THINKING, Riker began calling for help.

He quickly realized how pointless that was, because his shouts only agitated the hellish fish squirming under his raft. They were as large as walruses, but sleek, with sucker mouths ringed by rows of teeth. In their agitation they no longer had the will for concerted attack, but they smashed and jarred the raft until it was little more than a bundle of driftwood tied together.

Riker snapped off his mast and used it as a spear to ward off the beasts, although that had little effect. As the raft broke apart, he curled up on a last door, hoping he would drown before the giant lampreys mauled him to death.

From the shore, Riker heard a cacophany of sounds: high-pitched screams, shrill tongue trills, and the frenzied slapping of water. He turned to see Shelzane, about fifty meters away, standing in the lagoon hip deep in water, making a terrific racket. She ducked her head under the waves, while she continued to slap the surface, and Riker figured she was shrieking underwater.

Whatever she was doing, it was working, as the huge lampreys peeled off one by one to slither in her direction. Riker wanted to shout to her to watch out, but she had to know what she was doing. He quickly grabbed a good-sized plank and used it as an oar to row the door like a boat. He was very careful to ease his oar gently in the water, realizing that movement and sound attracted the creatures. Fortunately, he couldn't compete with the unearthly racket that Shelzane was making.

He watched nervously as she flailed in the water, attracting certain death. "Get out! Get out!" he yelled at her. She managed to crawl out onto what was left of the pier just as black waves roiled under the waters of the quiet lagoon.

Riker lifted his oar out of the water, realizing that he had to be still. But Shelzane dragged herself to a spot on the east side of the island and began to create her diversion all over again. With darkness fast approaching, he could no longer see the awful creatures, so he just kept rowing—slowly, calmly—toward the beach. Incoming waves picked up the door and propelled him the last twenty meters, until he fell off in the surf and staggered onto shore.

"Shelzane! Shelzane!" he called, stomping through the wet sand.

He found her, lying unconscious in the damp marshes near the lagoon. She was soaking wet, her frail body wracked with shivers and burning with fever. Riker picked her up and carried her into the house. He carefully undressed her, dried her, and laid her in her bed. After cleaning up the room, he stood by the French doors, alternately watching Shelzane and the double moons float on the dark sea.

"Lieutenant!" came a hoarse voice.

He rushed to her side. "Are you all right? Can I get you anything?"

"Some broth, in a while," she whispered. "But first, I have a request."

"Anything."

"When I die, please feed my body to those creatures."

"What?" asked Riker, in shock.

"Like most Benzites, I believe in renewal. So give my body to the sea creatures ... they can benefit from my death. Don't worry, I heard the doctors say that the animal life is unaffected by the plague."

"You're not going to die," said Riker without much conviction.

"You're a bad liar, Lieutenant," she rasped, her voice degenerating into a ragged cough. When she recovered slightly, she added, "My altered lungs will probably fail first. I may die of suffocation."

"You won't—" He stopped. "What do you want me to do?"

Her rheumy eyes looked sick but oddly peaceful. "If my lungs fail in this atmosphere, it should be quick."

Riker looked down, unable to say anything for the lump in his throat. Finally he croaked, "You saved my life ... I want—" He tried, but he couldn't get more words out of his mouth.

"I know." She nodded her head weakly. "There is one thing ... you never did tell me why Starfleet security thinks you're a commander."

Riker laughed in spite of himself. "Now that's a story. If

you think *this* is a mess, wait till you hear about what happened to me ten years ago—"

B'Elanna Torres and Tuvok stood outside the gleaming metal door in the northern gate of the IGI complex on Astar. She was literally stamping her foot, because they had been waiting here for fifteen minutes—with no response to their presence. It didn't seem as if the powers within would ever recognize them and let them enter. Tuvok stood calmly at attention, aggravating her impatience even more.

"Let me go get Klain," she muttered. "Maybe *he* can get them to let us in."

"The fact that they are avoiding us is very revealing," said Tuvok.

Torres scowled, "Well, you may want to stand here all day and find that revealing, but *I'd* like to get some work done."

He looked at her and cocked an eyebrow. "Were you getting work done when I hailed you?"

"No," she admitted. "I was eating my way though the Dawn Cluster. These people have real food."

"We must verify the information I received."

Torres scowled. "Do you really think that the Helenites are killing each other with the plague?"

"You are half-human," said Tuvok. "Humans used to inflict biological warfare upon one another with appalling regularity."

"But these aren't humans! Helenites are much more refined." B'Elanna shook her head. "I'm sorry, but it sounds like this Ferengi was just trying to get something out of us—like a ride."

"That is possible," conceded Tuvok. He looked directly at the area just above the door and spoke loudly. "If we cannot verify this information with Dr. Gammet, we will have to contact the smaller genetic companies. Perhaps they will be more open with us. Let us go."

Abruptly the Vulcan turned and walked away. Before B'Elanna could even take one step to follow him, the metal door whooshed open.

"Well, it's about time," she complained as she charged into the complex. Tuvok strode briskly behind her.

They walked down the sloping green corridor, now more familiar than strange, and entered the sleek turbolift. Tuvok surprised Torres by immediately opening up his tricorder. She watched him study the device as she went through the usual disorientation.

"As I thought," said Tuvok. "We have been transported."

"What?" asked B'Elanna. "Are you sure?"

"The shielding makes it difficult to obtain an exact reading, but we are deep under the surface of the planet—*not* a hundred meters, as we were told. If my suspicions are correct, the IGI complexes spread throughout Helena are nothing but empty monuments, with defense systems. There is only one IGI facility, and all the imitation turbolifts feed into it through transporters."

The door whooshed open, and a morose Dr. Gammet stood before them, looking more stooped than he had before. "You are correct, Mr. Tuvok—yes, you are. Except for a few scattered recovery homes, this is IGI. We have fooled and bamboozled our fellow Helenites for over two hundred years, and now we're paying for it. We call ourselves 'miracle workers,' but when our people come to us looking for a miracle, we're fresh out. We're phonies . . . with big buildings and a lot of parlor tricks."

"Somebody on this planet has created and unleashed a very sophisticated chimera," insisted Tuvok.

"Well, it wasn't *us!*" snapped the diminutive doctor. "IGI has been ruined by this thing. We've lost the confidence of the people, and our operations have been exposed to strangers. The pyramid on Padulla is under seige by Cardassians, and we've lost control in half-a-dozen other cities. In fact, our most secure wing—this one—is no longer safe."

"How many rooms are there like this?" asked Tuvok.

"Eighteen. Five of them have been cut off—even I can't get in. We've had serious sabotage."

"Why didn't you tell us any of this before?" demanded Torres.

The little man gulped. "Pride. Disbelief. We've controlled this planet for centuries, and we maintained control even when the Cardassians came in. We bribed them and shared our research with them—they weren't a problem. Yes, we had a few competitors, but nothing we couldn't handle . . . until the plague came. Now, overnight, it's all crumbled down around us."

"So who's doing this to you?" asked Torres.

Gammet shook his head, his spotted forehead crinkling in thought. "I would have said it was our competitors, but I don't think so. The scope of this is beyond them . . . somehow."

"Who are your competitors?" asked Tuvok. "Do you have a list of them?"

The little man nodded and crossed to his stylish desk. From a drawer, he removed a small computer padd, which he handed to Tuvok. "Here they are, plus the information I have about them. I thought about confronting them, but I kept thinking it wouldn't get worse. Well, it has."

As he read the data, Tuvok raised an eyebrow. "One of them is Prefect Klain."

"Yes, yes," said Gammet with a wry smile. "We only tolerate each other. And starting an operation like this, even on a small scale, requires considerable capital. You'll find Helena's finest families on that list."

"This is ridiculous," grumbled Torres. "Prefect Klain is not going to devastate his own planet for a business advantage."

"That's the conclusion I reached," said Dr. Gammet, scratching his unruly mane of white hair. "So who's doing this to us?"

Suddenly, the floor under their feet trembled, and the lights in the waiting room flickered. Dust and paint chips floated down from a crack in the ceiling. Torres and Gammet looked around nervously, while Tuvok closed the padd and put it safely in his belt pouch.

"What is happening?" asked the Vulcan calmly.

"Cardassians!" Dr. Gammet moved toward the turbolift. "We've already evacuated the patients, and there are just a few of the staff left. As you pointed out, our facility is linked by transporters, so once they've breached one of our pyramids, they can attack anywhere. They must be smashing their way from one wing into another."

The little man stopped in front of the turbolift door, looking expectantly at it. When the door didn't open, he pounded on it. "Something's wrong!"

The room shuddered even more violently, and the lights went off and stayed off, plunging them into absolute darkness. A lantern beam finally pierced the blackness, and Torres trained her light upon the turbolift door. It was frozen like a glacier.

"Is there another way out of here?" She strode across the room to the revolving bookcase. "Where does this go?"

Gammet hurried after her. "Yes, yes! Come on!"

Leading the way, the little man in the lab coat ducked

into a passage behind the bookshelf. Torres and Tuvok followed, and they found themselves in a featureless corridor that ended in a junction with five similar corridors. At the end of one of the hallways, sparks glittered on the wall. When Torres pointed the light in that direction, it became clear that someone was cutting through the panel with a beamed weapon.

Dr. Gammet whirled around, looking stricken with fear. "They're here!"

"Which way?" she demanded.

"It doesn't matter . . . we're doomed!"

Torres grabbed him by the collar and pushed him down a third corridor, heading in the opposite direction of the sparks. Her light caught colored stripes on the corridor walls, which probably would have told her where to go if she only knew the code. She just moved forward, pushing the diminutive doctor ahead of her. Tuvok drew his phaser and brought up the rear, protecting their escape.

They reached a door, which probably should have opened automatically but didn't. Tuvok applied his tremendous strength and pushed it open, while Torres and Gammet slipped inside. She expected to end up in another waiting room, but a quick flash of her light showed they were in some kind of operating room, with huge metal bins on the walls.

Dr. Gammet shuddered. "The morgue."

"Are those bins empty?" she asked.

"Probably."

From behind them came a clattering sound, as a chunk of metal fell into the corridor. Loud voices sounded, followed by thudding footsteps. Tuvok immediately shoved the door shut, as Torres shined her light around the room, trying to find anything that could help them. Her beam caught the doctor opening a bin on the bottom row. It was empty.

Torres moved her light to the left to reveal a large sign on a pedestal—universal symbols for "Biohazard! Danger!" superimposed over an impressive skull logo. She grabbed the sign and placed it directly in front of the door, so it would be the first thing anyone saw when they opened the door even a crack.

A metallic thud sounded, and she turned to see Dr. Gammet climbing into the body locker. He waved just before he shut it and went into hiding. Tuvok walked briskly around the large room, stopping at a metal door that looked like one of the fake turbolifts. He began fiddling with his phaser; B'Elanna couldn't tell what else he was going to do, because at that moment she heard voices on the other side of her door. She padded across the floor as quietly as she could, turning out her light as soon as she reached Tuvok. In absolute darkness, they flattened themselves on the floor and waited.

*These Cardassians have come from Padulla,* she told herself. *The plague is bad there, and they may not even know where they are in this labyrinth.*

Grunting, groaning, and scraping sounds issued from the darkness, followed by a clang as the Cardassians slammed the door open. A strong light struck the sign, and from a distance she could see it reflected on their shiny black heads, which were covered with gas masks. They shined their lights around the room, bouncing off the gleaming lockers, but they didn't advance into the morgue. Despite the crisscrossing light beams, the room remained as still as the death promised on the sign.

Nearby an explosion sounded, and the ground trembled. When an officer barked orders, the lights retreated into the corridor. Amid grunting and groaning, the door was pushed shut, and the room was returned to merciful darkness.

Torres rolled over and turned on her light, shining it at Tuvok. He squinted at his phaser, making an adjustment to the weapon. "This will have to do. Please hand me your phaser."

"But they may come back any minute," she protested.

"I need our phasers to supply power to this transporter," he replied. "We will exhaust our weapons, but it may enable us to reach the surface."

Torres couldn't argue with that, and she turned over her weapon. "Do you need a light?"

"No, I have my own. But you can help me get the door open. I have to find the override controls."

Putting her hip into it, Torres was able to help Tuvok get the turbolift door opened. The enclosure was similar to the others, only larger, in order to accommodate gurneys. Tuvok used his tricorder to locate the access panel, then he set up his light. He removed a compact tool kit from his pouch and set to work.

Muttering under her breath about Cardassians, Torres went back into the morgue to unearth Dr. Gammet from his body locker. When she pulled out the drawer, he blinked at her. "Is it over?"

She whispered, "I'm afraid not. But Tuvok is trying to get us out of here. Are the turbolifts the only way up?"

"There are vents, but we're so far down, I'd hate to imagine how long that would take." He whimpered pathetically.

Torres scowled at him. "Is there anything else you haven't been honest about?"

"No," muttered Gammet. "We've reached the end— there's nothing left to protect or hide. Now we're dependent upon you to save us."

"Great. You've got the plague, a mass murderer, and Cardassians running amok—and only the Maquis to save you." B'Elanna Torres offered a hand to pull him out of the body locker. "Let's hope your luck changes, or you're going to need one of these for real."

Gul Demadak laughed lustily at the antics of the Olajawaks, a troupe of comedians who followed centuries-old traditions in their costumes and routines. Although he had seen this troupe before, their clownish acrobatics had the old gul slapping his knee. The rest of the audience was just as appreciative, laughing and applauding in all the right places. Until he had gotten to the theater, Demadak hadn't realized how much he needed this evening of diversion. Considering what he had been through lately, it was understandable.

Besides, he always enjoyed coming to the Primus Theater, an outstanding example of a baroque period in Cardassian architecture. With its numerous statues and busts, thick velvet curtains and chairs, and intricate murals, the Primus looked nothing like most of Cardassia's gray, utilitarian buildings. It always seemed a bit naughty to come here, particularly since the Primus had once been used for more lascivious entertainment. He had a private box, of course, as befitted his station.

He glanced at his long-suffering wife and smiled. It had been her idea to come to the theater tonight, and he was appreciative. Although he mostly ignored the woman these days, she persisted in maintaining the semblance of a marriage. At times like this, thought Demadak, his marriage was comforting. Perhaps he would reward her by inviting her into his bed tonight.

In the middle of a guffaw, he felt a tap on his shoulder.

Demadak turned angrily to see a wizened old usher. "What is it?" he snapped.

"Sorry to interrupt you, sir," answered the old man, quaking in his boots. "We have a hail for you on our public communicator."

"That's ridiculous!" snarled Demadak. "Nobody knows I'm here. I'll have your job for annoying me."

The old man gulped and took a step back. "I'm sorry, sir, but he was quite insistent. He knew exactly where you were sitting, and he said that if you refused to come, I should mention a word."

"What word?"

"Helena."

Demadak stared at the old usher, and it would be hard to say which of the two men looked more frightened. He turned to his wife and manufactured a smile. "I'll be right back, my dear."

"What is it?"

"Nothing important." Demadak rose quickly and followed the usher into the ornate lobby. With the show in progress, the lobby was empty, and the usher conducted him to a small booth near the refreshment counter. As soon as he entered the booth and closed the door, soothing lights came on.

"Demadak?" asked a raspy voice that had been electronically altered.

"Yes?" The gul swallowed hard and balled his hands into fists.

"Do you know who this is?"

"I can guess. I don't know why you should be bothering me here. I've sent you all the pertinent—"

"Silence!" roared the altered voice. "You presume to think you can fool *me*. Let this be a warning that I know

191

where you are every minute of the day, and I know everything you do—and *don't* do. Against my explicit orders, you've sent a fleet to Helena—to destroy it!"

Demadak lowered his voice, hardly believing they were discussing these matters aloud. "I am not the entire government of Cardassia," he insisted. "I delayed sending ships for as long as I could, but the Detapa Council is up in arms. All they can think about is the plague and the Maquis—"

"No excuses!" thundered the voice. "I could find a million failures who make excuses, but you were chosen for your independence and ruthlessness. Sending a fleet to Helena endangers the entire experiment and my best operative. Now I will be forced to rescue my operative and end the experiment early—before your ships blunder in and destroy the planet. You had better pray to your gods that our records are recovered as well."

"Or what?" snapped Demadak defiantly. "I don't like to be threatened—even by *you*."

"I never threaten," said the voice with a steely calm. "I only promise. In fact, I promise you this—when you return home tonight, you will find your prized riding hound dead in its kennel, its throat slashed."

"What!" wailed Demadak with a mixture of outrage and horror.

"And the next time, it will be your grandson, or your daughter. Or *you*. Do I make myself clear?"

The gul started to protest that his estate was protected, under high security—that they couldn't have gotten in and killed his prized hound, Marko. Then he remembered with whom he was dealing. "Yes, it's clear," he muttered through clenched teeth.

"Good. You have to delay the destruction of Helena as

long as possible. Exaggerate the number of Maquis vessels, if you must. I'll inform you when it's safe to proceed. And call off your garrison—they're wreaking havoc with my operation."

"Yes, sir," answered Demadak in a hoarse whisper. He wasn't going to mention that he might not be able to hold off the fearful cowards on the council or in Central Command. They could always replace him with someone more amenable. But his benefactor knew that and was counting on Demadak's considerable political skills.

"Don't keep anything hidden from me again," warned the scratchy voice. "Good-bye."

When the gul stepped out of the booth, he finally unclenched his fists and found that his palms were clammy and sweaty. Few beings had such an effect on him.

Still in a daze, he returned to his seat in his private box. His wife smiled at him and pointed to the frantic players on the stage. "You missed the funniest part," she said, "when the harlequin tries to punish the servants."

"Yes, I like that," he replied absently.

When the rest of the audience howled with appreciation at a particularly wild stunt, Gul Demadak turned his attention back to the performers. But he was no longer able to laugh.

A light flickered on inside of the transporter/turbolift in the bowels of the darkened IGI complex. Tuvok motioned to Torres and Gammet to come inside. "Hurry," he urged. "We only have a few seconds."

They did as they were told, although Torres kept her light shining on the empty morgue and the door that they had forced open to get in. Although she hadn't seen the Cardassians since their brief visit, she had heard them ransacking nearby rooms. They couldn't be far away, and this sudden burst of power might alert them.

"Stand in the center," ordered Tuvok, reaching into the access panel. Torres could see their two phasers, jury-rigged to the circuits, with Tuvok about to connect two couplers.

"Are you sure this is going to work?" asked Dr. Gammet doubtfully.

"No," answered Tuvok as he continued to work.

"Then maybe we should—"

Suddenly there was a crash and the sound of angry voices. Torres peered out the door of the turbolit and could see three brawny Cardassians pushing open the door to the morgue. One of them pointed at her, and she quickly killed her light.

"Hurry!" she warned Tuvok.

"That is my intention."

The Cardassians stormed the morgue in force, and their lantern beams crisscrossed the room like a laser show. A phaser beam streaked over Tuvok's head and blasted a hole in the wall, but that didn't stop his nimble fingers from connecting more circuits and wires. Finally finished, the Vulcan took a step to join them in the center of the turbolift just as the lead Cardassians charged into view.

"Raise your hands," ordered Torres, hoping a show of having no weapons would buy them a few seconds.

It did, as the lead Cardassian leveled his weapon but didn't fire immediately. The odd feeling of disorientation gripped B'Elanna not a moment too soon, and the Cardassians were caught by surprise when the dormant transporter suddenly activated. They shouted and fired their weapons, but Torres, Tuvok, and Gammet disappeared in a curtain of sparkling molecules.

A moment later, they found themselves in the same place—the turbolift—only Cardassians were not threatening them with phaser rifles. The door was closed, and the lift was dark, forcing Torres to turn on her light. Tuvok immediately threw his tremendous strength against the door. "Help me, please."

Torres and Gammet also pushed, but the Vulcan did the majority of the work as they heaved the door open half a meter. Torres squeezed through first and dropped into a crouch, warily shining her light into the blackness. With relief, she saw that they were in a jade-green corridor that sloped upward, and she motioned to the others to follow her.

When they reached the next door, Dr. Gammet was able to open it with a pass card. "The outer wall is on a separate circuit," he explained.

Torres pointed her light back down the corridor, but she could see no indication that hordes of Cardassians were chasing them. After Gammet and Tuvok exited into the street, so did Torres, and she decided that warm sunshine had never felt so good.

She glanced around, but the streets appeared deserted. "Where are we?"

"Padulla, I believe," answered Gammet, frowning at that conclusion.

"Let's find some cover," said Tuvok, striding toward a deserted storefront across the street. Torres and Gammet hurried after him.

Once they were off the street, she tapped her combadge. "Torres to *Spartacus*."

"Seska here," came the reply. "Where have you been?"

"I'm worried more about where we *are*, which is Padulla," she answered. "Three to beam up."

"It will take us a few minutes to get into position. Stand by."

Torres tried the door to the shop but found it locked. She whirled around and kicked the shop door open, and it fell off its hinges with a cracking sound and crashed to the floor. "Let's get to higher ground," she ordered.

She led the way, not pausing until they had reached a stairwell which led to the roof. With a sigh, she halted their mad dash and slumped against the door. Gammet, who was panting heavily, sat on the top step, while Tuvok calmly took out his tricorder.

"I can find no lifesigns in the immediate vicinity," he reported. "We appear to be safe for the moment."

"Thank you for saving me," breathed Gammet.

"You're not safe yet," countered Torres. "How do we find out whether Klain—or any of your competitors—started this disease?"

The little doctor scratched his white whiskers. "I know what Prefect Klain fears the most—that the plague will strike Dalgren. If that happens, his reaction might tell us something."

"Hmmm," said B'Elanna, wiping a sheen of sweat off her forehead ridges. Before she could say anything else, her combadge chimed. "Torres here."

"Stand by to beam up."

"Gladly," she breathed.

All night long and all the next morning, Thomas Riker had been digging a hole on the north side of the island, using pots and pans as shovels. Fortunately, the sandy earth was fairly soft, and his makeshift tools were good enough for the job, if slow. Riker paused every few minutes to catch his breath and listen for sounds from the house. He had found an old dinner bell and had hung it by Shelzane's bed, hoping she would use it to call him, if she needed him.

He felt guilty, thinking he should stay by her bedside until the end. But Shelzane had insisted that he pursue his latest escape plan, although it was the craziest one yet. They both knew that the clock was ticking for him, too, and he was beginning to feel tired. Hours of digging and no sleep were making him feel that way, Riker told himself, because he refused to acknowledge that he was infected by the disease. Nevertheless, a sense of urgency propelled him to crouch on his knees for hours on end, digging this monstrous hole.

The long hours paid off when he reached a metal box containing machinery—the valves, gears, and circuits that controlled the flow of fresh water from the pipeline into the house. While getting Shelzane a glass of water, he had realized that life on the island wasn't static—fresh water came and went everyday. The pipeline came from somewhere, carrying water, then kept going . . . somewhere else. From observing the pipeline in the ocean, he guessed that the pipe itself had to be about two meters in diameter, large enough to accommodate him if it wasn't completely filled with water. He wouldn't find that out until he broke into the pipe.

When he looked up to wipe the sweat from his brow, Riker spotted something in the crystal blue sky. Shading his eyes, he peered at what appeared to be a large white bird, soaring high above him. When he looked closer, he realized it was a sea-glider, similar to those he had seen floating in the bay at Padulla.

He bounded to his feet and waved frantically, yelling at the top of his lungs. The plane, however, never deviated from its course or altitude. Even if the pilot were looking directly at the tiny island, Riker told himself, it was doubt-ful he could see him from that distance. Nevertheless, spot-ting the glider gave him hope, just knowing that not everyone on Helena was dead or dying.

As soon as he began digging again, he heard the peal of the bell inside the house. Riker tossed down his tools, jumped to his feet, and rushed inside. Even before he reached the master bedroom, he heard horrible wheezing, and he rushed inside to find Shelzane writhing on the bed, gasping for breath. He rushed to her side and hugged her trembling body.

Somehow his presence calmed her, although her frail chest continued to heave with the struggle to breathe. He felt her hands grip his back, as if trying to hang on.

"I'm here!" he assured her. "I'm here."

"I know," she rasped. Shelzane gave him a final squeeze, then her fingers loosened and slipped from his back. Her entire body went limp, and he gently laid the Benzite on the bed. Despite the ravaged state of her body, she wore a look of peace on her face.

Riker stood up, wiping the tears from his eyes. Enraged, he yelled at the top of his lungs, "Are you happy—you bas-tards! What did you achieve by killing her?"

He whirled around, half expecting to see the little white-haired hologram, gloating at them. But no one was there—he was alone in the stylish beach house. A breeze ruffled the curtains and blew through the bedroom; despite the warm sunshine outside, the air was strangely cold.

It was time to go.

Riker wrapped Shelzane in her bedcovers and carried her to the lagoon. He unwrapped her body in the waist-high water, then tossed the sopping blankets into the water. As Shelzane had done for him, he slapped the water, calling the creatures. Gazing intently at the surf, Riker finally saw black shapes moving beneath the creamy blue, edging closer to the sounds. He climbed out of the water a few seconds before the sea creatures reached Shelzane's body. The water began to churn, and he turned away.

Fighting back tears, Thomas Riker strode toward the pit he was digging. Before he returned to work, he stopped to look at the endless horizon of two-tone blue. He didn't know who the perpetrators of this terrible disease were, or why they were doing this to Helena, but he knew one thing: he was going to stay alive long enough to stop them.

# Chapter Thirteen


AFTER HEARING A REPORT from Torres and Tuvok, Captain Chakotay stroked his chin thoughtfully and looked at Dr. Gammet. "So it's possible that your own people—former colleagues of yours—planted this terrible disease on Helena?"

The little man sunk into a chair in the mess hall of the *Spartacus*. He looked extremely embarrassed. "Yes, it's possible. All of our research would suggest that *somebody* planted this disease on Helena, and I've wracked my brain trying to figure out who. And why. The Cardassians could have done it, but why? If they wanted to destroy the planet, there are more effective means that are less dangerous to them. On the other hand, if somebody wanted to destroy IGI, they've accomplished that."

Chakotay nodded and looked at Tuvok. "Any thoughts?"

"Only that we cannot hope to be successful if unknown parties continue to introduce this disease. Even those who have been treated can contract it again."

"We're fighting an entrenched battle against this thing," said Chakotay, "trying to find a place to draw the line and contain it. Padulla is under control, but the number of people left there is relatively small. If the disease spreads across Dalgren, Santos, Tipoli, and the other continents, we'll be overrun. And now you're saying we don't have IGI to help us?"

"I'm sorry," muttered Dr. Gammet. "None of us were prepared for a disease like this . . . and the repercussions. Most of the people on our staff are already helping you, but the Cardassians have ransacked our facilities. I don't know what else to do."

Torres frowned, as if reaching a very unpleasant decision. "I've got an idea for testing Prefect Klain's honesty, but it's risky. It might cause a panic."

"The whole planet is already an armed camp," said Chakotay. "Dr. Kincaid and her staff were fired upon when they landed on Santos. The Cardassians are liable to pop up anywhere. All in all, I'd say it's too late to worry about panic. While the medical teams do their work, we've got to do whatever it takes to track down this mass murderer."

"Agreed," said Tuvok.

Dr. Gammet nodded solemnly. "B'Elanna and I can go to the Dawn Cluster tonight and try her plan on Prefect Klain. If it's not him, we'll keep looking."

"Captain," said Tuvok, "you and I have been invited for dinner at the Velvet Cluster, a lodge for unibloods. Since the Ferengi already gave us valuable information, we might learn more by going there."

"All right, but let's all be careful and keep in contact,"

said the captain. "Riker and Shelzane are still missing, and I don't want to lose anybody else."

He looked at B'Elanna and managed a smile. "Where do I get some fashionable clothes like yours?"

Standing in the middle of a large, mucky hole in the ground, Riker looked with satisfaction at an access panel he had uncovered atop the main pipe. It was large enough for him to fit inside, just barely. More importantly, the panel would mean he wouldn't have to punch his way into the pipeline, an action he didn't think he had the strength to perform. Using a spoon handle as a screwdriver, he opened the access panel to reveal a rapid flow of dark water surging past on its way to some unknown destination.

Although there appeared to be some clearance between the top of the pipe and the water level, Riker wanted as much clearance as possible. So he went back to the control box, where he had already removed the cover. Putting his back into it, he cranked the outlet valve all the way open, siphoning as much water as possible into the beach house.

Then he jogged inside the house and turned on every faucet full blast. Water was soon gushing into the tub, shower, and various sinks at an enormous rate, and Riker laughed, thinking that the exquisite house would be ruined in a few minutes. He felt giddy, slightly feverish, and he tried to tell himself it was mere exhaustion.

Now he needed a float. There was a small wooden table in the living room that he had not used building the doomed raft. With his spoon, he unscrewed the legs from the table and hefted the tabletop, glad it was a fairly substantial chunk of wood. It would have to carry him a long way— how far he didn't know.

Riker gathered some food from the reserves and wrapped

them in the waterproof shower curtain. He thought about changing from his muddy clothes into clean clothes, but what was the point? Anything he wore would get soaked. It would also be dark soon, but there was no reason to wait, as day or night would look the same inside that pipe.

With a last glance at the beach house—and final thoughts about his fallen comrade, Shelzane—he walked out the front door of the house and didn't bother closing it.

A minute later, Riker stood astride the pipeline, gazing into the rushing water and thinking he was about to take the ride of his life. There was a good chance he would drown, or get chewed up in a hydroelectric plant, or meet some other such fate, but he couldn't worry about that. It would be a faster death than the alternative. At least in the pipe he wouldn't die of thirst, he thought ruefully.

Taking a deep breath and a firm grip on his tiny raft, Riker plunged into the pipe full of rushing water. The raft was nearly ripped from his hands by the initial surge, but he managed to hold on and right himself. Soon he was speeding along in absolute darkness, and the sensation reminded him of two pursuits from his youth. One was bodysurfing at the beach, and the other was riding the hydrotubes at an aquapark.

Riker was pleasantly surprised to find that the water in the pipe wasn't that cold. Warmed by ocean currents, it was about the same temperature as the lagoon. He had no idea how much clearance there was above his head, which he kept firmly planted on the tabletop. Besides, there was nothing to see but darkness and water—and nothing to do but hang on, stay awake, and ride it out.

As darkness embraced the city of Astar, Chakotay and Tuvok materialized on Velvet Lane, just outside an ostentatious mansion that bore a golden sign proclaiming "Velvet Cluster." A uniformed doorman, who appeared to be Argelian, looked curiously at them, then he broke into a grin.

"Ah, you are the Maquis unibloods," he said with pride at his own powers of observation. "Member Shep has been waiting for you." With a grand flourish, he opened the door and ushered them inside.

For some time, Chakotay had been accustomed to spartan living conditions, and he was frankly amazed by the opulent splendor of the Velvet Cluster. Crystal chandeliers, rich brocaded furnishings, and centuries-old tapestries graced the sumptuous foyer. Several grand rooms opened off the foyer, and Chakotay peered with interest into the open doorways. Laughter and the clinking of glasses came from what appeared to be a restaurant filled with people. In a darkly paneled library, patrons indulged in the quieter pursuits of reading and card playing. A ballroom with a high vaulted ceiling appeared to be empty.

"So this is how the underprivileged live," he whispered to Tuvok.

"It would appear so," answered the Vulcan. "One can only imagine what the Dawn Cluster is like."

"Well, these people are trying to prove something, so it may not be as grandiose as this."

"Mr. Tuvok!" called a voice.

They both turned to see a stocky Ferengi rushing toward them, a snaggletoothed grin on his face. "And this must be Captain Chakotay. What an honor!"

The captain smiled back. "Meeting a Maquis captain isn't usually considered a great honor."

"But you people are heroes. Everyone says so. Without you, Helena would be alone in this moment of crisis." He lowered his voice to add, "Thanks for coming. This should be good enough to get me another month's worth of credit here."

"Glad to oblige," said Chakotay.

"Let me introduce you around." Slipping between them, Shep eagerly grabbed their arms and steered them into the dining room. What followed was a rapid-fire round of introductions with merchants and uniblood dignitaries. Chakotay tried to determine whether any of these people could furnish them with useful information, but most of them asked whether there was any room on the *Spartacus* for passengers.

"Lay off," grumbled Shep to a persistent Andorian named Bokor. "These are *my* friends—if anyone gets off this planet, it's *me*."

"We're not taking on any passengers," said Chakotay. "Believe me, the life expectancy on a Maquis ship is shorter than it is on Helena."

The Andorian laughed heartily, and his antennae twitched. "I suppose it is. But you don't have to worry—the Cardassians like you."

"Why do you say that?" asked Tuvok.

"Because they're letting you operate unfettered here, even after you destroyed their ship," answered the Andorian. "I sell supplies to the Cardassian garrison on Tipoli, and they're under orders to leave you alone."

"What?" asked Chakotay, taking a seat at the Andorian's table. "You're sure of that?"

"Yes. I just flew there myself by sea-glider two days ago, and they don't know what to make of it. Gul Demadak, the military commander of the DMZ, gave the orders himself."

"But they just recently attacked the IGI complex," said Tuvok.

"Well, you aren't the IGI, are you? They don't trust the IGI, and I can't say I blame them."

Chakotay asked, "Did you see two prisoners in the Cardassian camp? Two of our people?"

"Aren't you listening to me?" muttered Bokor. "Although they don't like it, they're under orders to leave you alone. If you've lost two people, somebody else must have them."

The Andorian sipped a tall glass of ale and smiled smugly. "However, they told me something else which you would pay dearly to find out."

"What is that?" asked Tuvok.

He laughed. "When I'm safely aboard your ship on my way out of here, I'll tell you."

"That's not going to happen for a while," replied Chakotay.

"Better not wait too long," warned the Andorian. "Meanwhile, I'll keep looking for some other way off Helena. If you want to do business, you know where I am."

"Come on, let's eat," said Shep, guiding Chakotay and Tuvok to an empty table. He rubbed his hands together. "I don't suppose you brought any latinum with you?"

"No," answered Chakotay. "Being in the Maquis doesn't pay very well."

The Ferengi sighed. "Well, let's see how good my credit still is."

Chakotay lowered his voice to ask, "Is that Andorian trustworthy?"

"Yes, and well connected . . . for a uniblood."

"Can you guess what his information is?"

Shep tugged thoughtfully on a gigantic earlobe. "Let's see . . . he speaks privately to Cardassians, and he wants desperately to get off the planet. Maybe he knows that a big fleet is coming to blow us to smithereens."

"A logical conclusion," agreed Tuvok.

The Ferengi sat down at an empty table and rubbed his hands together. "Who's hungry?"

"All of a sudden, I'm not," said Chakotay.

"Oh, sit down," insisted Shep. "It does no good to die on an empty stomach."

B'Elanna Torres smiled politely at the well-wishers who greeted her when she entered the Dawn Cluster with Dr. Gammet in tow. The two of them were afforded the royal treatment and escorted to Prefect Klain's private booth at the rear of the dining hall.

"The prefect has been notified and will join you in a moment," said the servant, smiling and bowing obsequiously.

"Thank you," answered B'Elanna.

"Can I get you something to drink and show you a menu?"

"No, thank you, we won't be staying for dinner."

The Helenite looked crestfallen. "That's unfortunate."

"We're only here to see Prefect Klain," said Dr. Gammet, looking and sounding very grave.

"I see," answered the confused waiter. "Perhaps I will have the honor of serving you next time."

When he was gone, Gammet whispered to Torres, "I hope you know what you're doing. Klain is a very powerful man."

"I know we can't sit around and wait—we've got to find out who's behind this. There's an old Klingon proverb: You don't know who your friends are until you start a fight."

The conversation in the dining hall rose several decibels, and Torres turned to see Klain cutting a swath through the room, shaking hands and greeting people at every table. With his olive skin, jet-black hair, and impressive build, he was a magnificent male specimen, the finest being that genetic engineering could produce.

"Did you have anything to do with Klain's birth?" she asked Gammet.

"Oh, my, yes," he answered, beaming with pride. "Beautiful, isn't he? But I could combine the same species a hundred more times and not get one like him. I just wish he didn't know how special he is."

The little gnome's eyes twinkled. "Of course, *you* are his equal. The children you two could have, even naturally—"

"Some other time," she grumbled, cutting him off. Maybe there would be another time when she could return to Helena to stay—to live in grand style with a perfect man like Klain. Much of that depended on what happened in the next few minutes.

The prefect approached their table, flashing his incredible smile. "B'Elanna, you're looking unusually beautiful tonight. And, Doctor, this is a pleasant surprise."

Gammmet scowled. "It's about to become considerably less pleasant. Please have a seat."

"What's the matter?" asked Klain, slipping into the booth beside Torres. He gazed with concern at the Maquis officer, as if fearing the news concerned her. This made her feel guilty about the lie she was about to tell, but she was committed to her plan.

With her voice a barely audible whisper, she said, "We've found cases of the plague here on Dalgren. I'm afraid there's going to be an outbreak."

"What?" he gasped.

"Please," cautioned Dr. Gammet, "we've got to keep this news secret for now. We don't want to start a panic, and there's a chance that we can contain the disease where we found it."

Klain looked like a man who had been struck by a Ferengi stun whip. "Are you sure they're native Dalgrens? Perhaps they came from Padulla, or Tipoli—"

"No, they're from right here," insisted B'Elanna. "Actually from several outlying villages."

"Several!" Klain buried his face in his hands.

Gammet patted the big man's shoulder. "It was rather unrealistic to think that Dalgren would be spared this malady, but perhaps we've caught it early enough."

"What can I do to help you?" asked Klain nervously.

"For the moment, nothing public," said B'Elanna. "You might want to prepare whatever emergency procedures you had planned to use, but I warn you—the IGI complex is shut down."

"What?"

"It's been ransacked by Cardassians," said B'Elanna. "Tuvok, Dr. Gammet, and I barely escaped with our lives." At least that much was true, she thought ruefully.

Dr. Gammet had been right—Klain looked like a man who had just seen his worst fear become a reality. If it turned out they were wrong about him, and he had nothing to do with this, then her lie would probably come back to haunt her. She could probably forget about any more spectacular meals at the Dawn Cluster.

"You have a genetic company," said Dr. Gammet. "With IGI out of commission, we'll need your facilities."

"But we have only a few beds," muttered Klain. He rubbed his handsome face, still convulsed with disbelief. Torres assumed that he would be upset with this information, but she found his surprise to be somewhat strange.

"I'm sorry, Klain, but we have to be going." She rose to her feet, and he quickly followed suit.

"When . . . when will I see you again?"

"I don't know, but maybe this will hold you over." B'Elanna reached up, wrapped her arms around his broad shoulders, and gave him the kiss he had been desiring for days. His mouth met hers in a bittersweet mixture of passion, sweetness, and desperation. She knew that even if she had lied to him about the disease, there was no lie in her kiss.

He was so distracted that he didn't notice when her hand curled under his floppy collar and affixed a tiny tracking device to his shirt.

Torres pulled away from Klain reluctantly, unsure whether she had made a terrible mistake or had just saved millions of lives. There were hushed whispers in the dining room as the patrons voiced their approval of this fairy-tale romance. Little did they know that the romance had just ended.

She hurried out of the room before her emotions betrayed her, leaving Klain to stare after her in disbelief. Dr. Gammet rushed after Torres, but he didn't catch her until she was in the street, striding down the sidewalk.

"That must not have been easy," he said softly.

"It wasn't." She stepped around the corner into a side street and took out her tricorder. Even in the darkness, she could see the blip that was attuned to the tracking device, and it was moving. "He's going somewhere. He just left the Dawn Cluster."

Gammet peered around the side of a building. "I can see him—he's in a hurry, headed the other way."

She tapped her combadge. "Torres to Chakotay."

"Chakotay here."

"The target is on the move."

"I've got him," said the captain. "We'll meet you en route. Good job, B'Elanna."

"Yeah, real good job," she muttered bitterly.


"You promised me this wouldn't happen!" barked Prefect Klain, pounding his fist into his palm as he paced the back office of a carpet store in the old section of Astar. "You *guaranteed* it."

"Oh, please," came the snide response. "There are no guarantees in an experiment like this. Besides, you got what you wanted—IGI is history."

"We'll *all* be history if this keeps up! Padulla was bad enough, but did it have to happen here? When are you going to deliver the antidote?"

"Soon. We need a few more days." The speaker knew this was a lie, as there was no magic antidote—never would be. "Those idiot Cardassians upset several experiments when they attacked IGI—I wish I knew who caused that. But if the disease is spreading this fast, we'll be done soon."

"*Now!* I demand you put an end to it now!"

"Or what?"

"Or I'll tell the Maquis everything! I'll . . . I'll tell the Cardassians. I'll *expose* you."

The other party's eyes narrowed. "That would not be a good idea. For one thing, you would be ruined."

"I don't care anymore!" snapped Klain with exasperation. "This has got to come to an end, do you hear me?"

"I hear you . . . all too well."

Suddenly a loud beep sounded in the unkempt back office, followed by a pounding on a distant door. A voice broke in over the comm channel: "Intruders at the public entrance!"

"Delay them!" Furious, the speaker turned to Prefect Klain. "You *fool!* You were followed!"

"I don't see how that's possible. I took side streets and watched out for—" Klain's dark eyes widened in horror. "What are you going to do with that phaser?"

"What I should have done long ago."

The phaser spit a red beam, which gnawed a burning hole in Klain's stomach. With a groan, he staggered to the door but collapsed halfway there. His assassin pressed a button, opening a secret panel, and hurried out the exit into the alley.

# Chapter Fourteen

"USE YOUR PHASERS!" ordered Chakotay when the door to the carpet store wouldn't budge.

As several Helenites watched with horror and curiosity, Torres and Tuvok stepped back and blasted the metal security door with full phasers. It began to sizzle and melt.

"What are you doing?" demanded one of the onlookers, a burly Antosian/Catullan.

"It's all right," said a small man in a white lab coat. "I'm Dr. Gammet from IGI, and this is official business."

His words appeased the crowd for the moment, although it was unlikely the quiet row of shops ever saw this much excitement. As the door crumbled into molten gobs, a phaser beam streaked from the store, barely missing Tuvok. The onlookers gasped and ran for cover, but the Vulcan stood his ground and calmly returned fire. A groan issued from within.

Tuvok kicked what was left of the door off its hinges and leaped over the molten metal on the ground. Chakotay, Torres, and Dr. Gammet charged into the store after him, and they found a brawny Helenite sprawled across a dozen rolls of carpet, a gaping wound in his chest.

Tuvok knelt down and felt for a pulse, then he shook his head. "He is dead. I regret that my phaser was on full."

"You had no choice," said Chakotay. He turned to Torres, who was studying her tricorder. "Where is Klain?"

"Not far." She led the way through the carpet store to the rear, where she found a door marked with symbols meaning "Private. No Admittance." Leveling her phaser, Torres pushed the door open and charged into the room.

A moment later, Chakotay wished he had been the one to go first. Lying in the middle of the small, unkempt office was Prefect Klain, crumpled on the floor like a pile of rags. Distraught, Torres bent over the body and put her head to his chest, listening for any sign of life. From the severity of his wound and the pool of blood, Chakotay doubted he was alive.

Still he tapped his combadge. "Chakotay to *Spartacus*. Stand by to beam one to sickbay."

"That won't be necessary," said Dr. Gammet, feeling for a pulse. "He's beyond us now."

"Belay that order," said Chakotay sadly.

B'Elanna jumped to her feet, fierce anger and tears in her eyes. "I killed him . . . as surely as if I had pulled the trigger."

"No, you didn't," said the captain, putting his arm around her trembling shoulders. "But we'll find who did it."

"How could his murderer have escaped?" asked Tuvok, scanning the small room with a tricorder.

"By Mizrah!" gasped a voice. Chakotay turned to see a

female Helenite standing in the doorway, her hand covering her mouth and a look of horror on her face.

"What's on the other side of this wall?" he asked, pointing to the wall opposite the door.

"An alley," she rasped.

"Tuvok, you're with me," ordered the captain. "B'Elanna, you'll probably want to stay here and—"

"No!" she said through clenched teeth. "I want to come with you."

"I can handle this mess," muttered Dr. Gammet. "I'll take a look around, too. The three of you go ahead."

There was no time to argue, as Chakotay led the way out the door, through the shop, and into the street. Since they were in the middle of a block of stores, he motioned Tuvok to go one way, while he and Torres ran the other.

An onlooker yelled at him, "What are you people doing?"

"Have you seen anyone suspicious, running?"

"Just you."

Figuring no one at the front of the store had seen anything, Chakotay dashed to the corner with Torres on his heels. They took a right onto a side street and ran to the alley behind the carpet shop. There was no one in the vicinity—not the murderer, not a witness, not anyone they could question.

Chakotay had seen dark alleys before, but none more foreboding than this. He drew his phaser and a handheld lantern, but B'Elanna charged ahead of him, rage in her eyes. The captain almost called after her to wait, but he knew she wouldn't when she was in a state like this.

He tapped his combadge. "Tuvok, where are you?"

"Making my way east down the alley," answered the Vulcan.

"Keep an eye out for Torres—she's headed right for you."

"Acknowledged."

Since the alley was covered from both ends, Chakotay looked around the area, trying to figure out where they were in the unfamiliar city. While in pursuit of Klain's tracking signal, they hadn't paid any attention to where they were going. He had to admit that they were lost.

A cool breeze brushed his face, bringing with it the earthy scents of salt, fish, and rotting seaweed. Chakotay followed the breeze to the end of the block and saw that the street stopped at the wharf. Lights twinkled on the dark water of the bay, where several boats and sea-gliders floated in peaceful repose. Some of the docking slips were empty.

*Our prey escaped via sea-glider,* he thought to himself. *That's why they chose this place as their headquarters—to be close to the sea-gliders.*

His combadge chirped, jarring him out of his reverie. "Torres to Chakotay."

"Go on."

"We've finished searching the alley—there's no one here."

"I think they escaped via sea-glider," said the captain. "Let's go back to the ship and run some scans—"

"There's a problem," Torres cut in. "Tuvok's been arrested."

When Chakotay got back to the front of the store, he found Torres and Dr. Gammet arguing with two Helenites wearing tricornered hats and blue uniforms with gaudy piping and epaulets. A large hovercraft was also parked in front of the store. Tuvok was nowhere in sight, although several of the onlookers had remained to watch the continuing drama.

"What happened?" asked Chakotay.

"I tried to explain to them," said Gammet with exasperation. "I told them that we were fired on first, and that your man returned fire in self-defense."

"Excuse me," said a stout official, "are you the Maquis captain?"

"Yes."

"We have to arrest you, too."

"Wait a minute," replied Chakotay, trying to stay calm, "are you going to give us a chance to explain?"

"We have accounts from several witnesses. They all tell us that you were trying to break into this shop, and the shopkeeper was trying to protect his place of business. No one denies that you fired first at his locked door, and that the Vulcan killed the shopkeeper. Not only that, but we found our prefect dead inside. In my thirty years of service, this is the worst case of violence we've ever had on Dalgren."

"Do you understand who these people are?" asked Gammet. "And what we're trying to do? We were chasing the people who are responsible for unleashing the plague on Helena!"

The official glowered suspiciously at him. "Are you saying that Prefect Klain was responsible for the plague?"

"I'm afraid so," said Gammet.

"Do you have any proof to back up this slanderous claim?"

"If you'll allow us to search his genetic company, perhaps we can find proof."

"There will be a full hearing," the other official assured him, "and plenty of search warrants. Which one of you killed Prefect Klain?"

"None of us!" shouted Torres. "Oh, this is pointless. People are dying by the thousands, and you're worried about *two* people."

"He was our *prefect*," insisted the official. "That's the highest office in the land."

"I *know* who he was," said Torres, glaring at him.

Her distress and reddened eyes had some effect on the officials, who evidently knew who she was, too.

"You're not a suspect," the official said with sympathy. "But until we find out what happened here, we have to hold the Vulcan and your captain."

Chakotay briefly considered making a run for it and ordering Seska to beam him back to the *Spartacus,* but they needed cooperation, not more strife. As unibloods, he and Tuvok were obviously at a disadvantage.

"I'll go with you," he told the officials, "as long as you realize that these arrests could further the spread of the plague."

The officials scratched their chins and looked at one another with indecision. Chakotay had the impression that their jobs were mostly ceremonial on the normally peaceful planet.

"Listen to him," pleaded Dr. Gammet. "Captain Chakotay's ship and the medical teams he brought with him are the only things standing between us and disaster."

"But he ordered them to fire their phasers!" shouted an onlooker. "I saw him!"

The stout official, who was the elder of the two, took a deep breath and came to a decision. "Dr. Gammet, if you will vouch for the captain, we'll allow him to remain on his own cognizance until the hearing. But we have to hold the Vulcan, because he admits to killing the shopkeeper."

"I'll vouch for all of them," said Gammet. "They only want to help us."

"Where is Tuvok being held?" asked Chakotay.

"In the Ministry of Public Policy," answered the official. "You can visit him in the morning."

Dr. Gammet strode up to the officials and said, "Right now, we've got to go to Genetic Enhancement—Klain's company—and search it."

"We can't get a search warrant until morning," said the stout official obstinately.

Torres snarled with anger. "A few days from now, when you're lying in bed—dying a miserable death—I hope you'll remember these delays you caused us. Better yet, I hope you come to us to save your life—or the lives of your children—and we say, 'Sorry, can't do anything until the morning.' "

The official's dark complexion paled several shades. He finally motioned to the hovercraft and growled, "Get in."

They could see the fire burning in the night sky from blocks away, the flames rising above the silhouette of the city like rocket thrusters. Helenites were running to and fro, pointing helplessly at the conflagration, and their driver stopped the hovercraft and stared in amazement. The air smelled like burning tar, and sparks floated in the darkness like erratic meteorites.

"That can't be!" he exclaimed. "The automatic sprinklers and transporters . . . the flame retarders . . . we haven't had a fire in Astar in a hundred years!"

He tapped a button on the instrument panel of the hovercraft and shouted over the commotion, "This is Chief Mufanno calling headquarters. There's a fire in section twelve, near the corner of Cosmos and Unity—"

"In the Genetic Enhancement building," said Dr. Gammet, drawing the obvious conclusion.

"Yes," agreed the official, staring at his passengers and realizing that they might have been telling him the truth about Prefect Klain. "Call out the Coastal Watchers and rush them to—"

"I wouldn't do that," cautioned Dr. Gammet. "Don't get anywhere near that building, unless you're wearing an environmental suit. You don't know what might be in there. The safest recourse is to keep people away, and let it burn to the ground."

The official stared in shock at the doctor and licked his blue lips worriedly. "Belay that order. Let's cordon off the block and keep people away. Just let it burn."

"Let it burn?" asked an amazed voice on the comm channel.

"That's right. Don't let anyone get near it, unless they're wearing an environmental suit. There are, uh . . . biohazards."

Chakotay sighed wearily and hopped out of the hovercraft. "I don't think we're going to find any information in that building. B'Elanna, contact the ship and head back as soon as you can. I'm sure Seska could use some relief on the bridge." He started walking away.

"Where are you going?" she asked.

"Back to the Velvet Cluster. There's a man I've got to see. I have a feeling our time is running out."

Gul Demadak breathed a tremendous sigh of relief as he read the coded message on the hidden screen in his library. At last, he was free to do what had to be done. He had also survived the most dangerous partnership he had ever undertaken. If this message hadn't come, he was probably only days, perhaps hours, away from from losing his post as military commander of the DMZ. He would make the Detapa Council and Central Command very happy with his next order.

"Experiment cut short," read the message. "Move in and clear out Maquis. Await my order for final resolution."

Demadak knew what that final resolution was—the end of the thorn in his side known as Helena. Now his place in history and the next great reign of the Cardassian Union was assured.

He quickly sent another message: "Await my arrival, and begin Phase Two. Prepare for Phase Three."

All during the night, Thomas Riker hurtled through the darkness, clinging to a chunk of wood and shivering in his wet clothes. Inside the pipe, he didn't know if it was night or day, sea or land, hell or heaven—whether he was ill or merely exhausted and half-crazed. All he knew was that the instincts for survival and revenge were stronger than the temptation to let go and end it, although that thought was never far from his mind.

*Did you survive all those years, put up with all the ridicule and unfairness, give up everything you worked for, and come all the way to Helena . . . just to die?*

*No!* Riker answered the voice within him. *I have to make my life—and my death—mean something. I'm alive for a reason, and there's something I have to do.*

Riker wasn't sure he was destined for success in Starfleet anymore, as he had once been convinced. He thought about the love of his life, Deanna Troi, and how he should never have let her get away. He had given her up for what? A career! What was a career but a bunch of disconnected, often incomprehensible events from which a person tried desperately to make some sense? The only thing in his life that had ever made any sense was Deanna, and he had willfully given her up.

His fingers and legs were painfully cramped as he clung to his board, and he had lost his meager supply of food in the rushing water. But none of that seemed as important as the realization he had just reached. When he got out of this, he would redeem himself. He would no longer let life drag him along like this current—he would bend it to his will.

To his surprise, Riker took comfort from a fact which he had resented bitterly for two years. *I'm not alone. There is another William T. Riker on the* Enterprise. He would let that other Riker scale the heights and have the incredible career that he had always considered to be his due. Tom Riker would be the altruistic and unselfish one—the one who thought and acted for other people.

He had taken the first step by giving up his high-profile bridge position to become a medical courier, then he had gone one step further by shipping out with the Maquis. He wondered what he would do next to further his development as a person.

Without warning, the artificial river dropped away beneath him, and Riker plunged headfirst into darkness. Involuntarily, he yelled and flailed his arms, losing his tiny life raft. At the last second, he ducked his head, put his arms out, and dove into a cold, dark pool of water. He protected his head, certain he would smash into a shallow bottom, but he came out of his unexpected dive in water that was plenty deep enough to swim in. Riker stroked and kicked with all his might, and he broke the surface, sputtering for breath.

Treading water, he looked up and saw a million stars, sparkling like the brightest lights of San Francisco or

Anchorage. "Yes," he breathed gratefully, slapping his hand on top of the water. As his eyes adjusted to the night sky and its tiny but vibrant bits of light, he could see that he was swimming in a small reservoir, with a dam looming on one side and a lower embankment on the other.

*I made it!* Where he was hardly made any difference, as long as it wasn't that damn island.

Knowing he was too weak to tread water for very long, Riker swam toward the low side of the reservoir. He finally found a ladder and dragged himself out of the chilly water. Collapsing on the concrete embankment, he lay there for several minutes, letting the water drip off his shivering body. He was only half-alive, but he was alive.

Riker staggered to his feet and looked around, unable to make out much in the darkness. If anyone was manning the reservoir, he couldn't see them, and no one seemed interested in him. In the distance was a wavering light—it looked like no more than a campfire, but that was enough to give him a new destination. Now he wished he hadn't lost his food.

Picking his way carefully through the dark, Riker walked away from the reservoir and found himself on a dirt path. The closer he got to the wavering light in the distance, the more it actually looked like a campfire, and hope spurred him to walk faster. Soon he heard voices, talking rather loudly, as if they expected no one to be nearby. He couldn't tell if it was friend or foe, but he doubted if his tormentors from the island would amuse themselves with anything as low-tech as a campfire. He was hoping these were Helenites—either rural workers or people who had fled the cities.

As he staggered through the brush, he could see their seated silhouettes huddled around the campfire. With their backs to him, he had no idea who they were, but from their voices, he assumed they were mostly males. Riker figured he had better not charge into their midst without announcing himself, so when got close enough he cleared his throat loudly.

"I'm Lieutenant Riker," he said, his voice sounding hoarse and hollow in his own ears.

The men jumped up as if a bomb had gone off, and he could see them grabbing what looked like weapons. In the dim firelight, he still couldn't see their faces, but he wanted to appear harmless. So he held up his hands and said, "I'm with the Maquis. I got separated from my—"

One of the men charged toward him, rifle leveled at his chest. In seconds, he got close enough for Riker to make out his bony face, black hair, and gray uniform.

*Cardassians!* Riker thought momentarily about trying to escape, but how far could he run in his condition? In fact, he felt so weak that he didn't think he could stand on his feet for much longer. But he kept his hands raised high and a smile glued to his bearded face.

Unfortunately, Cardassians were not known for responding well to human charm. This one raised his phaser rifle and fired a searing beam that hit Riker in the chest. That was the last thing he remembered before he pitched forward into the dirt.

# Chapter Fifteen

"I TOLD YOU, CAPTAIN CHAKOTAY, I won't give you any information until you take me away from Helena. That is my firm price."

The speaker, an Andorian named Bokor, sat stone-faced at his table in the Velvet Cluster dining room. Chakotay sat across from him, his hands folded before him and his face just as implacable as the blue-skinned alien's. The Ferengi, Shep, sat between them, and he was the only one who looked animated, except for the servers who bustled around them importantly.

"Don't agree to anything," Shep cautioned Chakotay. "Let *me* negotiate for both of us."

The Andorian laughed. "What have you got to bargain with, Ferengi? You don't know anything, and you don't have anything. All your goods are floating in orbit around the planet."

"I have my *mind*," answered Shep, tapping his large frontal lobes. "And a strong desire to get out of here myself. Besides, I was right about Prefect Klain, wasn't I?"

"Yes, you were," agreed Chakotay, his voice barely audible over the clink of glasses and ricochet of silverware. "That's why I came back here—to see what else I could find out."

Bokor arched an eyebrow and waited until an older Catullan couple shuffled past. "Terrible thing about the prefect. Who ever thought *he* could be involved with this tragic disease? Everyone is talking about it. As I told you, Captain, I have a very valuable piece of information, but I won't part with it for free."

"Bokor doesn't know anything," scoffed Shep. "So he talked to a few Cardassians who are also stranded here—big deal. Those boneheads don't know any more than the rest of us! Captain Chakotay is the only one with a starship—he's the only one in a strong bargaining position."

The captain shrugged. "Actually I have *three* ships under my command, all of them in orbit: the *Spartacus,* the *Singha,* and a warp-drive shuttlecraft."

Now the Andorian leaned forward with avid interest. "A shuttlecraft, you say? Now *that* is something worth negotiating for, especially on Helena. How much gold-pressed latinum do you want? Name your price."

Chakotay smiled and leaned back in his chair. "Latinum doesn't do me a bit of good—no place to spend it. Your information isn't all that valuable either, because any fool could guess at it. The Cardassians must be planning to come back here with more ships—maybe a whole fleet. And when they do, we'll run for it, and you'll still be here. If the plague doesn't get you, they will."

The Andorian scowled. "Make your point, Captain. What do you want?"

"Don't hurry him," said the Ferengi, smiling. "A good negotiation must be savored, like good wine."

Chakotay leaned forward and whispered, "I need four things. It would be good to know exactly when Cardassian ships are returning, and in what strength. I also need to know what happened to my two missing crewmen. Just because you didn't see them doesn't mean the Cardassians don't have them. We need to ask them point-blank if they know anything about Lieutenant Riker and Ensign Shelzane."

"What else?" grumbled the Andorian, not enjoying this tough negotiation as much as the Ferengi.

Chakotay's tattoo grew three-dimensional in the furrows of a deep frown. "Tuvok, the Vulcan on my crew, has been arrested for killing a man who was working with the people who brought this plague to Helena. If there is any sort of influence you could bring to bear on the officials, it would be appreciated."

Bokor snorted, and his antennae twitched. "Anything else, while we're at it?"

"Yes. Whoever takes that shuttlecraft has got to return it and the medical team to the Federation."

The Andorian groaned and slumped back in his chair, while the Ferengi nodded with satisfaction. "What will you say to that, Bokor?"

"I'll say that this human wants an awful lot for his shuttlecraft."

"That's all I want from *you*," said Chakotay. "From you, Shep, I want someone to gather information about Klain's company, Genetic Enhancement. He's still got confederates here on Helena, and we've got to run them down."

"I'm going on the shuttlecraft, too?" asked Shep excitedly.

"Yes, because I reward those who help me." Chakotay rose to his feet and looked at the Andorian, sensing other diners glancing at him. "Bokor, you still have your seaglider, don't you?"

"Yes."

"Good. I'll meet you at the bay in an hour, and we can take a little flight to look for my missing crew."

The Andorian scowled. "It will take us a day or two to get there."

"I have a shortcut," promised the captain.

"But I haven't agreed to any of this yet!"

Chakotay smiled. "You haven't said no, so I'm taking that as a yes. You might want to load up some supplies to make it look good. See you in an hour."

The Maquis captain strode away from the table, with many of the members of the Velvet Cluster watching him go. Shep nodded his head in admiration. "For a hu-man, he's an awfully good negotiator. Wouldn't you say so, Bokor?"

"A month ago, we would have laughed him out of the cluster." The tall Andorian rose to his feet. "Now I had better put some supplies on my glider."

Tuvok sat in a cell with a force-field grid protecting the open door. There were three other cells linked with his, all of them opening onto a central corridor, but the other cells were empty. His jailers had left him reading material, food, and water, but he ignored these niceties to sit in silence and contemplate the actions that had landed him in this predicament.

He had killed a man. The killing had clearly been in self-defense, but that knowledge didn't assuage his conscience at all. For a Vulcan to take a life was a serious matter, a cause to doubt one's training and commitment to logic. For Tuvok, it was a cause to wonder what he was doing on the Maquis crew—a group of people who lived a life so dangerous that it might be called suicidal.

He realized that he was only here because he was a spy, but that was also an illogical role for a Vulcan. For that very reason, he had been the logical member of Captain Janeway's crew to infiltrate Chakotay's ship. A Vulcan never lied, except when it was more logical than telling the truth, which was very seldom. Until this mission, his role as a spy had never troubled him much, because the actions of the Maquis were both illegal and illogical. But their actions on behalf of the inhabitants of Helena were noble and logical. The absence of the Federation was the only thing that was illogical.

He was not ready to forsake his allegiance to the Federation, but for the first time he questioned the wisdom of a treaty that left innocent people so vulnerable. After recent events, he had no doubt that Helena had been chosen by unknown parties as a breeding ground for this disease for the very reason that it was isolated and vulnerable. A civilized society derived from the Federation, it was a perfect microcosm of the Federation as a whole. If anything, the mixed-species Helenites were more disease-resistant than a typical populace, which made them the perfect proving ground for a biological weapon. If the disease could succeed here, then no Federation planet was safe.

But who would endanger millions of people for an experiment? Not even the Cardassians were so vile.

That question brought him back to the life he had taken. A Vulcan never killed, except when it was absolutely necessary, and he could not say the death of the shopkeeper had been absolutely necessary. Had the shopkeeper lived, he might have furnished valuable information. Dead, he was nothing but a mystery, and a reason for the Helenites to distrust the Maquis. He was also the cause of Tuvok's incarceration and imminent trial.

Try as he might to justify his actions, Tuvok now saw that he had acted rashly. He thought back to his youth, when he had nearly rejected Vulcan philosophy in favor of passion and love. A wise teacher had steered him back onto the proper path, but the doubts always remained. Was he prone to acts of passion and poor judgment?

Tuvok lay back on his narrow bunk, realizing that he couldn't answer these questions himself. Perhaps he wouldn't survive his stay on Helena, which made his introspection moot. One thing was certain—there was nothing like being incarcerated in a cell, awaiting trial for murder, to make a person think.

Thomas Riker squinted into the blazing sun and licked his parched lips, wishing it was still night. He was lying in hot sand on the beach, imprisoned in a crude cage about a meter high and three meters long, made of sticks and wire. Had he any strength, he could probably smash his way out of this handmade cage in a few seconds, but he was extremely weak. His throat felt raw and his glands swollen; he couldn't see himself, but he imagined from his peeling skin that he looked fairly awful.

Riker knew he was dying of the plague.

About thirty meters away, under a canopy that gave them ample shade, a group of ten Cardassians sat in a circle playing a dice game. Every now and then, one of them would look in his direction with a jaundiced eye, noting that he was still there, and still alive. Behind them on the bluff loomed a small fortress, which he assumed was the actual garrison, but it appeared eerily quiet, perhaps deserted.

Riker turned to look at the vast ocean, glistening in the sunshine, incongruous in its beauty in the middle of his personal hell. He had always thought of oceans as a symbol of life and freedom, but this one seemed like a mirage, beckoning him to a freedom he could never attain. It mocked him with its ageless splendor, telling him that it would go on for eons and eons after he was gone. If this was to be the last thing he saw before he died, he almost wished it could be something not so achingly beautiful.

He licked his lips again and rubbed his throbbing head. Riker felt as though he had been unconscious for days, but it had probably only been a few hours since the Cardassians had stunned him and tossed him into this cage. Looking around his enclosure, he figured it was some dead fisherman's lobster trap, or whatever the Helenite equivalent of lobster was. Would they make him die like this, staked out in the heat? Or would they at least give him the succor of food and water? Maybe he could goad them into killing him outright.

"Hey!" Riker shouted, his voice sounding as rough as his shaggy beard. "Give me some water!"

When the Cardassians did nothing but glance at him, he shouted, "Come on, you cowards! Afraid of an unarmed man?"

The guards looked at him and laughed, but one of them stood and shuffled toward him. His phaser rifle was slung casually over his shoulder, as if he knew he needn't fear this prisoner.

He stopped about ten meters away from the cage and sneered. "We're betting on how long it takes you to die.

I've got you down for twenty-six hours. Think you can hold out that long?"

"Maybe if I have a drink of water," rasped Riker.

The Cardassian shook his head. "Sorry, but we're not allowed to aid you either one way or another. We can't give you any food, drink, or medicine; and we can't beat you senseless either. This has got to be a fair contest."

"What makes you such experts?" grumbled Riker. "Maybe I'll live for a week."

"I don't think so. I've watched sixty percent of our own garrison die, so I have some experience. I'd say twenty-six hours is just about right, although you look pretty strong. Maybe I should've taken thirty."

The guard laughed, sounding oddly jovial and half insane. "I might not even be here in thirty hours to see you die. It's just as well that I took twenty-six."

"Where are you going to be?" asked Riker hoarsely.

"Far away from this pesthole." He turned and shuffled back to his comrades.

Riker laid his head on the hot sand and wondered if he could burrow into it for some protection from the sun. But the wooden bars extended underneath the cage, and he didn't have the strength to break them. He supposed he could untwist the wires that held the structure together, but his captors were sure to notice him working on it.

Bored, he turned back to look at the endless sky, stretching across the blue sheen of the ocean. Yes, he was going to die—and the way he felt now, he didn't think it would even take twenty-six hours. It was best to sleep, he decided, and conserve his strength, while waiting for a miracle to happen.

*Who am I kidding?* thought Riker. *Miracles happen to other people, not to me. What did the old blues song say? "If it wasn't for bad luck, I wouldn't have no luck at all."*

Just before he closed his eyes, he caught sight of something in the clear blue sky. Riker rubbed his eyes and peered into the glare, wondering if it was real or only his fevered imagination. After several seconds, the apparition was still there—it looked like another one of those sea-gliders, headed their way.

A sudden babble of voices made him turn to look at the Cardassians under the canopy. They had seen the glider, too, and a few of them rose to their feet and took up arms in apparent defense of this lonely stretch of beach. Others remained seated in the sand, lethargic and apathetic; they looked every bit as resigned to death as he was.

He struggled to listen to their conversation against the gentle flow of the waves to the shore. "It must be Bokor," said one. "Did we order more supplies?" asked another.

*Supplies?* Riker turned to watch the white glider make its graceful approach. Hope sprang unbidden to his heart, although he knew such hope was pointless. Anyone who dealt with the Cardassians wasn't likely to save him, or even care if he lived or died.

The approach and landing of the seaplane was quite impressive as it glided across the creamy water and set down on its sleek pontoons with barely a splash. Half of the ten Cardassians formed a line in the sand, although they kept a safe distance away from him. There appeared to be two people in the craft, and one of them opened the hatch.

The visitor threw something into the water—it was a compressed-air raft, which instantly expanded to its full size. Riker watched with interest as a gangly Andorian stepped gingerly into the raft, oar in hand, and began rowing leisurely toward the shore. The Cardassians on the beach began to relax, apparently not viewing this new arrival as a threat. Some of them went back to their dice game.

The raft scraped into the sand, and the Andorian climbed out, trying to maintain his dignity as best he could in the tiny boat. As he strolled past Riker, he looked at him with mild interest, although he didn't stop to talk. His destination was clearly the Cardassians and the fortress on the hill.

"Bokor!" shouted one of them with disapproval. "What are you doing here?"

The Andorian shrugged. "Just making my rounds. I thought I'd see if you needed anything. I've got some nice salted fish and a case of Rigelian ale."

"Go away, you scavenger!" yelled another Cardassian, although he didn't sound very angry. "We don't need anything, except to get off this lousy rock."

"I can't help you there," said the Andorian with a resigned smile. He pointed to Riker in the cage. "I see you've found some entertainment."

"Yeah, one of those meddling Maquis. But he's not going to last long—he's got the plague."

"Oh," muttered the visitor. "Are you sure you don't need anything? Your great fleet hasn't shown up yet."

"They will. They're on their way. Now get out of here, before we put you in a cage, too!" At that remark, there was a round of laughter among the Cardassians.

"Okay," said the Andorian, holding his hands up. "I'm not looking for trouble, just customers."

"Who's that in your glider?" asked another guard, peering suspiciously at the sleek craft floating in the surf.

"Just my new pilot. I'm showing him the route."

"Well, there's no sense coming back here again. We'll be gone before we need any more supplies."

"Lucky you," muttered the Andorian, sounding as if he meant it. "I'll cross you off my list. So you're sure?"

"We're sure," growled a big Cardassian, hefting his phaser rifle. "Now if you don't get out of here in ten seconds, I'm going to use your glider for target practice."

"I'm going!" To another round of laughter, the Andorian hurried toward his raft. As he passed Riker, he gave him a wink, which was an odd thing for him to do. *He probably caught a grain of sand in his eye,* thought the prisoner.

"Help me!" groaned Riker, but the Andorian was already pushing his raft into the surf to make his escape.

The lieutenant watched forlornly as the merchant rowed back to his craft and climbed aboard. He hauled his raft in after him, letting out the air as he did. Without further ado, the sea-glider floated majestically into the air; like a giant kite, it caught a wind drift and soared away.

Riker watched the glider sail into the sky, a feeling of despair gripping his chest.

"That's definitely your man down there in the cage," Bokor told Captain Chakotay as the glider cruised away from the Cardassian garrison. "But he's sick."

"How sick?"

"Not that bad—he's still talking."

Chakotay took a deep breath, grateful that they had at least found Riker. "There was no sign of a Benzite in their camp?"

"None. And there's no more time to look for her. They sounded like their fleet could show up any minute."

Chakotay punched some numbers into his computer padd. "Are we out of their range of fire yet?"

"Yes—just barely."

The captain tapped his combadge. "Chakotay to *Spartacus.*"

"Torres here," answered a familiar voice.

"I'm sending you some coordinates—it's Riker, and I want you to beam him up immediately. Tell Kincaid that he's got the plague, and she's got to drop everything to save him. Stand by." Chakotay took off his combadge and plugged it into the padd. He watched intently as a stream of lights showed the data transfer.

"We've got the coordinates," said Torres. "Initiating transport." After seconds that stretched forever, she reported, "We've got him!"

The captain let out a long sigh of relief. "Okay, that's two items crossed off our list. Bokor, are you ready to take command of that shuttlecraft?"

"Right now?" asked the Andorian, aghast. "We're flying over an ocean. Who's going to fly my glider?"

"We're going to abandon it."

Bokor gulped, and his antennae twitched. "Abandon it? Right here . . . in the middle of the ocean!"

"If you're leaving Helena, you won't need it anymore."

"All right," muttered the Andorian. "You're a very decisive man, Captain."

"I have to be." He pulled his combadge off the computer padd and affixed it to his chest. "B'Elanna, do you still read me?"

"Yes, sir."

"Lock onto the two of us and beam us up. And alert Danken on the shuttlecraft to stand by for a shift in personnel."

"Yes, sir."

The dour Andorian looked extremely displeased to be losing his fine sea-glider. Chakotay reached forward from his co-pilot seat and patted him on the shoulder. "Think of it as a trade-in for an even better shuttlecraft."

"Right."

A moment later, they disappeared from the cockpit of the sea-glider, while it continued its graceful flight, sailing unmanned into the blue horizon, like a great white albatross.

When they materialized on the transporter pad in the cargo hold of the *Spartacus,* now converted into a sickbay, Chakotay rushed immediately to the bed where Lieutenant Riker lay. Dr. Kincaid and her assistants were working on him with their medical equipment, plying him with hyprosprays.

Riker lifted his head and stared at Chakotay in utter amazement. "Have I died and gone to heaven? Or am I dreaming this?"

"Neither one," answered Chakotay with a smile. He looked at the doctor. "Is he going to be all right?"

"We got him not a moment too soon," answered Kincaid. "The biofilter took care of the multiprions, but he has some tissue damage and secondary infections. He's going to be laid up for a while."

"Not too long, I hope. We need him badly." The captain gazed down at Riker. "Where is Ensign Shelzane?"

"Dead," said Riker hoarsely, tears welling in his rheumy eyes. "We broke into IGI . . . and then—"

"Tell me later. Right now, you have to get well." Chakotay patted his comrade on the shoulder.

"I got a miracle," rasped the lieutenant. "I never thought *I* would get a miracle."

"Let's hope for a few more." Chakotay returned to the transporter platform, where the Andorian stood in shocked silence, gazing around at all the equipment and bustle of activity. "You'll take command of the shuttlecraft and fly straight toward Federation space at maximum warp. When they hail you, stop and tell them exactly what's happening here—that a Cardassian fleet is massing to destroy Helena. Tell them the Cardassians are breaking the treaty in a big way."

Bokor gaped at him. "The Maquis are going to call Starfleet for help?"

Chakotay nodded grimly and motioned at the medical teams in action around them. "For some jobs, you can't beat Starfleet—facing down a Cardassian fleet is one of them. That is, if they even bother to show up."

"What about Shep? And the doctors you wanted me to take back?"

"There's no time for that now. Don't let me down, Bokor. The lives of everyone on Helena depend upon you." A metal pan clattered to the deck behind them, as if underscoring the urgency. A weary doctor picked up the pan, then teetered woozily on his feet until a colleague helped him to a chair.

The tall Andorian nodded gravely. "I won't fail you, Captain Chakotay. You have impressed me greatly—I'm glad you drove a hard bargain." He stepped upon the transporter platform and squared his shoulders.

Chakotay turned to the transporter operator. "Beam him to the shuttlecraft, then beam Danken back here. Energize when ready."

"Yes, sir," answered the Bolian on duty.

The Andorian gave him a regal wave as he vanished in a column of sparkling, swirling lights. The captain immediately left the cargo hold and hurried the length of the scout ship to the bridge, where B'Elanna Torres was on duty at the conn. The peaceful blue curve of Helena filled the viewscreen, giving the false impression that all was well on the watery world beneath them.

"Any emergencies?" he asked, slipping into the seat beside her and turning on the sensors.

"The struggle goes on," she answered. "Two members of the medical team on Padulla came down with the plague, and they're being treated along with everyone else. I see the shuttlecraft has just taken off. What's their destination?"

"Federation space. I hate to do this, but it's time to send for the cavalry."

"Why?" asked Torres, with an edge to her voice.

"Because I've learned that a Cardassian fleet is headed this way." He started scanning the land masses on the planet beneath them, looking for kelbonite deposits, or anything that could mask the presence of a small starship. "We've got to find someplace down there to hide this vessel."

"Wouldn't it be easier to run for it?"

"Yes, but we're not going to leave without Tuvok and our doctors. We'll hide this ship and leave the *Singha* in orbit. When the Cardassians show up, the *Singha* can run for it, so they'll think all the Maquis have left."

"That's risky," muttered B'Elanna. She snorted a laugh and gave him an ironic smile. "Maybe this will be our first step toward retirement."

"What do you mean?"

"Prefect Klain offered to let us stay here, remember? Even Tuvok said it was a good idea for us to start planning how to get out of the Maquis. He's right, you know. We can't keep up this crazy life forever. If the Helenites protected our identities, this would be a good place to hide from both the Cardassians and Starfleet."

Chakotay shook his head. "There's too much left to do. Besides, they'll keep hunting us to our graves. Do you think we could go from being Maquis to being law-abiding citizens just like that?" He snapped his fingers.

Torres shrugged. "Maybe. Given the right circumstances."

"It's only a pipe dream," said Chakotay. "But I'll keep it in mind."

"How's Riker?"

"Worse for wear, but he's going to live. But he says Ensign Shelzane is dead. We need to contact Dr. Gammet and see when Tuvok's hearing is."

"Gammet checked in, and he said that the hearing is tomorrow." Torres lowered her head, and her voice sounded far away. "Klain's funeral is in less than an hour. I wouldn't mind going to that."

"You were really starting to care for him, weren't you?" asked Chakotay, knowing that if B'Elanna didn't feel like answering, she wouldn't.

Her shoulders sagged, and the tough facade faded just a little. "It's hard not to like a man who worships you and wants to give you the world. Like most of the men I like, he turned out to be rotten. Why am I always attracted to the rotters?"

"Because you're a rebel at heart. Despite that, someday you'll find a man who deserves you." Chakotay continued working his console, but he scowled when all his scans turned up empty. "Gammet can probably tell us a good place to hide. Let's take this ship down to the surface right now."

"What about the Cardassians down there?"

"The ones who are left are sitting around, waiting to be picked up. They're no threat anymore."

The captain opened a channel and contacted the *Singha,* telling Captain Rowan all that had happened, and all that was about to happen. She was not adverse to the idea of running for it when the Cardassians showed up in force. He also contacted their mobile clinics and filled them in.

That accomplished, Chakotay took over the conn and eased them onto a reentry course.

Captain Chakotay landed the *Spartacus* in the same field they had landed in on their first visit to Dalgren. Although that had only been a few days before, it seemed like several lifetimes ago. Dr. Gammet and a driver met them in a hovercraft, and Chakotay, Torres, and Echo Imjim made up the official contingent from the *Spartacus,* leaving Seska in charge of the grounded ship.

As they rode to the cemetery, Chakotay turned to Echo and said, "You've been a big help to us, and I'm very thankful. But I think you can return now to your son ... and your life."

The Helenite gave him a warm smile. "Are you sure you don't want to come with us? You could be a very good glider pilot ... with a few more ocean crossings under your belt. And I've been thinking about having *two* gliders in my flock."

"Thank you, but not now," he answered. "I'll try to come back sometime, after things have calmed down in the DMZ."

"There will always be a home for you here," she assured him.

"I concur," said Dr. Gammet. "After all the effort you've put in, and all the risks you've taken for us, it would be a shame if you had to leave. Stay with us—we'll protect your crew from the Cardassians and the Federation. I know that's what Prefect Klain wanted, too."

"Well, we are going to stay for a while," said Chakotay. "We may have turned the corner, but we're still a long way from conquering this disease. I wanted to ask you if you know of any isolated place on Helena where we could hide our ship for a while. When I say 'hide,' I mean hide from sensors as well as from view."

The diminutive doctor stroked his long, white beard. "Yes . . . yes! I know just the place—Flint Island in the Silver Sea. It's colder there than it is here on Dalgren, but they have kelbonite reefs and silica deposits that would mask your ship completely. So many shuttlecraft and gliders have been lost on Flint Island that it has a reputation for being haunted. But that's good—people seldom go there."

"Sounds perfect," said Chakotay.

Torres took a computer padd from her pack and turned it on. "I've got an atlas here—can you show me where it is?"

"Yes, my dear, I can."

While they consulted and the hovercraft cruised along, Chakotay watched the rolling countryside on one side of the craft and the charming city of Astar on the other. Helena was a remarkable planet—worldly yet unspoiled. Could they actually find refuge here from the turmoil in the DMZ? He had no doubt that the Helenites would accept them with open arms, especially B'Elanna, whom they would probably crown queen. Perhaps it wasn't fair of him to force her to leave when she would never be as warmly accepted anywhere else as she was here. Maybe Tuvok was right, and they should have an exit strategy.

Throughout this entire mission, Chakotay had the urgent feeling that time was running out for them. He didn't know what to do about it, except to plunge ahead with the task at hand. Maybe he needed to slow down and withdraw from the conflict.

By the time they reached a picturesque cemetery on a grassy knoll, Chakotay had nearly talked himself into staying, if their mission proved successful. He saw the hundreds of people waiting to attend Klain's funeral, and he realized that the Helenites were a warm, forgiving people.

When they exited the hovercraft, the crowd parted to let them approach the grave site. B'Elanna took the lead, accustomed to all the attention. Chakotay felt someone tug on his sleeve, and he turned to see Shep, the little Ferengi.

"Captain," he whispered. "I knew you'd be here."

Chakotay stepped aside, allowing the others to walk ahead. "Have you found out anything else?"

"Only that Klain recently got a large infusion of latinum into his company and was poised to compete with IGI. It really would seem that he did all of this for profit, which makes me have some sympathy for him." Shep looked around at the large crowd and whistled. "Imagine how many people would be here if he had been a *good* man."

The captain's combadge chirped. *"Spartacus* to Chakotay!"

"Go ahead, Seska."

"Captain! A huge starship has just entered orbit, and the *Singha* is under attack!"

# Chapter Sixteen

In orbit over the shimmering blue planet, a mammoth starship bore down on a tiny Bajoran assault vessel, peppering it with a withering barrage of phaser beams. The *Singha* tried valiantly to return fire while swerving back and forth, but the highly advanced starship had taken her by surprise. The Maquis ship quivered from one blast after another, and her aft sections were aflame, spitting vibrant blue and gold plumes.

"All power to rear shields!" shouted Patricia Rowan on the bridge. Her scarred, gaunt face was haunted with fear. "Continue evasive maneuvers!"

The ship shuddered violently, and the conn officer had to grip his console to stay in his seat. "We've lost all power to the helm. Shields down to six percent!"

"Hail them!"

"They're not answering!" shouted tactical. "We're dropping into the atmosphere—"

Another blast jolted them, and sparks and acrid smoke spewed into the cabin, causing Rowan to gag. The captain dropped to her knees to avoid the worst of the smoke, but she felt herself floating as the ship lost artificial gravity. The deadly barrage never stopped for an instant, and the tiny ship absorbed blast after blast. The scorched, bloodied face of her helmsman floated past her stinging eyes.

"Long live the Maquis!" yelled Captain Rowan with her last breath.

Upon entering the atmosphere, the assault vessel turned into a flaming torch, and a moment later it exploded into a riot of silvery confetti and burning embers. What was left of the *Singha* fluttered through the upper atmosphere of Helena like a gentle snowstorm.

On the ground, Chakotay shoved his way through the crowd and grabbed B'Elanna Torres by the arm. "We've got to get back to the ship—the *Singha* is under attack!"

"What?"

He tapped his combadge. "Seska! Beam us back—now!"

"There's no rush," came a subdued response. "The *Singha* is gone."

Chakotay's jaw dropped, and B'Elanna scowled and ground her boot into the dirt. All around them, Helenites gaped, not understanding what had happened.

"How many Cardassian ships are there?" asked Chakotay, certain that the enemy fleet had arrived.

"Only one ship," answered Seska. "But she isn't Cardassian. At least she isn't like any Cardassian ship we've ever seen before."

"What is she?"

"Unknown. Her warp signature doesn't match anything in our computer."

"That doesn't mean much," grumbled Chakotay, knowing how out-of-date their ship's data was. "What's she doing now?"

"She just beamed one person up from the planet." A tense pause ensued as they waited for more information. "The ship is leaving orbit . . . they're powering up to go into warp. Whoever they are, they're gone."

Chakotay scowled, wishing now that he had kept the *Spartacus* in orbit. "If we had been up there, could we have made a difference?"

"I don't think so. Maybe a Federation starship could have handled them, but not us."

"Well, that's it," said a voice behind Chakotay. He turned to see Shep, the Ferengi, shaking his bulbous head. "It sounds like Klain's murderer has just made his escape."

Anger and frustration surged through Chakotay's veins, and he looked around for the gaudily uniformed officials who had arrested Tuvok. When he spotted the portly one, Chakotay strode toward him and glared at the Helenite. "Klain's murderer—the one most responsible for the plague—has just gotten away in an unknown starship. And they destroyed our sister ship. I want Tuvok released from your prison this instant."

The Helenite looked flustered, but he held his ground. "We can't do that—the hearing isn't until tomorrow."

Chakotay tapped his combadge. "Seska, do you read me?"

"Yes, sir."

"I want you to take off and fly over Astar, destroying buildings at random. In fact, go ahead and level the entire city. You can start with the Dawn Cluster."

"Yes, sir. Preparing to launch."

The Helenite official blanched, paling several shades. "You can't do that! It's . . . it's against the laws of decency!"

"I make my own laws," snapped Chakotay. "I'm Maquis."

The stout Helenite gulped, then he looked around at his fellow citizens, whose expressions made it clear that they didn't want their city destroyed in order to make a dubious point. They slowly backed away, except for Dr. Gammet, who pushed through the crowd.

"Let the Vulcan go, will you!" pleaded the doctor. "These people are *dying* for us. They've risked their lives and their freedom for us. Our own Coastal Watchers are shooting down gliders that try to land here. Our own Prefect Klain was partly responsible for this horrible disease. These are *not* normal times."

After a moment, the official heaved a sigh. "All right, come with me." He motioned them toward his hovercraft.

Chakotay tapped his combadge. "Belay that last order, Seska."

"Yes, sir," she answered, sounding relieved. "What's the real plan?"

"Right now, we're going to get Tuvok out of jail. Stay prepped for launch, because we're taking the ship into hiding. We're going to keep helping sick people for as long we can. Chakotay out."

Dr. Gammet stepped up to the captain and warmly shook his hand. "Captain, I don't think we can ever express our gratitude for what you've tried to do for us. No matter how it turns out, we know you've done all you can. We may not be able to erect any statues to you, but the Maquis will always be heroes to us."

"Hear! Hear!" yelled someone in the crowd. Spontaneous applause erupted, and several Helenites patted Chakotay on the back. He could still see fear and uncertainty in their eyes, but there was also genuine affection.

"I'll keep the clinics open," vowed Gammet. "You leave it to me."

Chakotay nodded, unable to find words to express his own feelings. Moments like this were few and far between for the Maquis, although they were the only reason the Maquis existed at all. When he turned to follow Torres and the official to the hovercraft, he felt a familiar tug on his shirtsleeve. It was Shep.

"What about the shuttlecraft?" asked the Ferengi. "When do we leave?"

The captain looked down at his small confederate and shook his head. "I'm afraid I had to send Bokor in the shuttle already, but you can come with us."

"You'll be the first Ferengi member of the Maquis," added Torres.

Shep thought for a moment, then replied, "No, thank you. I think I'd rather take my chances here. These people aren't so bad after all. Good luck to you, Captain Chakotay."

"You, too," replied the captain.

A moment later, as they settled into the hovercraft, he turned to Torres and said, "So he would rather stay on a plague-ridden planet than join the Maquis. What does that say about us?"

"After what just happened to the *Singha,* I can't say I blame him."

"I'm sorry you didn't get to see Klain's funeral."

"I've got a feeling I'll see more funerals before this is all over," she answered glumly.

\* \* \*

Tuvok squinted slightly when he stepped from the huge ministry building into the sunshine after being incarcerated in a dim cell for sixteen hours. "What is our status?" he asked Chakotay.

"Not good, I'm afraid." He told Tuvok about the destruction of the *Singha* by unknown forces, the escape of Klain's murderer, and the imminent arrival of a Cardassian fleet.

The Vulcan raised an eyebrow. "Perhaps I should go back to my cell."

"On the good side," said Torres, "the captain rescued Lieutenent Riker. Near death, but still alive."

"What about Ensign Shelzane?"

She shook her head. "Riker says she's dead."

"I don't know whether it will do any good," said Chakotay, "but I sent the Andorian back to the Federation in Riker's shuttlecraft. Maybe they'll come, maybe not."

"Are we retreating from Helena?"

"No. Our medical teams still have work to do, and we're not deserting them, or the mission. But we are going into hiding." Chakotay tapped his combadge. "Seska, three to beam over. Prepare for launch."

As the *Spartacus* swooped over a dismal, gray ocean with small ice floes bobbing in the pale water, Chakotay knew why it was called the Silver Sea. When the sun caught it, the ocean might have looked quite beautiful, but under a cloudy sky it looked cold and foreboding.

A bleak, rocky island lay ahead of them, and Chakotay knew without looking at the coordinates that it was Flint Island, also aptly named. "What kind of readings are you getting from that island?" he asked Tuvok, who was seated beside him.

The Vulcan studied his instruments and cocked his head.

"High kelbonite and silica readings are disrupting our sensors. I presume there must be some vegetation, but I cannot get any readings."

"Perfect. I'm slowing down to make a pass over the island—we'll have to use visual to find a place to land."

Tuvok nodded and sat forward in his seat, ready to use his sharp vision. The *Peregrine*-class starship swooped over a rugged island that looked surprisingly large when seen from close range. Spindly gray mountains rose above rocky bluffs and cliffs, and there were a few scattered clumps of vegetation clinging to the bare stone. In the center of the island was a lagoon filled with brackish water, and a few stunted trees grew there. Flint Island's bays and black beaches lacked the sea-gliders and boats they had seen on the rest of Helena.

"There," said Tuvok, pointing. "Under that ledge."

Chakotay brought the ship around for another pass over the area Tuvok had indicated. Now he spotted it, too—a great ledge carved by crashing waves in the side of one of the cliffs. Under the ledge was a shiny wet chunk of bedrock. It would be tricky to land there, but he thought he could do it. The advantage would be that the ledge would obscure the *Spartacus* from prying eyes, should any of their enemies fly over Flint Island.

The captain hit his comm panel, and his voice echoed throughout the small ship. "All hands, brace for landing. It may be a little rough."

"Allow me, sir?" asked Tuvok.

Chakotay looked at his capable first officer and nodded with relief. "Yes, take the conn."

Under Tuvok's sure hands, the landing was not rough at all. He piloted the *Spartacus* under the ledge and hovered for a second, thrusters blasting away. Then he eased her onto the bedrock like a mother putting her baby down for a nap.

When Tuvok killed the thrusters, Chakotay finally let his breath out. A wave splashed a sheen of water against their front window, and it dribbled down like a veil of tears.

"Now what?" asked the Vulcan.

"Now we wait," answered the captain. "If we put a communications array on top of the cliff, do you think we could monitor subspace transmissions?"

"I believe so. I will attend to it." Tuvok rose from his seat and strode off the bridge, leaving Chakotay to ponder the gray sea that lapped at their precarious perch.

They were safe . . . for the moment.

Eight hours later, Chakotay sat alone on the barren cliff, warming his hands by a small campfire and watching the twin moons of Helena try to shine their way through dense cloud cover. Although the clouds were gloomy, he knew they were keeping the night temperature on Flint Island warmer than it had a right to be. A few meters away, the communications array hummed busily, listening for voices of doom behind the swirling clouds.

The campfire, made from driftwood, was his own small conceit. They had portable heaters that would probably be more efficient, and they could monitor the subspace traffic just as easily from the ship. But Chakotay had felt a need to sit and commune with fire, the ground, and the night. Until this mission, he hadn't realized how much he had missed being on land. He loved space, but he knew he was a visitor there; he felt connected to the land, even this forsaken, haunted island.

Hearing footsteps behind him, he whirled around to see two people approaching. One of them was walking stiffly with a cane, and the other was helping him. When they reached the circle of light from the campfire, he was surprised to see that it was Riker using the cane, and B'Elanna helping him.

"What are you doing up?" he asked Riker, with a mild scold in his voice.

"I couldn't lie in that bed a moment longer," said the lieutenant with a smile. "You look like one of your ancestors, sitting up here by the fire. Except that you used a lighter to start it." Riker pointed at the device.

Chakotay smiled wanly. "I'm sure they would have used more appropriate technology. But however I accomplish the aim, sometimes I need to speak to my ancestors, and this is a good place to find them."

"I don't blame you," said Riker, easing himself to the ground with some difficulty. "I grew up in fairly wild country on Earth, and I miss sitting outside by the campfire."

"Where are you from?" asked Torres.

"Alaska. It's beautiful—forests, lakes, rivers, glaciers, lots of wildlife. Most of the year, it's cold, like this. I miss it."

"Why don't you go back?"

The big man shrugged. "There's not much call for a Starfleet officer in Alaska. Besides, there are some memories I'm not so fond of. But maybe I will go back someday."

Suddenly, the communications array crackled with activity, and several voices broke in at once, overlapping. Chakotay jumped up from the campfire to adjust the equipment, and a moment later they heard a male voice order, "All ships, assume standard orbit, six thousand kilometer intervals. Cruiser *Gagh N'Vort*, coordinate scanning activity. Warship *K'Stek Nak*, coordinate targeting."

"Targeting?" breathed Torres. "They're going to destroy

the planet! We've got to get back to the ship."

"Wait a minute," said Riker puzzledly. "Those aren't Cardassian ship names."

"Cloak on my command," the voice continued.

"Cardassians don't have cloaking," said Chakotay. "They're *Klingon* ships!'

A grin spread across Riker's face. "I think the Cardassians are in for a surprise."

# Chapter Seventeen

GUL DEMADAK RUBBED his hands together and smiled, thinking how good it would feel to finally be rid of the obstacle known as Helena. Destroying the planet would not only please his superiors and squelch the plague, but it would destroy any trace of his involvement with his secret benefactor. It would also rid the Cardassian Union of a worthless planet that was more trouble to govern than it was worth.

And he would do the deed himself, to achieve the maximum recognition and credit.

"Coming out of warp in thirty seconds," the captain of the *Hakgot* reported to him.

"Excellent," Demadak said with a satisfied smile. He had only been able to scrounge up eight ships on the spur of the moment, but he figured that would be enough to scorch the planet. If they didn't kill everyone and everything with their weapons, the nuclear winter they caused would destroy everything in a few days. From what he knew of the planet, the inhabitants were peaceful and had no working starships, so they wouldn't be prepared for an all-out conflagration. They would have no place to hide.

"Coming out of warp," reported the captain of his flagship.

Gul Demadak rose from his seat and stood before the viewscreen. *What an ugly little planet,* he thought when it came into view—*all blue and watery, like a human's weak eyes.* "Any sign of the Maquis?" he asked.

"None," answered the officer on ops. "There are no ships in orbit."

The gul nodded, thinking that the cowardly Maquis had run for it. Or perhaps they had all succumbed to the plague. It was just as well, because his crew needed all of its firepower for the task at hand.

"What about the garrison?" asked the captain.

Demadak frowned, his bony brow knit with concern. "According to their last report, most of them have already died from the plague, and the rest are getting sick. We have no facilities to care for them, and we don't want to stay here any longer than absolutely necessary."

The captain nodded. Nobody wanted to risk getting the plague, and the whole purpose of this operation was to make sure that the plague died on Helena.

"I'll make sure that they are all decorated for bravery," said Demadak. "Posthumously."

He looked at another viewscreen and could see the other seven ships in his fleet spread out behind him, ready to execute his commands. "Power up weapons," he ordered.

"Yes, sir."

Before they could even fire a shot, his ship was jolted by a powerful blast, and the gul staggered on his feet. "What was *that?*" he demanded.

"Port nacelle damaged!" reported a frightened ops officer.

"Look!" barked the captain, pointing at the viewscreen. A massive Klingon Bird of Prey had materialized from nowhere—dead ahead of them. Behind them, two more Klingon ships came out of cloak.

"Return fire!" yelled Demadak.

"Belay that order," said the captain, fixing a jaundiced eye on the gul. "In total, there are *thirteen* Klingon ships ringing the planet. Gul Demadak, I have to remind you that *I'm* in command of this ship and her crew. I really don't care to die over this stupid planet."

"They're hailing us," reported the tactical officer.

"On screen," muttered Demadak, slumping into a seat. He knew at that moment that his career was over. He would probably be executed.

A rugged, bearded Klingon appeared on the viewscreen. "Cardassian vessels, turn around and leave. I am General Martok, and the planet of Helena is under the protection of the Klingon Empire."

"You . . . you have no right to be here!" sputtered Demadak.

"Neither do you," replied the Klingon.

"This is in direct violation of the treaty!"

"*We* have no treaty with you," sneered General Martok. "However, you are clearly breaking your treaty with the Federation. I have been instructed to deliver a message to you from the Federation. They will overlook this serious transgression if you will leave the Demilitarized Zone immediately. In exchange, they will send a fleet of unarmed personnel carriers to evacuate the population of Helena. This will effectively end your concerns over the disease that has infected the planet. I can see no reason why you should refuse this gracious offer."

"Neither can I," said the Cardassian captain, stepping in front of Demadak. "General Martok, we will take our leave. End transmission."

After the screen went blank, the captain turned to the helmsman and ordered, "Take us home. Maximum warp."

Fuming, Demadak glared at the captain. "I'll have your head for this!"

"No, you won't. They *knew* we were coming. You are responsible for a serious security breach, and I'll make sure Central Command hears about it."

Gul Demadak leaned forward and buried his face in his hands.

A week later, Chakotay and his crew were still hiding on Flint Island, monitoring the evacuation of Helena. They were unable to leave because of all the ships in orbit. Although their mission was a success and most of the Helenites had been saved, there was a bittersweet feeling of defeat. It had never been their intention that a civilization hundreds of years old should be uprooted and taken back to a place from which they had fled. Chakotay could only imagine the sorrow of Dr. Gammet, Echo Imjim, and so many others who had to leave their homes, businesses, and unique lifestyles. In a way, they had won the battle but lost the war.

Also, they were troubled by the knowledge that the real masterminds of this biological weapon had gotten away. Where they would strike again, no one knew; but Chakotay was certain that they *would* strike again.

Night after night, members of the crew sat on the cliff by the campfire, listening to radio traffic from the personnel carriers. At least, thought Chakotay, there was no more talk about B'Elanna or anyone else retiring from the Maquis and living happily ever after on Helena. When the last ship left, Helena would again be the exclusive property of the birds, fish, and animals. Cardassians would be free to settle there, but he doubted they ever would.

He watched Thomas Riker, who seemed to be the most troubled of all of them. The Maquis were used to the Federation messing things up, but the lieutenant had never gotten such a vivid demonstration of its heavy-handed interference before. It had come as something of a shock.

All of the Starfleet doctors had left with the others, but not Riker. He refused to leave the *Spartacus*. One night, Chakotay found himself alone on the cliff with the lieutenant. He hadn't broached the subject yet, but it was time.

"Riker," he said, "the evacuation is almost complete. If you're going back to Starfleet, you've got to go now. We'll beam you over to one of the other islands."

The lieutenant gritted his teeth. "I can't stand what they're doing here. All of it is just to make life easier for *them*. They don't give a damn what happens to the Helenites."

"Why do you think we formed the Maquis? The Federation's appeasement of the Cardassians has destroyed more lives than you can ever imagine. What's a few million Helenites down the drain, as long as it keeps the treaty intact. If you're not going back to Starfleet, are you going to stay with us? Are you ready to join the Maquis?"

The big man nodded slowly. "I can't believe it, but I think I am. What am I going to do in the Maquis?"

"*You* can do a lot for us, since you can impersonate that

other Riker. There's a mission we've talked about, but we've never had the right person until now."

"What is it?"

He looked around, just to make sure they were alone. "I think I can trust everybody in my crew, but I'm not entirely sure. So I want you to keep this between you and me."

"That's no problem."

Chakotay smiled. "Ever been to Deep Space Nine?"

**Pocket Books**
**Proudly Presents**

### Double Helix #5

# DOUBLE OR NOTHING

### Peter David

**Available in August from Pocket Books**

**Turn the page for a preview of**
*Double or Nothing. . . .*

Gerrid Thul was eminently pleased as he looked around the room of dead men.

That might not have been the most accurate of terms, he reasoned. Not all of them were men, for starters. A goodly number of males of the species were there, yes, but there was a vast array of females as well. All equally deserving, equally titled, equally dead. And to be absolutely, one hundred percent correct, he would have to admit that none of them were actually, in point of fact, dead.

Yet.

Never had the word "yet" been so delicious, held so much promise. Yet. Definitely, indisputably, yet.

As he walked through the grand reception hall that hosted the first of what was intended to be a number of gatherings celebrating the bicentennial, he couldn't help but be satisfied, and even amused, at the way that others within the Federation were reacting to him. There were nods, smiles, a polite wink or two. And many, ever so many requests for "just a few moments" of his time that invariably expanded into many minutes.

He had been careful, so very careful in making his contacts. And what had been so elegant about the entire matter was that those poor, benighted fools in the Federation had a tendency to side with the underdog. And that was something that Thul had very much seemed. A man who was once great, who had lost everything, and who was now trying to build himself back up to a position of strength and influence. He had come to people seemingly hat in hand, unprepossessing, undemanding. And he played, like a virtuoso, upon one of the fundamental truths of all sentient beings: Everyone liked to feel superior to someone else. It made them comfortable. It made them generous. And best of all, it made them sloppy and offered a situation that Gerrid Thul could capitalize upon.

Of course, Vara Syndra had helped.

"Where is Vara this fine evening?" assorted ambassadors and high muck-a-mucks in the Federation asked. But Thul had held her back, and not without reason. Best to build up anticipation, to get them to want to see her, ask about her, look around and try to catch a glimpse of her. Vara knew her place, though, and also knew that timing was everything. She would remain secreted away until the appropriate time had presented itself, and then he would send for her.

He had a feeling that the time was fast approaching.

"Thul! Gerrid Thul!" came a hearty voice that Thul recognized instantly. He turned to see Admiral Edward Jellico approaching.

He did not like Jellico. That, in and of itself, was nothing surprising; he didn't like any of them, really.

But Jellico was a particularly pompous and officious representative of humanity. Thul hoped against hope that he might somehow actually be able to see Jellico when the death throes overtook him, but that didn't seem tremendously likely. He would have to settle for imagining it. Then again, Thul had a famously vivid imagination, so that probably wouldn't present too much of a difficulty.

"Edward!" returned Thul cheerfully, perfectly matching the pitch and enthusiasm of Jellico's own voice. He had to speak loudly to make himself heard over the noise and chatter of the packed ballroom. Furthermore, all around him the scents of various foods wafted toward him. Thul had a rather acute sense of smell, and the array was nearly overwhelming to him. Some seemed rather enticing while others nearly induced his gag reflex, so it was quite an effort to keep it all straight within him. "It is good to see you again, my friend."

"And you as well, Gerrid." He gestured to those who were accompanying them. One was another human, a tall and powerfully built human female. The other was a rather elegant-looking Vulcan with quite dark skin, graying hair, and that annoying serenity that Vulcans seemed to carry with them at all times. "This is Admiral O'Shea," he said, pointing to the female, "and this is Ambassador Stonn. Admiral, Ambassador, Gerrid Thul of the Thallonian Empire."

"The late Thallonian Empire, I fear," said Thul. He bowed in O'Shea's direction, and then gave a flawless Vulcan salute to Stonn. "Peace and long life," he said.

"Live long and prosper," replied Stonn.

*One of us will,* thought Thul.

"I'm familiar with your good works, Thul," said O'Shea. "As I recall, you were working just last month to seek more humanitarian aid for refugees from Thallonian space."

"Actually," Thul told her, "I have been looking into expanding my efforts. You see, in exploring what needs to be done to help our own refugees, I have stumbled upon other races that could use aid as well. Aid . . . which is sometimes hampered by the Federation."

"Hampered? How so?" asked Stonn.

"It is . . . ironic that I would bring this up now," Thul said, looking quite apologetic. "We are, after all, here to celebrate the signing of the Resolution for noninterference, one of the keystone documents of the entire Federation."

"Yes. So?"

"So, Admiral O'Shea . . . it may be time to revisit the entire concept of the prime directive. All too often . . . and I truly do not wish to offend with my sentiments . . ."

"Please, Gerrid, say what you feel," Jellico urged him.

"Very well. It seems that, all too often, the intent of the prime directive is corrupted. The letter is followed when the spirit is violated." He noticed that several other people had overheard him and were now attending his words as well. Superb. The larger audience he had, the better he liked it. "The fact is that the prime directive was created specifically so that more advanced races would not *harm* less developed races. But too many times, we encounter situations where it is specifically cited as a reason not to *help* those races. Starfleet stands by, watches them fumble about, and simply takes down notes while observing from hidden posts. Think, my friends. Think, for example, of a small child," and his voice started to ache with imagined hurt, "a small boy, dying of a disease . . . the cure for which is held by those who look down from up high. But do they help? Do they produce a medication that will save him? No . . . no, my friends, they do not. They bloodlessly watch, and take down their notes, and perhaps they'll log the time of death. And who knows if that child might not have grown up to be the greatest man, inventor, thinker, philosopher, leader of that race. The man who could bring that race into a golden age, cut off . . . in his youth. What would it have hurt . . . to help that child? And what tremendous benefit might have been gained. Who among you could endorse such a scenario . . . and believe it to somehow serve a greater good?"

There was dead silence from those within earshot. Finally, Stonn said, "A very passionate observation, Thul. At its core, there may even be some valid points. However . . . interference invites abuse. It was an earthman who stated that power tends to corrupt . . . and absolute power corrupts absolutely. For all of the positive scenarios that you can spin, I am certain that I would easily be able to create plausible hypotheticals of abuse of that selfsame power."

"What Ambassador Stonn is saying," said Admiral O'Shea, "is that if the noninterference directive is, as you postulate, an error . . . isn't it better to err on the side of caution?"

"Two hundred years ago, perhaps. Perhaps, I will certainly grant you that. But of what use is experience if one does not learn from it?" replied Thul. "There are people who need help and don't even know that they do. Besides, is not human history rife with such 'interference'? Were there not more advanced members of the human race who went to less-developed, undernourished or undereducated areas and brought them technology . . . advancement . . . even entire belief systems?"

"And in many instances did as much harm as good," Jellico said. "There was also conquest, to say nothing of entire races of people who were annihilated by germs and strains of diseases that their own immune systems were completely unequipped to handle."

"Ultimately, however," and Thul smiled, "things seem to have worked out for you."

"Yes, because we found our own way."

"Or perhaps in spite of finding your own way. Think, though. If older, wiser, more advanced races such as yours, and all those represented in this room were to use their experience, their knowledge of the mistakes that they themselves made to avoid mistakes in the future . . ." He shook his head. "Don't you see. Here, around you, you can very well think of this as a sort of golden age for the Federation. But when there is want and need by other races who have never even heard of the Federation, and who could benefit so tremendously by the help . . ."

"You're saying that perhaps it's time to abolish or reframe the prime directive?" said Jellico.

"At this time? Two hundred years after the signing of

the document that was its genesis? Yes, that is exactly what I am saying."

There were thoughtful nods from all around, like a sea of bobbing heads. Finally it was Jellico who said, "You may . . . have some valid points there, Gerrid. Obviously I can't speak on behalf of Starfleet, and certainly not the Federation . . . but perhaps some serious study should be done as to whether it's time to rethink our intentions and perhaps expand upon—"

"You hypocrite."

The voice had come completely unexpectedly, and the words were slightly slurred. As one, everyone within earshot turned and saw the rather remarkable sight of a Starfleet captain, holding a drink and glaring at Admiral Jellico with as open a glare of contempt as Thul had ever seen.

"You are some piece of work, Admiral. You are really, truly, some piece of work." He took another sip of the blue liquid that was swirling about in his glass.

Thul couldn't quite believe the change that had come over Jellico's face. He had gone from thoughtful to darkly furious, practically in the space of a heartbeat. "Captain Calhoun . . . may I ask what you're doing here?"

"Listening to you reverse yourself," replied Captain Calhoun. "The number of times I've had to listen to you pontificate and talk about the sanctity of the prime directive . . . of how unbreakable the first, greatest law of Starfleet is . . . and how you've used that selfsame law to second-guess and denounce some of my most important decisions. But now here you are, all dressed up at this extremely important gathering," and he added exaggerated emphasis to the last three words, "and this . . . person . . ." and he waved in a vague manner at Thul, ". . . suggests the exact same thing that I've been saying for years now . . . and suddenly you're ready to listen. You act like this is the first time you've heard it."

"Perhaps Gerrid Thul simply has a way of expressing his concerns that is superior to the belligerent tone you usually adopt, Captain," said Jellico. Quickly he said to the others around him, "Gerrid, Ambassador Stonn, Admiral O'Shea . . . I'm terribly sorry about this. I'm not entirely certain what this officer is doing here . . ."

"I'm here because I was ordered to be here," Calhoun said. A number of other guests were noticing the ruckus, which wasn't difficult since Calhoun's voice was carrying.

"That's strange. My office should have received a memo on that," Jellico said, his eyes narrowing with suspicion.

"Really. Perhaps someone simply forgot. Or perhaps you were too busy getting ready for this little get-together that you didn't have a chance to stay current with your memos. Look, Admiral," and Calhoun swayed ever so slightly. Thul could tell that this rather odd individual had clearly had a bit too much to drink. "Make no mistake. I'd rather be on my ship. But I was ordered to be here because I'm supposed to be representing the Federation's interests in Thallonian space. One of the new frontiers that we brave individuals are exploring and protecting. Here's to us," and he knocked back more of the drink, leaving about a third of it in the glass.

"Of course," said Thul in slow realization. "Captain Calhoun . . . of the *Excalibur*. Am I correct?"

"Correct."

"I am very aware of your vessel's humanitarian mission. It is also my understanding that Lord Si Cwan is among the personnel of your brave ship. I met him once, when he was a very small child. I doubt he would remember me."

"Captain Calhoun was just leaving," said Jellico, "weren't you, Captain?"

"Oh, was I?" Calhoun smiled lopsidedly. "But Admiral, this is a party. Why are you so anxious to have me leave?"

"Captain," O'Shea spoke up, "I'm well aware that you have some . . . issues . . . with Admiral Jellico. But I submit that this is neither the time nor the place . . ."

"Or perhaps it's the perfect time and place," Calhoun shot back. Thul quickly began to reassess his opinion. Calhoun wasn't a bit drunk. He was seriously drunk. Not in such a way that he was going to fall over, but certainly whatever inhibitions he might have about speaking the truth were gone. "The fact is that the good Admiral here has had it out for me for years now. Just because he got it into his head that I was some sort of super officer, and then I didn't live up to the place that he'd set for me. I saved his life, you know," he said in an offhand manner to Thul. "This man would be standing here dead if not for me."

"And because of that, I protected you as long as I could," Jellico said, his body stiffening. "But you're the one who allowed the Grissom incident to get to you,

Calhoun. Accidents happen, bad things happen to good people. True leaders manage to rise above that."

"And leave their consciences behind?"

"I didn't say that. Look, Calhoun," said Jellico, his ire clearly beginning to rise, "you said you're here because you were ordered to be here. If you're actually obeying orders, it's going to be the first time that I can recall in ages . . . perhaps ever. That being the case, here's another order: Get the hell out of here before you embarrass yourself further, if that's possible."

"Gentlemen," Stonn said, "perhaps you might wish to take this conversation into a private area . . ."

It seemed to Thul that, at that point, everyone in the place was watching them. He also saw several men dressed in UFP security garb threading their way through the crowd.

"I'm sure he'd like that," Calhoun said. "That's how his kind best operates—in the dark, in private, alone, like any fungus."

*"That's enough,"* said Jellico, the veins on his temples clearly throbbing.

"You sway with the wind, Jellico," said Calhoun. "To your superiors and your pals, you say what you think they want to hear. And to the rest of us, you step on us like we're bugs. That's all we are to you. And you can't stand me because I actually stood up to you. Stood up! That's an understatement. I flattened you. I flattened him," Calhoun said to O'Shea. "One punch. I resigned from Starfleet, he tried to get in my way, I warned him, and one punch, I took him down."

"It was not one punch." Jellico looked around, clearly embarrassed. "Not one punch."

"It was. One shot to the side of the head, and you went down on your ass, right after you grabbed my arm . . ."

"All right, that's it. Security!" called Jellico.

He grabbed Calhoun by the arm.

Calhoun's smile went wolfish, and to Thul it seemed as if all the inebriation, all the fuzziness about the man, dissolved in a second. Whatever the man might have had to drink, he was able to shunt it aside in a split second. His fist whipped around with no hesitation, and caught Jellico squarely in the side of the head. Jellico went down amidst gasps from everyone surrounding him.

"That will suffice," said Ambassador Stonn, stepping between Jellico and Calhoun. At that moment, despite the superior strength of the Vulcan, Thul would not have wanted to place bets on just who would win an altercation between the Vulcan and Calhoun.

But Calhoun didn't display the least interest in fighting off Stonn. Instead he simply grinned and said, "See? Told you. One punch."

"Get him out of here!" Jellico said, rubbing his head. His eyes weren't focused on anything; Thul could practically hear Jellico's head ringing right from where he was standing.

The security guards converged around Calhoun and took him firmly by either arm. Calhoun didn't put up any protest. He seemed to be enjoying Jellico's disorientation immensely. "One-punch Jellico, they should call you. That's all it takes," Calhoun called. "That's all it takes to puncture a pompous windbag."

O'Shea helped Jellico to his feet, asking after his

health solicitously, but it didn't seem as if Jellico even heard her. Instead, across the room that had now become completely hushed, Jellico shouted, "I'll have your rank for this, Calhoun! Do you hear me? This is the last straw! I don't care who your friends are! I don't care what you've accomplished! I don't care if Picard backs you up! I don't care if the words, 'Calhoun is my favorite captain' appears on the wall at Starfleet headquarters in flaming letters twelve feet high! You are gone! You are finished! Do you hear? Finished!"

"I hear you, Admiral!" called Calhoun as he was escorted forcibly from the room. "And I heard you when you said it years ago! And I came back, didn't I? I keep coming back!"

"Not this time, Calhoun! Not this time!"

There was a long silence after Calhoun had been removed from the room. Jellico was flushed red in the face, clearly utterly chagrined at the turn of events. "You've nothing to be embarrassed about, Admiral," said Thul consolingly. "Obviously he was a madman."

"I could tell you horror stories, Gerrid, I really could," said Jellico. "Mackenzie Calhoun represents . . . I'm sorry, I should say 'represented' . . . everything that's wrong with the 'cowboy' breed of captain. No respect for rules or for authority. No respect for the chain of command. No . . ."

"No respect, period?" offered Thul.

"Yes. Yes, that's exactly right. He left the fleet once before . . . went freelance . . . did dirty work for whomever would pay him. The only reason he was brought back into the fleet was because he had well-placed supporters, but after this debacle, even they won't back him. Believe me, we're stronger without him."

"And he certainly seems to have no love for Starfleet . . . or even perhaps the Federation," Thul said slowly.

"The Mackenzie Calhouns of this world love only themselves and care about their own skins, and that's all. We were speaking of abuse of power before, Gerrid? He's exactly the type that the prime directive was created to ride herd on. Good riddance to him, I say." Jellico rubbed the side of his face. "Let him be someone else's problem."

"Excellent idea," said Gerrid Thul. "A most excellent idea."

**Look for**
*Double or Nothing*
**Available in August**
**Wherever Books Are Sold**

# STAR TREK®
## Strange New Worlds III
## Contest Rules

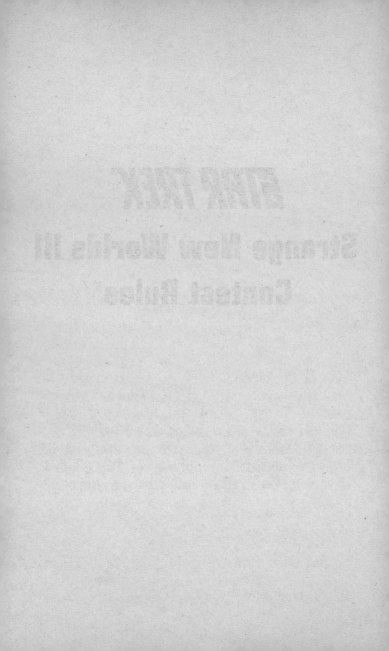

"professor," a note signed on one side of more corosable proof. Do not put proof else where on. The author's name, address, and phone number must appear on the last page of the entry. the author's name, the story title, and the page number should appear on every page. No originals of task submissions will be accepted. All entries must be original and the sole work of the entrant and the sole property of the entrant.

4) ADDRESS

## 1) ENTRY REQUIREMENTS:

No purchase necessary to enter. Enter by submitting your story as specified below.

## 2) CONTEST ELIGIBILITY:

This contest is open to nonprofessional writers who are legal residents of the United States and Canada (excluding Quebec) over the age of 18. Entrant must not have published any more than two short stories on a professional basis or in paid professional venues. Employees (or relatives of employees living in the same household) of Pocket Books, VIACOM, or any of its affiliates are not eligible. This contest is void in Puerto Rico and wherever prohibited by law.

## 3) FORMAT:

Entries should be no more than 7,500 words long and must not have been previously published. They must be typed or printed by word processor, double spaced on one side of non-corrasable paper. Do not justify right-side margins. The author's name, address, and phone number must appear on the first page of the entry. The author's name, the story title, and the page number should appear on every page. No electronic or disk submissions will be accepted. All entries must be original and the sole work of the Entrant and the sole property of the Entrant.

## 4) ADDRESS:

Each entry must be mailed to: STRANGE NEW WORLDS, *Star Trek* Department, Pocket Books, 1230 Sixth Avenue, New York, NY 10020.

Each entry must be submitted only once. Please retain a copy of your submission. You may submit more than one story, but each submission must be mailed separately. Enclose a self-addressed, stamped envelope if you wish your entry returned. Entries must be received by October 1st, 1999. Not responsible for lost, late, stolen, postage due, or misdirected mail.

## 5) PRIZES:

One Grand Prize winner will receive:

Simon and Schuster's *Star Trek: Strange New Worlds III* Publishing Contract for Publication of Winning Entry in our *Strange New Worlds III* Anthology with a bonus advance of One Thousand

Dollars ($1,000.00) above the Anthology word rate of 10 cents a word.

One Second Prize winner will receive:

Simon and Schuster's *Star Trek: Strange New Worlds III* Publishing Contract for Publication of Winning Entry in our *Strange New Worlds III* Anthology with a bonus advance of Six Hundred Dollars ($600.00) above the Anthology word rate of 10 cents a word.

One Third Prize winner will receive:

Simon and Schuster's *Star Trek: Strange New Worlds III* Publishing Contract for Publication of Winning Entry in our *Strange New Worlds III* Anthology with a bonus advance of Four Hundred Dollars ($400.00) above the Anthology word rate of 10 cents a word.

All Honorable Mention winners will receive:

Simon and Schuster's *Star Trek: Strange New Worlds III* Publishing Contract for Publication of Winning Entry in the *Strange New Worlds III* Anthology and payment at the Anthology word rate of 10 cents a word.

There will be no more than twenty (20) Honorable Mention winners. No contestant can win more than one prize.

Each Prize Winner will also be entitled to a share

of royalties on the *Strange New Worlds III* Anthology as specified in Simon and Schuster's *Star Trek: Strange New Worlds III* Publishing Contract.

## 6) JUDGING:

Submissions will be judged on the basis of writing ability and the originality of the story, which can be set in any of the *Star Trek* time frames and may feature any one or more of the *Star Trek* characters. The judges shall include the editor of the Anthology, one employee of Pocket Books, and one employee of VIACOM Consumer Products. The decisions of the judges shall be final. All prizes will be awarded provided a sufficient number of entries are received that meet the minimum criteria established by the judges.

## 7) NOTIFICATION:

The winners will be notified by mail or phone. The winners who win a publishing contract must sign the publishing contract in order to be awarded the prize. All federal, local, and state taxes are the responsibility of the winner. A list of the winners will be available after January 1st, 2000, on the Pocket Books *Star Trek* Books website, www.simonsays.com/startrek/, or the names of the winners can be obtained after January 1st, 2000, by sending a self-addressed, stamped envelope and a request for the list of winners to WINNERS' LIST, STRANGE NEW WORLDS III, *Star Trek* Department, Pocket Books, 1230 Sixth Avenue, New York, NY 10020.

## 8) STORY DISQUALIFICATIONS:

Certain types of stories will be disqualified from consideration:

a) Any story focusing on explicit sexual activity or graphic depictions of violence or sadism.

b) Any story that focuses on characters that are not past or present *Star Trek* regulars or familiar *Star Trek* guest characters.

c) Stories that deal with the previously unestablished death of a *Star Trek* character, or that establish major facts about or make major changes in the life of a major character, for instance a story that establishes a long-lost sibling or reveals the hidden passion two characters feel for each other.

d) Stories that are based around common clichés, such as "hurt/comfort" where a character is injured and lovingly cared for, or "Mary Sue" stories where a new character comes on the ship and outdoes the crew.

## 9) PUBLICITY:

Each Winner grants to Pocket Books the right to use his or her name, likeness, and entry for any advertising, promotion, and publicity purposes without further compensation to or permission from such winner, except where prohibited by law.

## 10) LEGAL STUFF:

All entries become the property of Pocket Books and of Paramount Pictures, the sole and exclusive owner of the *Star Trek* property and elements thereof. Entries will be returned only if they are accompanied by a self-addressed, stamped envelope. Contest void where prohibited by law.

# Look for STAR TREK Fiction from Pocket Books

## Star Trek®: The Original Series

## Star Trek: The Next Generation®

*Encounter at Farpoint* • David Gerrold
*Unification* • Jeri Taylor
*Relics* • Michael Jan Friedman
*Descent* • Diane Carey
*All Good Things* • Michael Jan Friedman
*Star Trek: Klingon* • Dean W. Smith & Kristine K. Rusch
*Star Trek VII: Generations* • J. M. Dillard
*Metamorphosis* • Jean Lorrah
*Vendetta* • Peter David
*Reunion* • Michael Jan Friedman
*Imzadi* • Peter David
*The Devil's Heart* • Carmen Carter
*Dark Mirror* • Diane Duane
*Q-Squared* • Peter David
*Crossover* • Michael Jan Friedman
*Kahless* • Michael Jan Friedman
*Star Trek VIII: First Contact* • J. M. Dillard
*Star Trek IX: Insurrection* • Diane Carey
*The Best and the Brightest* • Susan Wright
*Planet X* • Michael Jan Friedman
*Ship of the Line* • Diane Carey

#1   *Ghost Ship* • Diane Carey
#2   *The Peacekeepers* • Gene DeWeese
#3   *The Children of Hamlin* • Carmen Carter
#4   *Survivors* • Jean Lorrah
#5   *Strike Zone* • Peter David
#6   *Power Hungry* • Howard Weinstein
#7   *Masks* • John Vornholt
#8   *The Captains' Honor* • David and Daniel Dvorkin
#9   *A Call to Darkness* • Michael Jan Friedman
#10  *A Rock and a Hard Place* • Peter David
#11  *Gulliver's Fugitives* • Keith Sharee
#12  *Doomsday World* • David, Carter, Friedman & Greenberg
#13  *The Eyes of the Beholders* • A. C. Crispin
#14  *Exiles* • Howard Weinstein
#15  *Fortune's Light* • Michael Jan Friedman
#16  *Contamination* • John Vornholt
#17  *Boogeymen* • Mel Gilden

**Star Trek: Deep Space Nine®**

*The Search* • Diane Carey
*Warped* • K. W. Jeter
*The Way of the Warrior* • Diane Carey
*Star Trek: Klingon* • Dean W. Smith & Kristine K. Rusch
*Trials and Tribble-ations* • Diane Carey
*Far Beyond the Stars* • Steve Barnes
*The 34th Rule* • Armin Shimerman & David George
*What We Leave Behind* • Diane Carey

#1 *Emissary* • J. M. Dillard
#2 *The Siege* • Peter David
#3 *Bloodletter* • K. W. Jeter
#4 *The Big Game* • Sandy Schofield
#5 *Fallen Heroes* • Dafydd ab Hugh
#6 *Betrayal* • Lois Tilton
#7 *Warchild* • Esther Friesner
#8 *Antimatter* • John Vornholt
#9 *Proud Helios* • Melissa Scott
#10 *Valhalla* • Nathan Archer
#11 *Devil in the Sky* • Greg Cox & John Gregory Betancourt
#12 *The Laertian Gamble* • Robert Sheckley
#13 *Station Rage* • Diane Carey
#14 *The Long Night* • Dean W. Smith & Kristine K. Rusch
#15 *Objective: Bajor* • John Peel
#16 *Invasion #3: Time's Enemy* • L. A. Graf
#17 *The Heart of the Warrior* • John Gregory Betancourt
#18 *Saratoga* • Michael Jan Friedman
#19 *The Tempest* • Susan Wright
#20 *Wrath of the Prophets* • P. David, M. J. Friedman,
         R. Greenberger
#21 *Trial by Error* • Mark Garland
#22 *Vengeance* • Dafydd ab Hugh
#23 *Rebels Book 1* • Dafydd ab Hugh
#24 *Rebels Book 2* • Dafydd ab Hugh
#25 *Rebels Book 3* • Dafydd ab Hugh

**Star Trek®: Voyager™**

*Flashback* • Diane Carey
*Pathways* • Jeri Taylor
*Mosaic* • Jeri Taylor

- #1 *Caretaker* • L. A. Graf
- #2 *The Escape* • Dean W. Smith & Kristine K. Rusch
- #3 *Ragnarok* • Nathan Archer
- #4 *Violations* • Susan Wright
- #5 *Incident at Arbuk* • John Gregory Betancourt
- #6 *The Murdered Sun* • Christie Golden
- #7 *Ghost of a Chance* • Mark A. Garland & Charles G. McGraw
- #8 *Cybersong* • S. N. Lewitt
- #9 *Invasion #4: The Final Fury* • Dafydd ab Hugh
- #10 *Bless the Beasts* • Karen Haber
- #11 *The Garden* • Melissa Scott
- #12 *Chrysalis* • David Niall Wilson
- #13 *The Black Shore* • Greg Cox
- #14 *Marooned* • Christie Golden
- #15 *Echoes* • Dean W. Smith & Kristine K. Rusch
- #16 *Seven of Nine* • Christie Golden
- #17 *Death of a Neutron Star* • Eric Kotani
- #18 *Battle Lines* • Dave Galanter & Greg Brodeur

**Star Trek®: New Frontier**

- #1 *House of Cards* • Peter David
- #2 *Into the Void* • Peter David
- #3 *The Two-Front War* • Peter David
- #4 *End Game* • Peter David
- #5 *Martyr* • Peter David
- #6 *Fire on High* • Peter David

1252.01